RAWHIDE RUNYAN

Rawhide Runyan builds up a cow outfit in the Arizona Strip near the Utah border. A superb fighting man built of rawhide and whalebone, with an aversion to outlaws in general and cattle rustlers in particular. His ranch is well-known as the Double Diamond R.

Slow Joe Hill, Rawhide's right-hand man, is a reformed outlaw, and their fights and adventures occur in the Arizona Strip and the surrounding country near the northern end of the Grand Canyon.

RAWHIDE RUNYAN

Chuck Martin

GUNSMOKE

First published in the UK by Quality Press

This hardback edition 2007
by BBC Audiobooks Ltd
by arrangement with
Golden West Literary Agency

ISBN 978 1 405 68142 1

British Library Cataloguing in Publication Data available.

Printed and bound in Great Britain by
Antony Rowe Ltd., Chippenham, Wiltshire

CONTENTS

CHAPTER I

THE BUZZARD

RAWHIDE RUNYAN sat up in his blankets and put on his hat. His right hand reached for the .45-70 Winchester under the tarp cover as his eyes roamed restlessly across the little mesa where he had made camp. Some foreign sound had awakened him from a sound sleep, and a leaden sky told him that it lacked an hour until sun-up.

Finding nothing to verify his suspicions, Rawhide turned to study his black cow horse, Shadow, who had ears like an owl's. Shadow's ears pointed toward a bosque of scrub pine at the east edge of the little plateau. A beautiful pinto mare was tethered near the black, grazing contentedly on the bunch grass.

Rawhide Runyan laid the rifle aside and stretched lazily. If someone was watching him from the thicket, that party would be looking at him over the sights of a gun. Rawhide stood up yawning, working the kinks out of his supple muscles. In the Arizona Strip, his neighbours called him a cowboy's cowboy. Five feet nine, his sturdy frame carried a hundred and fifty pounds. All rawhide and whalebone, a veteran of the long trails though still in his early twenties.

When a man sleeps on the ground for long periods, he acquires a sixth sense which warns him of danger. He can feel the gaze of other men on the back of his neck, or the muzzle of a gun aimed at his back. Rawhide knew he was under scrutiny, but he also knew that if he betrayed that knowledge, his curiosity would never be satisfied. Whoever had trailed him knew his way around.

Shivering against the chill of early morning, Rawhide buttoned the collar of his heavy shirt. A dead tree lay near his bed-roll to furnish firewood, and it was the natural thing to start a breakfast fire. Gathering a handful of dry pine needles, Rawhide broke off some brittle branches and flicked a match to touch off his tinder.

He told himself that all his actions must be natural. A canteen hung from his saddle, which had served for a pillow. A spring dripped from the rocks at the west end of the mesa and, taking the canteen, Rawhide walked carelessly away from his fire. From the corner of one eye he saw Shadow watching the copse of timber, and he found the answer at the same time.

Rawhide Runyan invariably travelled light, but now he was returning home to the Arizona Strip with a pack mare. The beautiful animal was a present from an old friend, and the packs she had carried were composed mostly of silver ore. Nothing to get excited about ; the metal chunks would make good door-stoppers in Rawhide's comfortable house on the Diamond Double R.

Rawhide held his canteen under the dripping spring. He could feel the short hair prickle at the back of his neck ; could almost feel the muzzle of a gun against his broad back. Any sudden move might send bushwhack lead into his tough body.

Rawhide raised the canteen to his lips and drank deeply. Stooping slowly, he placed the canteen where it would catch the drip, stepped to the side, and walked around the out-cropping of rocks. Then he slipped quietly into the brush with a sigh of relief as he placed the unseen watcher on the defensive.

The minutes ticked away with only the drip of water in the canteen disturbing the early morning silence. The fire needed more wood, but Rawhide shrugged carelessly. When the fire died down, the other hombre might get impatient.

Rawhide Runyan crouched in his hiding-place where he could watch the entire mesa. The pinto mare raised her head and whinnied as the scent of water came down the wind. Shadow pawed the ground a time or two as though to signal Rawhide. Then the slight scrape of a boot ended the battle of nerves.

A tall man left the timbered fringe at the east end of the mesa, clutching a rifle in his slender hands. He moved like an Indian as his dark eyes darted to the spring and back to the fire. A lean six-footer wearing cowboy rigging, swift in all his movements, he was apparently confident of his own abilities.

Rawhide slipped his long-barrelled .45 six-shooter from his holster, but he did not raise the gun. The stranger circled the two horses, stopping to heft the packs the pinto had carried. A soft whistle keened from his lips, and for a moment the stranger forgot his caution.

Rawhide Runyan left his hiding-place and circled to the

east. His boots made no sound on the bunch grass, but Shadow raised his head suddenly and whickered.

"Drop that long gun!" Rawhide ordered, as he clicked back the hammer of his six-shooter.

The tall stranger dropped his rifle and turned with both hands raised. Rawhide stared and spoke unconsciously.

"You look like a buzzard!"

The stranger's long nose curved down over a thin gash of a mouth and almost hid his bloodless lips. His black eyes were steady and unwinking, with short, lashless lids. High cheekbones, heavy shelving eyebrows, and a head as bald as a skull.

"Good guess," he said in a rasping metallic voice. "I am Buzzard. You'll be Rawhide Runyan."

Rawhide stepped forward behind his cocked gun and emptied the stranger's holster. The weapon was a .44 Colt, Frontier model, balanced by a master. Rawhide shoved the gun in his belt, never removing his gaze from the prisoner's hawkish face.

"Never heard of you," he said carelessly. "Where do you tend bar?"

"An apt question, my young cow-punching friend," the stranger answered quietly. "I tend the bar of justice, and I was suspicious of the load you carried on the pinto mare. I'm John L. Buzzard, repping for the A.C.P.A."

"Says which?"

"Arizona Cattlemen's Protective Association," Buzzard explained. "There had been some rustling going on during your absence. You were my first suspect."

Rawhide Runyan trapped his lips together and stared at the dark piercing eyes which never seemed to wink. He admitted to himself that Buzzard was no novice. Buzzard could have killed him a dozen times. The nearest ranch was his own Diamond Double R, thirty miles to the north-east.

"I never heard of the A.C.P.A.," he told Buzzard coldly. "Must be a new outfit, and we don't need any up here in the Strip."

"That ain't the way Jim Williams of the Rafter W put it," Buzzard answered evenly. "Williams has signed up, and Tad Lancy of the Anchor T will do likewise."

Rawhide Runyan did not show the surprise he felt. The cattlemen in the Strip had always looked to him for leadership, but something happened every time he left home. He had been gone less than a month and, now, according to Buzzard, rustlers were once more active in the Strip.

" Why didn't you announce yourself before sneaking into my camp ? " Rawhide demanded. " And why all the interest in my packs ? "

" Rustlers shoot first and answer questions later," Buzzard said with a shrug. " As to your packs, they sounded like branding-irons to me. Any harm in making sure ? "

" I've seen men shot for less ! " Rawhide bit off the words. " And that ain't all. If you're a A.C.P.A. man, you know that most rustlers carry a running-iron, and mebbe a pair of saddle rings. They don't need any other branding-irons."

" I didn't know there was silver in these parts," Buzzard changed the subject abruptly. " That's mighty high-grade ore you are packing to the county seat."

" I make mine raising cattle," Rawhide said quietly. " I brought the stuff along to use for door-stoppers."

" Of course, of course," Buzzard agreed quietly. " I don't blame you for hiding your secret until you file your claims."

Rawhide Runyan raised his gun and centred his sights on the stranger's left shirt-pocket. The funereal face opposite him did not change expression, and the staring dark eyes reminded Rawhide of the eyes of a snake.

" Now you talk fast, mister ! " he barked. " Just who are you, and what's your real business up here in the Strip ? "

" The name is John L. Buzzard, and you won't shoot," the stranger answered. " Yonder comes a mutual friend riding up the trail."

" That's an old one, but I'll wait," Rawhide grunted, and then his eyes widened as the sound of shod hoofs came from the trail.

Shadow was also watching the trail with ears pricked forward. The black horse whickered with recognition, and Rawhide glanced swiftly around. He lowered his gun as Jim Williams rode out on the mesa with another mounted man following.

" Jim and Slow Joe Hill," Rawhide almost shouted. " Howdy ! "

Jim Williams, sixty-odd, was a big man who sat his saddle like a youngster. His Rafter W spread bordered the Diamond Double R on the south, and the old cattleman had always been one of Rawhide's supporters. Now he frowned as he stared at the gun in Rawhide's hand.

" Howdy, Rawhide. Put up your hardware and make the sign of peace. Make you acquainted with John L. Buzzard, representative of the Arizona Cattlemen's Protective Association. We've lost considerable stock since you went traipsing off to Nevada to help Jim Barbee."

" That's right, boss," Slow Joe Hill added. " I rode out to meet you, and picked Jim up on the way. I figgered you might tangle with the Buzzard."

" Hill, you were an outlaw before Runyan gave you a chance to go straight," Buzzard interrupted dryly. " You might be foreman of the Diamond Double R, now, but there was a time when you rode the owlhoot trail."

Slow Joe Hill was six feet tall, weighed two hundred pounds. He threw a thick leg behind his cantle to dismount, glaring at Buzzard with anger glowing in his little eyes.

" My past is behind me, and yours will be, right soon," he promised grimly, as he swung to the ground.

CHAPTER II

THE A.C.P.A.

KNOWING the terrible strength of Hill, his foreman, Rawhide stepped between Slow Joe and Buzzard. Suddenly an arm like a steel band wrapped around Rawhide's waist, and his lowered pistol was snatched from his right hand. It was Buzzard.

" Stand back, the two of you ! " Buzzard ordered in his brassy voice. " I came up here to render a service, and I don't aim to be manhandled. You make a move, Slow Joe, and I'll give you what you should have had years ago. Once an owlhooter they don't ever change ! "

Slow Joe pulled his head down between his incredibly wide shoulders, scuffed his boots to dig little holes, a sure sign that he meant to change. Buzzard watched coldly and cocked the gun in his right hand.

" Don't leave the ground, or I'll snipe you on the wing," Buzzard warned Slow Joe. " I'm a range detective, and I use your kind of people up mighty fast."

" Don't touch off your powder, Buzzard," Williams' growling voice warned. " Getting mad won't get us anywheres. You, Slow Joe. Lay your hackles and unhook your spurs out of those grass roots. Give Rawhide back his cutter, Buzzard."

" I will, when he hands me back my own," the A.C.P.A. man answered. " He's packin' it in his belt."

Rawhide Runyan nodded and reached in his belt. He

gripped Buzzard's weapon, flipped his hand, earing back the hammer as the .44 Colt turned a half circle.

"Lower your hammer, and we'll call it a draw," Rawhide said softly. "If you don't, we'll make it a draw, regardless."

"You can trust Rawhide," Jim Williams told Buzzard. "We wouldn't need any A.C.P.A. rep if he would only stay home."

Buzzard lowered the hammer of Rawhide's gun and reversed the weapon in his hand. His eyes widened a trifle when Runyan copied his every move and offered the captured gun with the muzzle turned toward himself.

Then, suddenly, Buzzard flipped the gun again in his hand, with the butt thwacking against his palm. Rawhide opened his fingers and dropped Buzzard's gun, diving at Buzzard's ankles before the A.C.P.A. man could level his sights.

The gun exploded harmlessly as Rawhide upset the detective. Rawhide rolled with the fall, coming to his feet like a mountain cat. Buzzard also rolled sideways and came up like a steel spring, his right hand slapping under his left arm, his fingers clawing air as Rawhide stepped in behind a straight driving right. Knuckles crashed against Buzzard's bony jaw, and the range detective was knocked backward to the ground under the battering blow.

Rawhide Runyan picked up his own gun and spun the cylinder to make sure against grit. His face was like sculptured granite as he turned to old Jim Williams.

"I don't like this vulture, and he better stay out of my way. He had a gun on me when I woke up this morning, and he went out of his way to make trouble with Slow Joe."

"I don't care what you like, Rawhide," the old cattleman answered stubbornly. "I lost fifty head of steers the week after you left for Nevada, and you lost the same number just last week. Tad Lancy lost twenty head, and then this Buzzard hombre drifted in and made us a proposition."

"What kind of a proposition?"

"He's reppin' for the Arizona Cattlemen's Protective Association. He'll recover stolen stock for twenty per cent. of market value, and collect the rewards on any rustlers he catches."

"Starting with Slow Joe and me," Rawhide said angrily. "I take a little trip, and he lets on I might have rustled the stock. Slow Joe was an owlhooter one time, so that makes him open season for a vulture like this Buzzard gent."

"Say!" Jim Williams whispered. "I never thought of that. Neither did Tad Lancy of the Anchor T."

"Joe," Rawhide said to his foreman. "Bring my canteen from the spring. We'll revive our scavenger man, and let him explain."

Slow Joe brought the canteen and sprinkled water in the unconscious man's face. John L. Buzzard groaned, then flipped to his feet with hand clawing for his gun.

"Come out of it, you living skeleton," Rawhide said quietly. "We are right back where we started from, and I have both guns. Now you start talking!"

Lifting his head slowly, Buzzard glared at Rawhide with a red glow in his lashless black eyes. He glanced at Slow Joe Hill, who grinned and went through the pantomime of a buzzard flapping its wings.

"I ain't talking," Buzzard croaked. "Go ahead and read my mind."

"I am, but I could be wrong," Rawhide said meaningly. "I might even join this A.C.P.A. Let's see your credentials."

John L. Buzzard opened his shirt and turned the left pocket to show a badge pinned inside. Rawhide's eyes widened as he saw the badge of a special deputy marshal. Buzzard then reached to his hip pocket, brought out a billfold and opened it. A card stated that he was the accredited representative of the Arizona Cattlemen's Protective Association with offices at Phoenix.

"Pay him no mind, boss," Slow Joe Hill growled. "One time I worked with a gang of rustlers, and we all had cards like that."

Buzzard turned and stared at Slow Joe like a snake charming its prey. His hat had fallen from his head, and his bald yellow skull gleamed in the early morning sun like old ivory.

"Some day you'll dig your own grave with your big mouth, you half-witted monkey," he warned Slow Joe. "I've seen animals like you in cages, but never running around loose in the hills!"

"I've never seen anything like you outside of a skull orchard," Slow Joe retorted, and doubled his big fists. "That ain't all, you skinny buzzard. There's a pard of yours running loose in the badlands. Gent about your size, only more meat on his bones, and his face all over whiskers!"

"Whiskers Snard!" Buzzard barked, and his brassy voice was like the tone of a metallic gong. "Where did you see that wide-looping rustler?"

Rawhide Runyan stared at Slow Joe, and then at Buzzard. Both seemed in deadly earnest, but Slow Joe stuck out his jaw to sneer at the range detective.

" Like as if you didn't know ! He was doggin' yore tracks like a hound dog trailing a skunk ! "

Buzzard turned to Jim Williams, who was listening with a puzzled gleam in his faded grey eyes.

" Now it comes out, Williams. Runyan lets on to make a trip to Nevada, leaving this owlhooter to ramrod the Diamond Double R. Hill takes up with Whiskers Snard, one of the most successful rustlers in the country. Runyan rides out to find a market, like as not with some pards of his over in Nevada ! "

Rawhide Runyan stared at Buzzard with a queer look in his eyes. Buzzard had told him to read his mind, but Buzzard was talking with his mouth wide open. If Buzzard and Whiskers Snard were in cahoots, they could work the plan Buzzard had outlined. If they were caught, Buzzard could collect twenty per cent. for the supposed recovery of the stolen cattle.

Rawhide Runyan told himself that a man had to be sure before accusing another man without proof. He nodded slightly, spoke quietly to Buzzard.

" I've been thinking, Buzzard. I've mebbe thought wrong of you, and you might have done the same thing about me. Now supposing we put it all together. The answer might still be Whiskers Snard and some of his pards. Your credentials look all right to me, and I might join up with your A.C.P.A."

John L. Buzzard turned slowly and fixed Rawhide with a steady stare. Rawhide returned the stare without winking, his hand flipping to the back of his belt again. He stepped up to the range detective and seated Buzzard's .44 Colt in the detective's empty holster.

" By dogies," Buzzard exclaimed, " I'll take a chance if you will ! I'll drop by the Diamond Double R and sign you up, and I'll either recover your stolen critters, or leave my bones here in the Strip ! "

He took a quick step forward and offered his right hand. Rawhide Runyan accepted the token of friendship, and then he winced. Buzzard's grip was like that of a steel vice. Rawhide twitched his right shoulder to bring his own muscles into play, and the range detective tightened his thin lips.

" I understand why they call you Rawhide, but I might need that hand again. Will you tell me something, Runyan ? "

" Fire ahead," Rawhide answered briefly.

" You went to see a friend over in Nevada. What's his name ? "

" Jim Barbee," Rawhide answered without hesitation.
" Jim was losing a lot of cattle, but we found every head."

" Now—that silver," Buzzard pressed his inquiry. " After
you file your discovery claim, could a man get in on the
ground ? "

" No," Rawhide answered shortly. " It's a closed concern."

" I was a miner one time," Buzzard said slowly. " I can
tell silver-bearing ledges when I see them. I mean to cover
this whole country, and I might come across your discovery."

Rawhide shrugged. " I'll saddle up if you are all talked out.
Stop by the Diamond Double R, and I'll join the Association."

CHAPTER III

RAWHIDE PAYS HIS DUES

Tom Owens of the T O Connected was waiting with Limpy
Watson, the Diamond R cook, when Rawhide Runyan rode
into the big yard with Slow Joe and John L. Buzzard. Owens
took off his old stetson, yelled a greeting—then scowled when
he recognized the A.C.P.A. detective.

" Mighty glad to see you home again, Rawhide," he said,
but his voice was sulky. " You travel in mighty poor company
these days was you to ask me."

Rawhide smiled and shook hands with the silver-haired
oldster. He and Tom Owens had fought together in most of
the battles of the Strip, and Rawhide valued the old cattleman's judgment. To make matters worse, Slow Joe added a
remark of his own.

" That's what I say, Tom. Buzzard by name, and Buzzard
by nature. Him and his twenty per cent."

" Better pay twenty per cent. than lose all the cattle that
have been rustled," Rawhide cautioned, watching Buzzard's
long bony face.

" Better tell that barn-shouldered ramrod of yours to
hobble his jaw," Buzzard said in his harsh voice. " I've
chewed up worse than him, and spat out the pieces."

" Let's you and Joe fight," Tom Owens suggested, his eyes
glinting with anticipation. He had seen Slow Joe in action,
and he added fuel to the fire with his next remark : " I'll
join your tinhorn club if Joe loses, and pay you double the
fee."

John L. Buzzard threw his black stetson on the ground
and shucked his spurs. Slow Joe cocked his head to glance

at Rawhide, who refused to meet Joe's eyes. Buzzard drew a line with his boot and stepped back.

"Cross that line, you bull-necked ape," he dared Slow Joe.

Joe made a leap before Buzzard had finished talking. He pistoned a right at the range detective's jaw, with all his weight behind the blow. Buzzard moved his head enough to let the big fist whiz over his shoulder. Then he half turned, grabbing Slow Joe's wrist with both hands. Joe swivelled around on the bony hip as Buzzard finished his turn. The A.C.P.A. man pulled down and bucked up at the same time, and Slow Joe flew through the air like a sack of spuds.

Buzzard turned loose his grip and followed the flight of his victim. Slow Joe landed soggily, sat up slowly and started to push up to his feet. Buzzard was waiting with his right fist cocked to deliver the crusher, but Slow Joe had learned a few of Rawhide's tricks. He lurched forward and ducked down at the same time, making a shoestring tackle which tumbled Buzzard to the thick dust.

Holding his grip, Slow Joe leaped to his feet and started a giant swing, holding to Buzzard's ankles. Rawhide Runyan watched with a grin on his tanned face, until he saw the look in Joe's little eyes, which gleamed red as fire in the eyes of some nocturnal animal.

Slow Joe continued his swing with Buzzard's body straight out like a flail. A gnarled pine stood near the house, and Joe was backing toward the tree. He meant to walk right into the tree with the range detective, and a shudder ran up Rawhide's spine.

"Joe!" he yelled. "Ease up!"

Slow Joe Hill was in another world, nothing but sudden death would satisfy his blood lust. Two more steps would put him close enough, and a third step would send Buzzard's head crashing against the gnarled pine.

Rawhide ran in close and stuck a boot between Joe's thick legs. Slow Joe stumbled and went to one knee, losing his hand hold as he tried to break his fall. Buzzard's body sailed through the air, hurtled to earth, and went spinning over and over until it brought up against the porch step.

Slow Joe got to his feet and started for the A.C.P.A. man, but Rawhide yelled to him to stop. Slow Joe backed away with a chuckle, holding up both hands.

"Don't you lower the boom on me, Rawhide," he yelled. "If you do, I'm hitting out for the owlhoot trails!"

John L. Buzzard sat up spitting and gasping. He was dust from head to foot, and his bony face was skinned from sliding through the grit. After dusting himself, he danced up to Slow Joe, looking for more fight.

"Bring it to me, you fat ape," he taunted. "The bigger they come, the harder they fall!"

Slow Joe jabbed viciously with his left fist and came in with the punch. Buzzard reached for a wrestling hold, but Joe belied his name when he crossed with a right to the jaw. The range detective grunted and fell face forward. Slow Joe could have caught the falling man, but he side-stepped and dusted his ham-like hands.

"The gent don't lack for guts," Owens said, coming up quietly, as he tugged at his white longhorn moustache. "Slop him down with a pail of water from the trough."

"And you shake hands with him, Joe," Rawhide said sternly. "If we are going to work with him, we don't want any hard feelings."

"I'll see him in . . . Awright, boss, I'll shake—if you say so."

"You heard me," Rawhide muttered, his face turned to hide the grin he could not hold back.

Slow Joe dipped a bucket of water from the horse trough, stepped across John L. Buzzard and dumped the pail. The range detective came up whooshing like a bear striking out for dry land. Slow Joe helped Buzzard to his feet, threw the water bucket aside and stuck out his right hand.

"Touch skin, you flappin' vulture," he said with a grin.

Buzzard stared for a moment and then thwacked palms. Joe yelled when the A.C.P.A. man tightened his grip, and he almost went to his knees under the pressure.

"Say uncle, or I'll break the bones," Buzzard said, as he grinned through the mud which almost hid his bony face.

"*Uncle*, you blasted crow!" Slow Joe yelled, and then he whacked Buzzard on the back. "No hard feelings, old skeleton?"

"That goes double," Buzzard came back instantly. "Would you mind telling me why they call you Slow Joe?"

"I just move slow to save my strength," Joe answered with a chuckle. "I can whip you now, pore and ganted the way you are. You stay around here a spell and eat some of Limpy's grub, and he'll put some tallow on your frame."

"When you two jiggers get done admiring each other's shortcomings, I'll jine up with the Association," Tom Owens called across the yard. "Free for nothing!" he reminded Buzzard. "But I'll pay twenty per cent if you get back those steers I lost."

John L. Buzzard walked over to his horse, fumbled in his saddlebags and produced a printed pad. Hooking a boot in the stirrup, he used his knee for a desk and wrote out two forms. He handed the pad to Tom Owens with a stubby tally pencil.

" Sign 'er right there, old-timer. After you, the big augur can affix his John Henry to the other blank I filled out."

Tom Owens signed and handed the pad to Rawhide. Buzzard watched with his head to one side, staring through slitted lids at the pack on the pinto mare.

" You want to pay me a hundred bucks in cash, or give me a couple of those door-stoppers ? " he asked quietly.

" Pick out a chunk that you can muscle out at the end of your arm," Rawhide agreed. " That ought to be about fifteen pounds."

The range detective walked over to the mare, threw off the diamond hitch which held the pack and dropped the heavy canvas to the ground. His dark eyes burned like live coals as he pawed through the silver ore until he found a chunk about the size of a man's head.

" I'll take this piece," he said quietly.

" Go on," Slow Joe sneered. " That piece weighs all of forty pounds, and you can't muscle half that much."

John L. Buzzard smiled and picked up the ore with both hands. After balancing the piece on his right hand, he slowly straightened his arm. The veins stood out on his bald skull, but the range detective bit down on his teeth and finished his stretch, holding the heavy piece of ore straight out from his shoulder.

" He held, eh," Slow Joe whispered. " The dang old skeleton must be all muscle and hard bone ! "

" You win," Rawhide said briefly, but even he was trying to figure where John L. Buzzard carried his amazing strength.

" Look, you big monkey," Buzzard said to Slow Joe Hill. " Catch, and let's see you muscle it out."

He tossed the heavy piece of ore at Joe, who caught it deftly and allowed the weight to bend his powerful arms. Joe hefted the ore, balanced it on his right hand and stretched out his arm without a jerk. Holding the piece at arm's length, Joe walked to the ore pile and picked up another chunk. This he muscled out with his left arm, then spat through his front teeth.

" There's only one like me," he boasted, with a grin at Buzzard. " When I was made, they busted the mould."

" That's something to be thankful for," Buzzard grunted,

as he took his ore from Slow Joe's hand. " I figure that chunk is worth about four hundred dollars, but I'll try to earn it. Where can a gent change his clothes and sluice the dirt from his weary frame ? "

" The crick is down in back o' the barn," Joe answered. " Is your name shore enough Buzzard ? "

" I signed it that way, didn't I ? "

" Reckon you did," Slow Joe agreed. " Well, let's go and swim the dirt off."

Tom Owens watched the two men walk toward the barn. They were almost identical in stature, but Buzzard was thin where Slow Joe was thick of limb. Tom Owens whistled.

" Look at the shoulders on the range detective," he said to Rawhide. " He's a big-boned jigger, and no mistake. What's your play, Rawhide ? " he demanded softly.

" I'm just going to keep my mouth shut and my eyes open," Rawhide answered, with a puzzled frown. " I used to be a range detective myself, but John L. Buzzard has a way all his own. And keepin' mum is the only way we'll find out what that way is."

CHAPTER IV

READING SIGN

It lacked an hour until daybreak when Limpy Watson beat on the bottom of a frying-pan to arouse Rawhide Runyan and Slow Joe Hill from their slumbers. Rawhide had enjoyed the luxury of his own bed after sleeping on the ground for more than a month. Cowboy style, he started dressing by first putting on his hat.

" It don't take a gent long to spend the night on this outfit," he complained to Slow Joe, as he tried to crawl out of bed. " I can't move my legs. They feel like lead."

" Try kicking that dog over to one side, boss," Slow Joe suggested. " He's been bedding down with me since you drifted to Nevada. You ought to see him work cattle ! "

A great bundle of fur leaped upon Rawhide and pinned him down. Then a long, pointed muzzle found his face in the dark, and Rawhide's face was licked all over before he could escape. He gathered the big collie in his arms and patted the wriggling body.

" Good old Shep," he said, with a hum in his voice. " You going to help us to-day, boy ? "

The dog barked joyously, jumped from the bed and ran to the front door. Limpy Watson struck a match to make a light, and grumbled that the dog was eating all the provisions on the Diamond Double R. But his eyes were warm with affection, and his rough voice was almost a caress.

"That dog will catch him a rustler, and it won't be the first time," the old cook prophesied. "Just find a place where Whiskers Snard has stood a while, put Shep to the scent, and get your shooting-irons ready."

Rawhide stomped into his boots and went to the back of the house to wash up for breakfast. His mind was leaping ahead to the twisting passages of the lava badlands, trying to locate some hidden canyon where the rustlers could hide the stolen stock. A hundred and twenty head would make a sizable bunch, but the badlands toward the Utah border were vast. Might take a week to find even a trace. Rawhide smiled as a tail whacked his legs.

"I believe that dog knows something, Rawhide," Slow Joe said eagerly. "We had to chain him up to keep him from hitting out to find you. But there goes the call for grub pile."

Limpy Watson always beat on his triangle, whether for one man or a dozen. He heaped ham and eggs before Slow Joe and Rawhide, took a seat at the head of the table and dumped a pile of salt-rising biscuits between the two hungry men.

"Say the word, and I'll bolt a hull on my pony and ride with you," he told Rawhide. "How many men you reckon this Whiskers Snard is rodding in his gang of owlhooters?"

"I forgot to ask John L. Buzzard," Rawhide answered with a grin. "I wonder where that range detective went?"

"He rode toward the notch when he left here yesterday," Limpy answered. "Come to think of it, boss, the rustlers might be drifting the rustled stock over there to Red Dog in Utah."

"Pass the syrup for these hot cakes," Rawhide mumbled, his mouth full of food. "You shore wrangle up a mean mess of vittles, Limpy."

"Thankee kindly, sir, he said with a graceful curtsy." The old cook sneered, but the smile on his weathered face told that he was pleased with the compliment. "Now getting back to that dry scrape leading over to Red Dog. How about setting Shep on the scent over behind the old dam above Dark Canyon? That's where we lost those two-year-old steers."

"My own idea exactly," Rawhide agreed, as he finished his

breakfast with another cup of steaming hot coffee. " Let's get going, Joe. It will soon be daylight, then noon. Half the day gone and us not started yet."

Rawhide was riding a big deep-chested bay horse, to give Shadow a rest, and Slow Joe straddled a chunky sorrel built like himself. The collie ran beside Rawhide with his flag held high, making no attempt to smell out a scent. His work would come later, and the trained dog made no attempt to take the lead.

Rawhide stopped at the entrance to Dark Canyon where the lush grass grew belly-high to a tall horse. He could see where the young steers had grazed, and he emptied his saddle like a relay rider as something on the ground attracted his attention. The object was a worn roper's glove, made to fit a big hand.

" I'll bet a chunk of silver ore this glove belonged to Whiskers Snard," Rawhide said to Slow Joe. " It's worth a chance. Watch the dog close when I give him the scent."

Calling the collie, Rawhide held the glove to the big dog's nose. Shep sniffed for a full minute, whined eagerly, and then began to circle with his nose to the ground.

" That won't work," Slow Joe said glumly. " When Whiskers jumps his saddle, that dog will be out of work."

Rawhide made no answer as he watched the circling dog. The man smell might be strong enough to guide the collie, especially if the man had handled his horse. Shep was a smart dog, and if he got those two smells—of Snard and his horse—together, he just might connect them in his mind. Many a time Shep had found Rawhide by tracking down Shadow.

The collie came to a trampled place and nosed about for a while. Suddenly he pointed his muzzle high and barked softly. Then he was away like the wind, pointing for the badlands down behind the old dam.

" Ride up fast and keep him in sight," Rawhide called to Joe, as he climbed his saddle.

Slow Joe put his sorrel to a hand lope and stood up in the stirrups. Rawhide caught up and circled off to the right, nodding his satisfaction as he saw a broken twig of mesquite here and there.

He wondered if Whiskers Snard was as bad as men painted the outlaw. Snard, known from Texas to the Canadian border as a man entirely without fear, was said to be a dead shot with either rifle or pistol. Rawhide felt the old familiar tingle in the fingers of his right hand. Snard was a big man—six feet and some, two hundred pounds of vicious killer, if all the stories about him were correct. Fast with his irons, too.

Rawhide drew his six-shooter and carefully checked the loads. Five cartridges with the hammer riding on an empty for safety. His left knee rubbed against the stock of a Winchester riding in the boot under his saddle fender. He wondered if John L. Buzzard was all he claimed to be. Had the range detective's senses been dulled by his desire to locate the rich silver mine which had provided Rawhide's door-stoppers?

Slow Joe yipped softly and pointed up ahead. Rawhide saw the collie's tail disappear through a narrow trail leading to the lava badlands. The horses came up fast and splashed through a shallow creek, just as the collie, circling near a clump of tamarind, wriggled through a small opening as Slow Joe rubbed his eyes.

" I always figured that was a blind draw," Joe said to Rawhide. " But if Shep can get in, we can squeeze through, too, one at a time."

Rawhide took the lead and rode up to the bushy barrier. Arriving, he leaned over the side of his saddle and pointed to a horse track half filled with water.

" Someone rode through here this morning or late last night," he said to Joe, as he took down his rope.

Slow Joe watched as Rawhide built a small loop and shot his twine at a hole in the brush. When the loop caught a limb and hung, Rawhide took his dallies and backed his horse. Slow Joe hummed softly under his breath as a section of the brush opened under the pull of rope.

Rawhide motioned for Joe to ride through, after which he followed and pulled the brush gate shut. The collie was waiting behind a stand of rocks, whining softly as he pointed to a bunch of cattle grazing on the tough dry land.

Rawhide rode behind the rocks and took a pair of old field-glasses from his saddlebags. Cupping them to his eyes, he focused on the cattle to read the brands and earmarks.

" Several head of Diamond Double R critters, Joe," he whispered softly. " Yonder are some Anchor Ts, and a scattering of Rafter Ws. Wait a minute! Get down, Joe. We're discovered! "

Slow Joe Hill dived from his saddle, and Rawhide Runyan was already on the ground, when a rifle shot barked flatly.

" That was close," Joe remarked carelessly. " Must have been Whiskers Snard. Slug nicked the top of my hat." Slow Joe picked up his old stetson and pushed a forefinger through a pair of holes in the high crown.

"Come back, Shep!" Rawhide called sharply to the dog. "Stay down, boy!"

The collie bellied down to thin the target he made as another bullet kicked up dust just to one side. Then he whipped around the rocks and sat on his haunches, his eyes watching Rawhide.

"I know this hide-out from the other end," Joe husked softly. "Narrow opening, just wide enough for a horse to squeeze through. Leads out to the Red Dog trail where one hombre could hold it against an army."

Rawhide reached up and pulled his Winchester from the saddle boot, hung his grey stetson on it out to the right, but nothing happened. Slow Joe grinned as Rawhide frowned.

"You're playing for keeps with an expert, boss," Joe said grimly. "That old trick wouldn't fool Whiskers Snard."

Rawhide poked a chink between the rocks and fitted his rifle barrel to the opening. He figured the range at five hundred yards, allowed for windage, centred his sights on a clump of brush where he had seen Whiskers Snard, and took a deep breath.

"Braam!"

Dust and rock splinters splattered Rawhide's face before he could trip the trigger of his rifle. Snard must have been watching through a pair of high-powered glasses, and his shot had been too close to make a man feel good.

Rawhide rubbed the red dust from his eyes, knowing that he was out-gunned. The roar of the outlaw's rifle suggested a Sharps or a heavy Henry buffalo gun, which threw an ounce of lead and threw it straight.

"Listen!" Slow Joe whispered, with his head cocked to the side.

Rawhide listened, cautiously peered through the crevice he had made as the drum of hoofs sounded across the valley. As a second set of hoofs took up the racing rhythm, Joe came out of hiding with a shout.

"I never did trust that skeleton man! Yonder goes Whisker Snard at a dead run, with John L. Buzzard making it a race. Those two owlhooters are in cahoots, and don't try to tell me no different!"

Rawhide grunted, called to the dog and walked into the open. He waved his right arm at the grazing steers as he gave a sharp command.

"Go round them, Shep. We'll open the gate and drive this stock back home. Take the left side, Joe. I'll crowd them from the right. Bring 'em up, Shep!"

CHAPTER V

GUN TRAP

TWILIGHT shadows were lengthening in the Diamond Double R ranch yard when Rawhide Runyan rode home with Slow Joe Hill. Sliding from the saddle, Rawhide turned quickly to give Shep the praise due him when the collie nuzzled his hand.

" Nice work, boy. For a reformed sheepherder, you make a right good cowhand. Ain't that right, Joe ? "

" Right as rain," Slow Joe agreed promptly. " With Shep bringing up the drag, we pushed those cattle critters all of fifteen miles. They'll bed down close to water while you and me get a good night's sleep."

" I think I'll ride over to see Tom Owens after supper," Rawhide said carelessly. " If Buzzard and Snard are the pards you seem to think they are, our boys ought to know about it."

He led his horse to the barn, stripped his riding gear and filled the mangers high with hay. Slow Joe watched as Rawhide poured grain in Shadow's feed-box and the black horse whinnied appreciation. Joe shrugged. Two quarts of oats usually meant a long hard trek, so evidently Rawhide was going to ride back home from the T O Connected.

After washing behind the house, the two men answered Limpy Watson's call to supper. Slow Joe told the old cook about the day's happenings, while Rawhide ate silently. Supper over, Rawhide pushed back from the table with a sigh of satisfaction.

" Your cooking improves every day," he complimented Limpy. Then he turned to Slow Joe. " I might stay over with Tom Owens, Joe. If I'm not back to-night, you start early in the morning with Shep. Move that bunch of steers up behind the dam and hold them near Dark Canyon."

Slow Joe nodded and walked to the barn with Rawhide. He watched his young boss saddle the big black, but he said nothing until Rawhide mounted up. Then Slow Joe spoke what was on his mind.

" If you ain't back at daylight, I'll turn Shep out to find you, Rawhide. Whiskers Snard and the Buzzard ain't going to like what we did to them to-day, and they might try to tally for you."

" Shadow can see in the dark," Rawhide answered with a smile. " I mean to run those two out of the country, but we might need some help from Tom Owens and Jim Williams. I'll be seeing you in the morning."

A rested horse travels fast in the cool of evening, and Shadow hit a high lope leaving the Diamond Double R. The T O Connected was five miles to the south if a rider followed the cattle trails through the scrub oak and catclaw. After running the kinks out of his muscles, Shadow settled down to a fast running walk, picking his sure-footed way through the velvety darkness.

Rawhide narrowed his eyes to stare at a pin-point of light over to the west. The T O Connected was a good two miles away, but there was a wooded rise between the two ranches. The light he saw did not come from a house ; it was more like the glowing embers of a camp fire.

Rawhide loosened his six-shooter from force of habit. If strangers were in the neighbourhood, he wanted to know about it—although it seemed unlikely that Snard and Buzzard would risk a fire.

As Runyan neck-reined his horse toward the light, he did a strange thing. Reaching to his saddlebags behind the cantle, he fumbled for a moment and then brought out the mate to the gun in his holster. Unbuttoning his heavy wool shirt, he seated the extra weapon in a shoulder holster under his left arm.

It was difficult to judge distance at night, but Rawhide estimated that he had covered two miles when he stopped his horse in a thicket of prickly pear. He dismounted, ground-tied Shadow with trailing reins, and pulled his stetson low over his eyes. The stars gave enough light now that his sight was accustomed to the dark, and Rawhide began to pick his way toward the little canyon where the dying fire made a soft red glow.

Only once did he step on a twig, but the sound was magnified to his sensitive ears. After waiting several minutes, Rawhide again began to creep forward, stopping only as he reached the edge of the sandy draw. He could hear a horse blowing from some hidden place back in the brush, and then his eyes focused on a bed-roll a few yards away from the fire.

It was spooky business busting into a man's camp in the dead of night, because the sleeper in the bed-roll might have a gun ready to his hand. Rawhide circled slowly, stopped at the edge of the brush near the head of the sleeper and drew his six-shooter.

" Hello in the camp," he said clearly but without raising his voice. " You're covered, so don't come out shooting ! "

" Drop that gun, Runyan," a harsh metallic voice warned from the brush behind Rawhide. " I figured you'd be night-riding, so I signalled you with my fire. Cast your eyes to the left, and you might see something else to lend you caution ! "

Only one man had a voice with that peculiar brassy twang. Rawhide Runyan knew that John L. Buzzard was behind him. He turned his head slightly to the left, caught a quick breath as he saw the barrel of a rifle pointing at him from the dense brush. The man behind the rifle would be Whiskers Snard, and Rawhide had tasted a sample of the rustler's shooting ability.

" Just as you say, Buzzard," Rawhide answered quietly, and dropped his gun to the grass.

" Now just put both hands behind your back," the range detective ordered gruffly. " I aim to hobble your wrists with a piggin' string. You might remember that I've got a gun at your back, in case you are tempted to go on the prod."

A man does not argue with a loaded gun, especially when that gun is in the hand of an expert. Rawhide sighed and put both hands behind his back, felt the loop of a piggin' string circle his right wrist. Three quick wraps and a half hitch completed the tie, after which Buzzard stepped around his captive and motioned for Rawhide to sit on the ground.

" I feel better standing up," Rawhide muttered.

The range detective took a quick step, grabbed Rawhide by the forearms and tripped him with a boot behind Rawhide's heels. Rawhide sat down hard with the hot blood surging through his veins.

John L. Buzzard grunted and crossed the clearing to the place where the hidden rifleman was concealed. Rawhide watched curiously as Buzzard reached out and grasped the rifle by the barrel. It came free from the brush as the range detective chuckled derisively.

" I want to see Whiskers Snard as bad as you do," he told Rawhide grimly. " Between you and him, you've ruined my business before I got a good start. Now you and me can talk."

" You talk and I'll listen," Rawhide suggested. " I don't even hold openers, so it's your say."

Buzzard took a seat on the other side of the fire from Runyan. Holding the rifle across his bony knees, he holstered his six-shooter.

" Believe it or not, the A.C.P.A. is a going concern,"
Buzzard began quietly, but his low voice was like the sound
of a brass cymbal. " I found that bunch of rustled cattle,"
the range detective went on. " About six thousand dollars
on the hoof, and my twenty per cent. for recovering same
would add up to about twelve hundred dollars. You and
that barn-shouldered ramrod of yours beat me out of just
that much."

Rawhide shrugged. " Keep on talking."

" I'll catch up with Whiskers Snard some day," Buzzard
went on harshly, his voice now vibrating like the tail of a
rattler. " I've hunted him for more than three years, but
he can wait. You owe me something, Rawhide Runyan.
I'd have had Snard to-day if you hadn't spoiled the play."

" Mark it down in the dust and let the rain settle it,"
Runyan answered with a shrug. " You and Whiskers Snard
are pards, so don't try to run a blazer on me."

" Pass that for now," Buzzard said with a sigh, and his
bony face grew hard. " I said you owed me something, and
it won't cost you much. Where's the discovery claim where
you found that silver ore ? "

Rawhide stared into the glowing dark eyes across the fire.
It would do no harm to tell Buzzard where the mine was
located, but first he would make a bargain.

" Man to man, if I tell you the truth, will you unhobble
my hands ? " he asked Buzzard.

" Your word is good enough for me, Rawhide Runyan,"
Buzzard answered without hesitation. " I've had enough of
the A.C.P.A. I'll stake out a silver claim of my own. The
Strip wouldn't need any help anyway, if you'd stay to home
and quit ramping around to see what's on the other side
of the hill. Where's the claim ? "

Rawhide pushed up to his feet, turned around and spoke
to Buzzard. " Turn me loose, and I'll unhobble my jaw."

The range detective caught the piggin' string and removed
the ties. Rawhide rubbed his wrists to restore circulation,
but he made no move to pick up his six-shooter.

" The silver I packed in came from a claim over in Nevada,"
Rawhide said honestly. " You'll find it on Jim Barbee's
ranch up in Iceburg Canyon."

The range detective stared at Rawhide without winking,
like a gambler who has placed a heavy bet, but takes his loss
without complaint. He picked up Rawhide's six-shooter,
jacked out the cartridges and seated the weapon deep in
Rawhide's holster.

" Get to your horse and ride," he said quietly. " After I complete some unfinished business of my own, I'll ride on out of the Strip ! "

CHAPTER VI

OLD JUDGE COLT

" You two hombres stand hitched ! "

John L. Buzzard was stepping away from Rawhide Runyan when the startling command came from the entrance to the canyon. Buzzard dropped his rifle, raised both hands level with his shoulders.

" You surprise me, Snard," he said quietly. " I could have shot you from the brush, but that ain't my way ! "

" Every man I've killed was shot in front," the deep voice said proudly. " Reach out and empty Rawhide's holster again."

Buzzard lowered his left hand and emptied Rawhide's holster. Without turning, he walked to the far end of the clearing with both hands high. Then he turned to face the big bearded man at the entrance of the canyon.

Whiskers Snard was braced firmly with his big boots spread wide, his black beard covering his throat, both hands hooked in his shell-studded belt.

" I brought you show-down," Snard said quietly. " How do you want it ? "

" I've trailed you for three long years," Buzzard answered, his voice like a rasping file. " You killed my brother, and you rustled a thousand head of our Circle Flying Bird stock."

" That Flying Bird was a buzzard," Snard taunted the range detective. " You've cost me plenty since then with your blasted Association ! "

Rawhide listened as he watched the two men. Now he was sure that John L. Buzzard had told the truth.

" One of us will stay here in the Strip," Buzzard whispered softly. " I've made a living by recovering stock you rustled, Whiskers Snard. You haven't done so well, but I never could bring you to the point of my gun."

" I'll make better than a good living after you quit kicking," Snard said coldly. " Rawhide Runyan will hold his hat over his head with his right hand. When he drops the hat, we draw our openers. Suit you ? "

" Keno," Buzzard answered promptly. " Prepare to meet the devil ! "

Rawhide Runyan stood between the pair, off to one side. His hard face did not change expression as he took off his stetson and held it above his head. He told himself that he had a stake in the game of draw—even if his openers were buried under his shirt. Without giving any warning to the two men who were staring at each other, Rawhide opened his fingers.

The old grey stetson fluttered from his hand and started its downward flight. Rawhide's right hand slapped for his left armpit and came out filled with lethal steel. The same movement carried the .45 six-shooter down and seated it in his empty holster.

Rawhide's slitted grey eyes watched the two gun fighters even as he filled his holster. Whiskers Snard moved like a tiger which has stalked its prey for the kill. He slapped for his gun, fired from the hip, beating Buzzard to the shot by that thin margin of time measured by the wink of an eye.

Buzzard got his shot away just as he was slapped into a turn by the battering shock of Snard's slug. The range detective slumped to the grass and straightened out his long legs.

Rawhide watched the fallen man, and the old familiar tingle of powder-smoke blood raced to the tips of his fingers. Buzzard's eyes were closed, a dead man's eyes were almost always open.

Whiskers Snard holstered his smoking gun and turned to stare at Rawhide Runyan.

" If you had a gun—" he started to say, and then his mouth popped open. It was just a round hole filled with gleaming white teeth in the black tangle of his heavy beard. " You have got a gun," he said in a low whisper of surprise, and his eyes darted to the ground where Rawhide's empty weapon gleamed from the grass.

" Yeah," Rawhide murmured. " I never was a two-gun man, but I always carry a spare for an emergency like this one."

" You mean—"

" What else ? " Rawhide countered. " I never did like a rustler none, and I've still got one bad habit I can't seem to overcome."

" One bad habit ? " Snard sneered softly.

" It is a bad habit," Rawhide answered grimly. " I hear

about some fast gun-swift, and I can't seem to take my rest until I've matched his cutter."

" Come to think about it, I've got that same habit," Snard admitted frankly. " I've met the fastest, and I haven't a scar on my body."

" With your size, I don't see how you've lived so long," Rawhide retorted evenly. " A man couldn't miss you at ten paces."

" John L. Buzzard missed me."

Rawhide changed the subject. " Buzzard ain't dead, if that's what you're thinking. Your slug just knocked him out. You shot too high, but point shooters do that most of the time."

Whiskers Snard made a grinding sound with his teeth. He wanted to glance at Buzzard's face, but he was afraid to take his eyes from Rawhide Runyan. The bearded outlaw shrugged his wide shoulders.

" He's as dead as he ever will be. Now about you and me . . . how do you want it ? "

" I'll play what I catch on the draw," Rawhide answered coolly. " We don't like rustlers up here in the Strip, but that's only an excuse. I'd have hunted you down anyway, after seeing you work with a rifle."

" I shot a mite to the right," Snard said. " I can tell from the scratches on your face where the rock splinters jumped."

" Look," Rawhide said softly. " There's a 'squite root nearly burned in two. It'll break apart and fall most any time. When it does—"

" That's the go-ahead," Snard agreed swiftly, and set himself for the draw, his wide shoulders hunched into a gunman's crouch.

Rawhide drew a deep breath and wondered if it would hold out until the charred root broke apart. His right hand was poised above the handle of his gun, steady as a rock. Hell was on fire with the devil's breath fanning the flames.

A soft wind from the south blew down the canyon and stirred the fire to make a dull red glow. Two silent men facing each other, killers both, with death riding in loaded holsters, they watched the mesquite root with eyes that did not dare to wink.

Rawhide felt the breath straining against his lungs, thrilled with the excitement that always came when the wings of death were brushing his shoulders. And then the glowing ember fell !

Two trained right hands sped down like striking hawks. Fingers curled round wood which had been whittled to fit the hands of fighting men, calloused thumbs notched back knurled hammers while completing their draws, and two six-shooters bellowed like one roaring gun. Or was there just a faint stutter between the two explosions?

Rawhide Runyan felt the tug of speeding lead against the edge of his calfskin vest, as his heavy gun bucked hard against his calloused palm. He watched the big outlaw as he eared back hammer on the recoil.

Whiskers Snard was swaying forward with his mouth wide open, a stunned stricken look widening his eyes as the smoking gun dropped from his nerveless fingers. His knees buckled to send him pitching forward, but the toes of his big boots did not rattle.

Rawhide advanced and turned the outlaw over. Snard's eyes were closed, and a red banner was spreading across his buckskin shirt just over the heart.

" Did you tally for the son, Rawhide ? " a rasping metallic voice whispered hoarsely.

Rawhide whipped round to face John L. Buzzard, who was propped up on his skinny elbows. The range detective seemed more than ever a skeleton as he smiled weakly.

" I ain't dead," he assured Rawhide. " His slug hit my badge pinned inside my shirt, but it went through my left shoulder. I've been hurt worse and still did a day's work."

Rawhide remembered the special deputy marshal's badge which gave Buzzard the authority of arrest wherever his searches took him. He hadn't been sure about the range detective, had never heard of the A.C.P.A. until Buzzard introduced himself. The wounded man smiled again and completed his confession.

" I'm the A.C.P.A. all by myself. Whiskers Snard was a cattle rustler, so I just followed his trail. I've been lucky."

" Some day you are going to crowd your luck too far," Rawhide answered grimly. " You'd be dead right now if that badge hadn't turned Snard's slug. Whiskers ain't dead either. I shot high just as I tripped my trigger. We'll turn him over to the sheriff down at Rainbow."

" You ain't a killer, Rawhide," Buzzard said softly. " Down inside, you've got a heart of silver. As big as that chunk you gave me yesterday."

Rawhide smiled with his face turned away. He had heard

about hearts of gold, but a wounded man could be mixed up
a little in his mind.

" Tie a rag around this scratch of mine, and then we'll pack
Whiskers out on his horse," Buzzard whispered.   " He was
faster than me, and I'm saying thanks."

" Forget it," Rawhide murmured, because gratitude always
embarrassed him.   " You can pick yourself out another chunk
of that silver ore when we get to the Diamond Double R.
There's been considerable gun smoke here in the Strip since
you rode in, but neither one of us are cold killers.   Turn over
this way so's I can bandage your wound."

CHAPTER VII

PAY DAY

BEEF roundup was drawing to a close in the Arizona Strip.
Bawling cattle were being bunched for a drive, in a pasture
below Dark Canyon.   They had been passed through the
tally men who made their counts on knotted strings
under the watchful eyes of Rawhide Runyan and Dave
Packer.

Rawhide Runyan always acted for the cattlemen here in
the high Arizona Strip where his own Diamond Double R
spread was located.   In his early twenties, he possessed the
undeniable qualities of leadership which made him stand out
in any gathering of cattlemen.

Dave Packer topped six feet by two inches, carried his two
hundred pounds easily, and kept most of his business under
his flat-crowned stetson.   He was a shrewd business man
who knew the cattle business from breeding to market, paid
cash for what he bought, and this year he was buying all the
shipping beef in the Strip.

Both men were in the saddle, marking their tally books
with blunt pencils.   Rawhide Runyan straddled his black
cow horse, Shadow.   The cattle buyer rode a tall rangy roan
which carried Packer's road brand on the left shoulder.
Packer mentioned the brand, pointed to part of his crew
which was working over fires out on the flat.

" I'm branding what I buy with my Sprawling D Bar P,

Runyan. You Strip fellers can make an inspection when my
boys string out the herd for the drive south."

Rawhide Runyan nodded. He pointed with his chin to a
pair of grizzled old cattlemen down by the creek crossing.
He also knew the cattle business and had appointed men for
the various jobs, such as thinning the herd for the tally
men, cutting out young she-stuff, and riding herd on the
cut-backs.

"Tad Lacy and Tom Owens will look over our critters,"
Rawhide told Dave Packer. "We're cleaning out the old
she-stuff and bulls this year, and we'll run those canners
and culls through separate. Tally five more for the
Anchor T."

"Tally five, Anchor T," Packer repeated, and closed his
book. "Call in the owners, and I'll pay off. Cash at the
graveside."

Rawhide Runyan had given his day orders during breakfast
at the chuck wagon. Slow Joe Hill was his *segundo*, a wide-
shouldered giant who matched Dave Packer for size and
weight. Slow Joe had been an outlaw until Rawhide had
shown him the error of his ways. Slow Joe sat his horse
solidly as he rode down to the crossing with cowboys from
the other crews.

Tom Owens of the T O Connected, Lacy of the Anchor T,
and Jim Williams of the Circle C rode toward Packer and
Runyan.

One of Packer's men left a branding-fire and rode toward
the group, leading a heavily laden pack-horse. He was a
tall, cold-eyed gun fighter of thirty-odd years.

"Slide down and throw off that diamond hitch, Turner,"
Dave Packer said, as the man rode up. To the cattlemen,
Packer explained: "Colt Turner is my cashier—and a good
one."

Colt Turner threw off his ties and spread a wool blanket
on the ground. He dumped two sacks of hard money on the
blanket, some packets of currency, and squatted on his high
heels—pay day in the Strip, with the travelling bank open
for business.

"Eighty head of three-year-old steers at thirty a round,"
Packer sing-songed the tally. "Pay Tom Owens twenty-four
hundred dollars. Forty head of cutters at fifteen; pay him
six hundred more."

Tom Owens tugged at his white moustache as he received
his pay. He signed the bill of sale provided by the cattle
buyer, dumped his money into a small sack, remarking with

3

quiet satisfaction that there would be grub on the T O table during the winter.

Tad Lacy took his place and was paid slightly more than four thousand dollars. Several other cattlemen were paid for small bunches. Rawhide Runyan waited until last.

" My boys made a count yesterday," Rawhide told Packer. " I've drawn up my own bill of sale to save time. What's your tally ? "

Big Dave Packer frowned and consulted his tally book. Colt Turner turned his sandy head to look Rawhide Runyan over from boots to stetson. No words were spoken, but Runyan felt a little tingle of anger stirring in his blood. He always felt this way when facing another gun swift, most of whom flashed him just such a silent challenge.

" Two hundred and eight head of prime beef at thirty dollars a round," Dave Packer read from his book. " Sixty head of cutters at fifteen."

" Here's the bill of sale all signed," Rawhide Runyan said, and handed the paper to Packer.

The cattle buyer took the paper and stared at the figures which were identical to his own. The bill of sale was written and signed with ink, properly filled out, with the purchase price included.

" Pay the Diamond Double R boss seven thousand, one hundred and forty dollars," Packer told Colt Turner. " Runyan's an expert accountant, and all the time I took him for a cowhand."

" Reading his brands and earmarkings, I taken him to be a fairly rapid gun hand," Turner said, and began to count out the money.

Rawhide Runyan clenched his teeth until his lower jaw jutted out like a reef of granite. His grey eyes were smoky with anger ; he could feel a pulse beating at the ends of the fingers of his right hand. He spoke very softly :

" I can say the same for you, Turner. You didn't get your front handle from breaking young horses ! "

Colt Turner stopped counting and came to his feet. His dark eyes were glowing and they changed colour. The sheaf of paper money was clutched tightly in his right hand.

Rawhide Runyan added fuel to the flames of the cashier's anger by calling attention to something Colt Turner had forgotten : " You ain't left-handed, Turner. Lay your hackles, and finish your count."

Colt Turner stared at the money in his gun hand, drew a quick breath, and resumed his squatting position. It was necessary for him to start all over, and after he pushed the money toward Runyan, Turner stretched again to his full height.

" Better count it," he sneered. " Mebbe I'm not honest."

" You'd know more about that than me," Runyan answered. " Just check over that dinero, will you, Tom Owens ? "

The cattleman nodded and squatted on his heels to make the count. Runyan faced Colt Turner across the blanket.

Dave Packer drew his horse back a step and spoke sharply to Turner : " Circle off there, Colt. This is a business deal, not a powder-smoke show-down ! "

" Show-down ? " Rawhide repeated. " You mean Turner is painted for war ? "

" Any time you say," Turner challenged. " When some riding hand lets on that I'm dishonest, I always call his hand ! "

" Start talking to yourself," Rawhide Runyan said coolly. " You called yourself names, and if the boot fits you, you might try it on for size ! "

Runyan watched the gun swift opposite, finding out many things. Colt Turner was a gun fighter—and a fast one. He wore his six-shooter tied down and toed in, and the weapon was balanced to fit his hand. Turner wasn't the first buscadero to come to the Strip hunting glory ; it required no imagination to read the purpose in his scowling features.

Rawhide Runyan was five feet nine, wide across the shoulders, and he weighed a hundred and fifty-five pounds. " All whalebone and rawhide," his neighbours described him.

" I've heard about you, Runyan," Turner said, his voice low and venomous. " You're said to be fast with your tools, and I don't mean ropes and branding-irons. Any time at all, cowboy ; any old time ! "

" Pay him no mind, Rawhide," Dave Packer interrupted. " Colt is working for me, and he either takes orders or he draws his time. Now get to work and sack up my money, Turner. I'm a business man, and you can take your pleasure after working hours."

" Like you say, boss," Turner growled, avoiding Runyan's glance. " Like as not I jumped at conclusions, and if this gent don't want to back up his wau-wau, I'm accepting his apology."

" I'm backing up my wau-wau," Rawhide Runyan said bluntly. " And I didn't offer any apology. I'll be around in case you still feel abused, but I never stop a man from doing his work."

Colt Turner was stuffing green-backs and hard money into sacks and made no answer. Old Tom Owens finished his count and told Rawhide that his money was right to the last dollar. The cowboy stuffed the money into a sack and tied it behind the cantle of his saddle.

"It's quite a drive to El Paso," he said to Dave Packer. "There's good feed all the way, and the rains are getting ready to set in."

"I might ship," Packer said with a shrug. "I'll talk it over with my ramrod, Bull Carter. We ought to finish road branding to-day."

Rawhide nodded and mounted his black horse. Tom Owens and Tad Lacy joined him as he rode toward the fires where Packer's crew was venting out old brands and stamping the trail herd with Packer's Sprawling D Bar P iron.

CHAPTER VIII

KNOCK-DOWN FIGHT

"WHAT you make of it, Rawhide?" Tom Owens asked Rawhide. "That gun slinger tried to pick a shoot-out with you."

Rawhide shrugged. "I dunno," he drawled, "unless Turner has powder smoke in his veins and an itchy trigger finger. We got a fair price, and we cleaned up our range of old stuff."

"Yeah," Tad Lacy said thoughtfully. "But if Packer is going to ship mebbe, why is he venting these brands and burning a road brand?"

"He bought our critters, and he paid cash," Rawhide answered, but his grey eyes were thoughtful, too. "What Packer does with them is his own business and none of ours."

"What Colt Turner does is going to be some of your business," Tom Owens reminded. "And I'm betting a cookie it has something to do with Dave Packer. Who's this lathy gent with the patch over his off eye?"

A tall lean man dusted the palms of his hands on the heavy bull-hide chaps which incased his legs. He wore a patch of black cloth on his right eye, over which he had pulled his battered stetson.

"That's Patch Watson," Rawhide explained. "He lost that eye in a saloon brawl down Laredo way, but he can see plenty good with the other one. Now he uses his head and lets Bull Carter do all the skull-and-knuckle work."

" Tally two Diamond Double R cows," Watson called over his shoulder to a short cowboy who was keeping the book. " Make 'em Sprawling D Bar P, and call it a day."

" Which means they've finished their road branding," Tom Owens remarked, as he lighted up an old briar pipe. " I'll be glad when this outfit has cleared out."

Rawhide Runyan was staring at a bunch of aged stock, and a peculiar expression was in his slitted grey eyes. He could tell one of his cows from a distance; they had been foundation stock when he had been building up his herd.

A big man left one of the fires across the clearing and bowlegged over to stand beside Patch Watson. He was Bull Carter, a mass of bone and muscle from thick ankles to his short bull neck, and his beefy face was scarred from many battles. He squared his incredibly wide shoulders, and addressed Rawhide : " Something wrong ? "

" Yeah," Rawhide replied crisply. " Cut those two young cows out of the bunch. They're coming three-year-olds this spring when they are due to calve. I sold your boss only the old she-stuff."

" We ain't cutting nothing," Bull Carter said flatly. " The boss took your tally and he paid cash at the graveside."

Slow Joe Hill came riding up from the forks of the creek on a deep-chested bay. He stopped near Rawhide, swung to the ground facing Carter, and spoke from the corner of his mouth.

" I knew you'd see those young critters, Rawhide. You cut out the cows—I'll take care of Bull Carter."

" You can take care of me first," Carter interrupted. " I've heard about you, owlhooter. You ain't changed much since you let on to ride the straight-and-narrow, but you can't rustle any part of our stuff."

Slow Joe Hill clenched his fists as he heard himself being called a rustler and an outlaw. He paused a moment, waiting for some word from his young boss, but Rawhide remained silent. This was a personal matter between Joe and Carter, involving Slow Joe's honour.

" How you want it ? " Bull Carter asked.

" No holds barred," Slow Joe grunted.

The ex-outlaw shed his laziness like an old coat. He leaped at Bull Carter who braced himself for the charge. Joe braked with his high heels and side-stepped, lashing out with his big left fist to clip Carter on the jaw. As the Sprawling D Bar P man was jolted off balance, Slow Joe crossed with a right which would have broken his opponent's neck, if it weren't so bull-like. Carter took the heavy blow and drew his head down between his powerful shoulders.

Rawhide Runyan turned slightly, hearing the sound of hoofs coming down to the creek.

Dave Packer and Colt Turner were watching the fight. Turner had a hand on his low-slung six-shooter.

" Stay out of it, Turner," Runyan warned him, with a chilling hum in his deep voice. " They're matched even, and no holds barred."

The cashier dropped his hand away from his gun, and Rawhide turned to watch the fight.

Bull Carter brought one up from his boot tops, but the blow never landed. Slow Joe beat him to the punch with a short left jab to the ribs, spinning Carter round in a half circle. Carter went with the blow to complete the circle, and Joe followed up with a driving right.

Rawhide caught his breath when Carter grabbed Joe's arm with both hands, pulled down and bucked up at the same time, and threw Joe crashing to the short grass.

The ex-outlaw landed on his back with the breath jarred from his lungs. He was stunned for a moment. Before he could get up Bull Carter was aiming kicks at his head with his sharp-pointed boots.

Slow Joe took one on the top of the head before he could cover up. Then his thick arms went about his face and head and he twisted sidewise and went into a looping roll. Carter was after him like a bulldog, kicking with both feet.

The downed man caught one of the boots and pulled with all his strength, jerking the Sprawling D Bar P ramrod's feet from under him. On his feet now, Slow Joe caught Carter behind the knees with both forearms, vising down with an elbow lock. Carter tried to kick himself free, but his opponent lifted him a foot off the ground.

Slow Joe jumped a bit and drove his captive's head down like a pile driver, adding his own weight to the plunge. Three times Joe repeated the punishment.

Then, a knife flashed in the right hand of Bull Carter ! Rawhide called a warning. Slow Joe saw the blade flash in the sun. He dug in with his heels, leaned back, and started to circle.

Colt Turner was swaying in his saddle, punching with both hands, as an excitable man will do when he sees an opening from the side lines. When the huge bulk of Bull Carter began to swing through the air, Turner slapped down for his six-shooter.

Rawhide Runyan was watching Slow Joe, and he did not see Turner's move until it was too late. Just as Turner's .45 cleared leather, Slow Joe Hill loosed his hold.

Bull Carter hurtled through the air like a sack of spuds. His body seemed to rise in flight with his bullet head tucked down between his wide shoulders. The gun exploded in Colt Turner's hand as Carter struck him waist-high and tore the gun fighter from his saddle. Both men crashed to the ground with Colt Turner underneath.

Carter came slowly to his feet, shaking his head. Slow Joe danced up to him, ignoring Colt Turner, who was lying motionless on the bunch grass. Joe put Carter in position with a short left jab to the chin, which was followed instantly by a resounding thud as Joe put all his weight and muscle behind his right fist, crashing it solidly against Carter's tilted jaw.

Bull Carter grunted and swayed forward. Slow Joe sidestepped, brought down a clubbing blow on the stunned man's head and Carter measured his length face down, ploughing a little furrow in the grass roots with his rocky chin.

" Drop it, Watson ! " The barking voice of Rawhide Runyan cut through the air. Patch Watson slogged his half-drawn six-shooter back into leather. Rawhide's gun had leaped to his hand with the hammer eared back for a shot.

Packer was sitting motionless in the saddle when Rawhide swivelled his gun to cover the big cattle buyer.

" Don't be a fool, Patch," Packer warned the one-eyed man. " It was a fair fight, and Carter got his needings. What caused the ruckus, Runyan ? "

Rawhide holstered his six-shooter and pointed to the two young cows in the herd of culls. Dave Packer stared at the vented Diamond Double R brand and turned on Patch Watson with a snarl in his voice.

" Cut that young she-stuff out of our bunch, Patch ! You and Bull both know better than to brand young strays just because they happened to drift into our herd. Don't give me any excuses. Cut those critters out ! "

Patch Watson clamped his lips together and mounted his horse. He was mumbling to himself as he rode into the herd of culls to obey orders. Packer made his apologies like a man.

" Sorry, Runyan. Watson and Carter should have known better, and I'm thankful you didn't kill them both."

" I'll talk for myself," a savage voice interrupted.

Rawhide Runyan turned in time to see Colt Turner come

to his feet. Turner was slapping for his gun, forgetting that it had been knocked from his hand. Rawhide spurred Shadow as he threw himself sidewise from the saddle.

Colt Turner threw up his right hand and slapped for a hide-out gun in a holster under his left arm. Rawhide's driving body hit the gun slammer shoulder-high, and Colt Turner was knocked sprawling for the second time. But a half turn had saved him from the full force of Runyan's drive, and Turner was the first on his feet.

Rawhide rolled up just in time to see the gun-proddy cashier launch a terrific kick with his right boot. Instead of going back, Rawhide dived at the kicking boot, breaking the force of the kick. He jerked up, spilling Turner backward. Rawhide's face was a cold mask as he waited for the treacherous gun fighter to get to his feet.

As he did, Rawhide danced in without saying a word. His flying fists battered Turner's face to a pulp, inflicting punishment without knocking the gun passer down. A sizzling right landed squarely on Turner's hawk-like nose, bringing a gush of crimson, and taking most of the fight out of Turner.

Rawhide feinted with his left, then lunged in behind his driving right fist. When Turner went down in a fog of unconsciousness, Rawhide turned slowly to face big Dave Packer.

"That's twice your cashier has made a gun play against me, Packer," he said. "That's one more chance than I usually give a glory hunter. If there's a third time——"

"I'll start my drive in an hour," Packer promised earnestly. "I can't figure out what's got into the boys, but I need them in my business. You, Patch!" he called to Watson, who was riding back from the creek. "Get a bucket from the cooky and slop down these two sleepers. We're starting our drive before noon, and I don't want any more trouble."

Patch Watson rode up with a bucket half filled with creek water. He dismounted, poured the water on Turner and Carter, and was back in the saddle before the two men came whooshing to their feet.

Dave Packer rode his horse between his two warriors and Rawhide Runyan. "Head for the wagon, you two buskies!" he roared. "Any more trouble from either of you and you draw your time!"

CHAPTER IX

RUSTLERS

RAWHIDE RUNYAN sat his Shadow horse in the middle of a ring of Strip cattlemen, watching Dave Packer start his trail drive. Bull Carter and Colt Turner rode at the point positions.

Eight D Bar P men were handling the strung-out herd, with the prime beef leading off, the she-stuff and the old bulls bringing up the drag. Dave Packer rode over to the cattlemen as the last culls crossed the creek ford.

" Sorry we had that bit of trouble, men," Packer said earnestly. " The boys were drinking last night, touchy as a she-bear with new cubs this morning. No hard feelings on my part, and I hope you'll consider trading with me again next fall."

" A feller can consider," old Tom Owens answered, but there was no warmth in his gruff voice. " It's none of my business, but I'd get a new cashier and ramrod if I was you. So long."

No one offered to shake hands and, after a pause, Dave Packer waved a hand and followed his trail herd.

Rawhide had lost some of his grimness when he turned to face his neighbours. " We've sold our shippers, pocketed the money, and now we better get back to our own outfits," he said with a smile. " Me, I'm staying close to the Diamond Double R until spring."

" That goes for me, too," Slow Joe chimed in. " I got a lot of sleep to make up when the rains set in. Adios, cow fellers."

It was nearing midnight when Rawhide and Joe rode into the big ranch yard, but a light was burning in the kitchen. Limpy Watson came to the door and called in his high-pitched voice :

" Grub's on the table ! Come and get it ! "

After filling the mangers with hay, the two saddle-weary men stumbled to the kitchen in the darkness. The old cook had thick steaks and shoe-string potatoes heaped on hot plates, salt-rising biscuits, and Dutch-oven beans. He was eager to hear the news, but Slow Joe told him to wait until they had ironed the wrinkles from their bellies. Then he pushed back his chair with a word of praise for the grub.

" Ain't a better *cucinero* than you in Arizona, Limpy. I

aim to lay around here all winter and get hawgfat. Me and
Rawhide had some trouble to-day, but we got it ironed out.
A couple of those D Bar P rustlers tried to get away with
some of our young she-stuff, but it didn't work."

" You know your business, boss," Limpy said slowly.
" But I wouldn't have sold off foundation stock if I was you."

" I didn't," Rawhide said. " I just got rid of all the old
culls."

" Come again," Limpy muttered. " Says which ? "

" Old stuff," Rawhide repeated. " That's what the fight
was about. Bull Carter and Patch Watson had vented two
of our young cows. By the way, is this one-eyed Watson
any kin of yours ? "

" Just my stepbrother," Limpy answered acidly. " I
wouldn't trust him with snow water, and let him melt it
himself. Now tell me why you sold a hundred head of our
young she-stuff to Packer. Three of his riders came up here
the day before yesterday with a note from you. They took
a hundred head of Diamond Double R cows and drove down
through Dark Canyon."

Rawhide Runyan sat very still for a long moment. He
stared at Slow Joe with eyes that did not see. After a long
silence, the cowhand spoke in a strained voice :

" Let's roll in and get a good night's sleep, Joe. It might
be our last for quite a while. Come daylight, you and me
are hitting the trail."

Slow Joe got up slowly, pushed back from the table and
walked to a pair of antlers over the fireplace in the big front
room. He returned carrying two heavy Winchester rifles.
He handed one to Rawhide and began to clean the one he
kept for himself.

" There's a hunter's moon, Rawhide," Joe said in his
rumbling voice. " That's when the wolves begin to run,
and it's always open season on wolves. This time you and
me're fighting for our own stock."

Rawhide, deep in thought, made no answer. He had
culled his herd thoroughly. His foundation stock was worth
fifty dollars a head on the hoof. His grey eyes narrowed
suddenly as Slow Joe's words struck him.

" Mebbe not just us, Joe," he said musingly. " If Dave
Packer rustled our critters, he'd do the same to the Anchor T
and the T O Connected. Let's hit the hay."

Limpy Watson had breakfast ready when the two men
rolled out of their blankets with the first grey fingers of daybreak tugging at their eyelids. Slow Joe mumbled about

what he was going to do to Bull Carter and big Dave Packer. Rawhide ate in silence, grim-faced, with a smoky glare in his narrowed eyes.

" I double-grained the hosses and fitted out a pack animal," Limpy remarked. " Loaded it with a greasy-sack outfit so's you and Joe could do your own cooking. Good huntin', and may yore shadows never grow less."

Rawhide walked to the barn without speaking. He mounted Shadow, stroking the black's sleek neck thoughtfully.

" We'll head for the Anchor T first, Joe. Mebbe I won't say so again, but when we come up on those rustlers, no holds are barred ! "

Slow Joe blinked. His young boss was changing for the better. This made the second time he had been given the go-ahead, like giving a blank cheque to a man you can trust all the way.

" Bend the lead, boss," Joe said slowly. " Big Dave Packer might be smooth, but he can be whittled down. You've got a score of your own fo settle with Colt Turner, so remember the promise you made to his boss."

" I'll remember," Rawhide answered grimly, and rode out of the big barn.

Tad Lacy rode out to meet them as Rawhide and Joe neared the Anchor T. Lacy spurred his horse, waving both arms, and slid his bronc to a stop in front of them.

" I've been robbed, Rawhide ! " Lacy yelled. " Colt Turner and Patch Watson laid for me as I was riding up Big Dark. They took my sack of beef money, shot my horse, and I had to hoof it the last three miles ! "

" How about your young cows ? " Rawhide asked.

" I said I'd been robbed ! " Lacy shouted. " They gave my cooky a note the day before yesterday and drove down the canyon with a hundred head. We've got to do something ! "

" Something besides yelling our heads off," Rawhide commented dryly. " Fall in, and we'll drop over to see Tom Owens."

The old cattleman came riding to meet them as they cantered down the trail to the T O Connected. Owens wore a bandage round his white head and carried a Winchester rifle in his gnarled hands.

" Rustlers ! " he shouted, as he came within hearing distance. " Bull Carter buffaloed me over the skull with his six-shooter. Another big gent covered me with a cocked gun from back in the brush. Looked like Dave Packer, but I couldn't be sure before the lights went out. When I roused round and rode home, one of my boys tells me I've sold a hundred and fifty head of young she-stuff to Packer, day before yesterday. I'm riding gun sign on that rustling crew, and they won't get far ! "

" Getting to be a habit," Rawhide remarked. " Ain't that old Jim Williams riding his spurs through the brush ? "

" I've been robbed ! " Williams yelled the bad news. " Fifty head of young cows and two thousand in money. The fellers were strangers, but they straddled D Bar P cayuses. Shore glad I met you rannies. We can start right out after those rustlers ! "

" Lay yore hackles, old mossy-horn," Tom Owens said gruffly. " Every one of us is in the same boat, and this here is a man hunt. It might be a long one, so me and Lacy will ride back and load pack-horses with some eating vittles. We'll meet down at the crossing and start from there. Keep your powder dry, and mind you don't spit against the wind."

As the two old cattlemen rode away, Rawhide nudged his horse closer to Jim Williams.

" We'll ride down to the Circle C, and you can pack a horse with grain," Rawhide suggested. " We might need it. I've got enough grub in my pack for you."

" By dogies, it's getting as bad as it was when you first rode up here to the Strip, Rawhide," Williams said testily. " The more outlaws and rustlers we clean out, the more comes in. You reckon we ought to notify Sheriff Jim Blaine over at Rainbow ? "

" Send a man to notify him after we're gone," Rawhide answered. " I don't aim to do my hunting this time from behind a law star. Unless my guess is wrong, I won't be riding for long with you fellers."

" You've got to stick with us, Rawhide," Williams argued, and it was evident that he was worried. " This whole outfit falls apart every time you go chousing through the brush and over the hills. Why ain't you staying with us ? "

" You remember that pack-horse loaded with money ? " Rawhide asked. " Dave Packer won't want to lose his cash. If he leaves his men, I'm leaving mine to run him down. Here's the Circle C. Joe and me will wait up for you at the crossing."

CHAPTER X

STAMPEDE

RAWHIDE RUNYAN looked over his forces gathered at the creek crossing at the lower end of Dark Canyon. Eight fighting men, including himself, all armed with six-shooters and rifles.

They would be outnumbered, but Rawhide intended to wage an offensive war. Dave Packer's crew would have to protect their herd to prevent a stampede. They could travel only as fast as their chuck wagon. Slow Joe Hill was telling some of the riding hands that the bars were let down with no holds barred.

Rawhide gave the go-ahead and led the way down the valley. Every mile counted, and they would make camp when darkness overtook them. Each man carried a blanket and his slicker behind the cantle of his saddle. Runyan's eyes brightened as he noted the oiled slicker covering Slow Joe's bed-roll.

The party made camp and cooked supper in a dry wash some twenty-five miles from their starting-point. Old Tom Owens remarked that the trail herd couldn't be more than ten miles ahead. Rawhide nodded. He asked Slow Joe to bring the pack-horses closer to camp, then explained a plan he had evolved while riding south.

" We want to keep our saddle horses fresh, men. Dave Packer will have to post night herders after he beds down his herd. We can give his crew plenty to do if we stampede the herd, and it won't take but three men to do it. Slow Joe, Tom Owens, and myself will saddle the pack-horses to do that little job."

Every man in the party wanted to ride along, but Runyan told them that too many cooks would spoil the soup. It was a part of his plan to keep Dave Packer in ignorance as to the identity of the night riders.

The three men stopped their horses on a little rise, after they'd been riding an hour.

" Camp fire below, Rawhide," Slow Joe murmured, but Runyan had already seen the blaze.

As they watched, three men rode up to the fire. Three more rode out to stand the graveyard trick.

After waiting until the rest of the D Bar P crew had rolled

into their blankets around the fire, Runyan jerked his head and rode wide to circle the sleeping herd.

Orders had been given ; each man knew what to do Slow Joe pulled the saddle strings which held his slicker, knowing that Tom Owens and Rawhide Runyan were doing the same thing. Those dry slickers would crack and pop like pistols when waved in the backwash of a running horse.

Rawhide was to ride in the middle with Tom Owens and Slow Joe to the right and left. The bunch grass deadened the hoofbeats of their horses as they approached the sleeping herd. Packer's night herders were singing softly to soothe the weary cattle as they rode around the far edges in a circle.

Rawhide Runyan pulled the neckerchief up over his chin and nose as he came close to the bedded herd. His six-shooter roared twice to signal Slow Joe and Tom Owens. The herd lurched up with bellows of terror. Rawhide began to wave his yellow slicker, yelling at the top of his voice.

Answering yells came from right and left as his two partners closed in with slickers popping. Now the herd was running madly, heading straight for the sleeping camp. The three D Bar P night herders were far out in front, trying to mill the stampeding herd in a circle.

Tom Owens was waiting over to the right, with Slow Joe angling over from the left. Rawhide rode between them, and the three men circled wide as they rode back to their own camp. Tad Lacy met the three stampeders as they rode into the dry wash and swung to the ground.

" We doused our fire with sand when we heard that stampede coming this way," he told Rawhide. " I'd say they were short-handed."

" That's the answer," Rawhide answered confidently. " Dave Packer split his crew up for a good reason. Part of them are driving the young stock they rustled from us, and right now we are between the two herds. We'll be moving south at daybreak. We should overtake our foundation stock before night."

" They've got a good three-day start on us," Tad Lacy said thoughtfully, and then he corrected himself. " Less than two days—the way we rode to-day—and we can travel more than twice as fast as they can, account of them walking the herd."

Rawhide rolled up in his blankets after pulling off his boots. He awakened four hours later as the moon was sloping down over the Western hills. His companions grumbled as they pulled on their boots, but the complaints stopped when Runyan told them that they would ride until daybreak and then make a breakfast camp. A fire now might lead the sleepless D Bar P crew to their hiding-place, and spoil any chance of surprising the other crew with Dave Packer.

Runyan felt certain that Dave Packer, Bull Carter, and Colt Turner were riding with the young stock. He talked quietly with Tom Owens and Tad Lacy when they stopped to cook breakfast beside a brawling stream. The water was clear, but both banks were trampled, sign of a trail herd travelling south.

Slow Joe was making meat sandwiches for lunch, using a double-edged hunting-knife to cut the heavy white bread. They would eat a hot supper if they were lucky. One of the Anchor T cowboys would follow slowly with the pack-horses. The saddle stock had been grained during the stop, and each man carried a measure of oats in a sack behind his cantle.

" Boots and saddles," Rawhide ordered, and swung aboard Shadow.

The chill of autumn made the horses travel up good, but Tom Owens complained that it didn't help the misery in his legs. The seven men halted for a noonday rest in a small canyon between two ridges. Rawhide Runyan urged his black cow horse up the south slope, shaded his eyes with his grey stetson and rode abruptly back to join his mates.

" Dust cloud to the south, not more than six-seven miles," he reported. " We can give the horses a good rest and still catch up with that trail herd by early afternoon."

Every man in the crew began to check his weapons. The horses munched their oats in the warm noonday sun. Rawhide Runyan ate his dry sandwiches, studying the faces of the other men. All were grim and silent as they figured their losses, sensing that show-down was near. Rifles were held ready in rope-burned hands as Rawhide Runyan gave the order to ride.

After riding an hour, Slow Joe and Tom Owens moved up to travel with Runyan. A fast half-hour ride would bring them close to the stolen herd of young cows, and the old cattleman asked for day orders.

" We'll fan out in a half circle, with each man picking himself a target," Runyan told them. " Don't shoot unless we're fired upon first, and let me do the talking to Dave Packer ! "

The word was passed back as the Strip cattlemen drew

closer to the rustled herd. A single rider was bringing up the drag. Rawhide identified him as Patch Watson when the cowboy turned in the saddle before racing up ahead to warn Dave Packer.

Rawhide Runyan smiled grimly when Packer dropped back with three men : Patch Watson, Colt Turner, and barn-shouldered Bull Carter. As the herd slowed down, another man rode out from a slanting canyon and joined the Packer crowd.

Rawhide eyed the newcomer narrowly as he stopped his horse a dozen paces from the Packer crew.

" You wanted to see me ? " Packer asked pleasantly. " I might warn you that I have six men hidden on both sides of this draw. You can see their rifles poking out of the brush."

" I want to talk to you, you blasted rustler ! " Tad Lacy exploded. " We came down here to get that young she-stuff you drove ahead of the beef you paid for ! "

" I have bills of sale for every head I drove out of the Strip," Packer replied confidently. " Will you look over my papers, Inspector Green ? "

The newcomer rode out and took a sheaf of papers from Packer. After looking them over carefully, he nodded his head. He wore the badge of a cattle inspector, but none of the Strip cattlemen had ever seen him before.

Rawhide Runyan said as much as he addressed Dave Packer. " This Green might be a ringer, Packer. John Parsons is the inspector for this district."

" Inspector Parsons has been transferred south," Green explained. " Do you question my authority ? "

" That's right," Runyan answered promptly. " I'd like to see the bill of sale I gave Dave Packer. Pay no mind to those rifles up the draw, boys," he told his companions. " They're dummies, and two of them have fallen out of the brush where they were planted ! "

" Here's your bill of sale," Green said quickly, but the Strip cattlemen had already seen the fallen rifles.

Rawhide took the paper, held it up to the light, and turned to Dave Packer.

" I wrote my bill of sale with pen and ink," he told the big cattle buyer. " Some of this writing has been rubbed out and the figures changed to give you a hundred head more of Diamond Double R stock than you paid for ! "

" Careful, Runyan," Packer warned. " Them's fighting words."

" That's right," Runyan answered evenly. " You're a rustler ; now make your fight ! "

When Dave Packer made no move to back up his war talk, Rawhide glanced to the side. A tall man was riding in from the south, a gleaming star on his faded vest. Runyan's jaw dropped. He knew the white-haired sheriff before the law-man introduced himself.

" Sheriff Matt Boulder of Pima County, gents. What's the ruckus about ? "

" I'm Inspector Green, taking over John Parson's place," Green interrupted quickly. " Here's my credentials, sheriff."

Sheriff Boulder looked over the credentials and nodded slowly. " They are genuine, Rawhide Runyan," he said stiffly. " I happen to know that Green switched jobs with Parsons. What's your grievance, young feller ? "

Rawhide explained the deal with the cattle buyer, giving facts and figures.

" I represent law and order in this county, Runyan," the sheriff said sternly as Rawhide finished. " If Inspector Green passes this herd, you have recourse in the civil courts. Looks to me like Packer bought your stock and paid cash for what he bought."

" That's right," Rawhide agreed. " He paid for what he bought, but not for what he *rustled* ! On top of that, he and his crew took back most of the money they paid out, at the points of guns ! "

A murmur went up from the Packer crew. Hands slapped at belt guns, stopping when the Strip cattlemen swung their rifles into position. Sheriff Boulder drew his .45 Peacemaker and covered Rawhide Runyan.

" Call off your war party, Runyan," he commanded sternly. " I'll empty your saddle if one of your men fires a shot ! "

Rawhide Runyan sat perfectly still, staring into the muzzle of the sheriff's cocked six-shooter. He had always helped the law, had never fought against it. The bills of sale, written with pencil, would probably work in favour of Packer in a civil court. The fate of the rustled herd would be decided by the evidence contained in the changed bill of sale written with pen and ink.

" You win this round, Packer," Rawhide finally conceded in temporary defeat. " Sheriff Boulder, you ramrod the law in Pima County. I insist that you hold this bill of sale of mine."

" I'll keep the paper," Boulder agreed.

" I'll take that paper, sheriff," Packer contradicted. " I'll need it to sell my stock."

" You've got law work to do, Matt Boulder," old Tom
Owens interrupted hotly.   " Arrest Colt Turner and Bull
Carter for robbery ! "

Sheriff Boulder held up his left hand as voices began to
murmur and grow louder.   He tucked the bill of sale in an
inside vest pocket and turned to Tom Owens, with his gun
still covering Rawhide.

" Have you any witnesses ? " he asked the old cattleman.

Tom Owens shook his head glumly.   Tad Lacy and Jim
Williams were in the same fix, but Owens did not give up
without a struggle.

" I've got witnesses about the rustling," he growled.   " It's
your duty to arrest these rustlers."

" You'll have to ride in and sign the complaint before I
can issue a warrant," the sheriff explained.   " It's quite a
way to Tucson."

" Fall back, men," Runyan ordered, without raising his voice.
" There's quite a difference between law and justice, and I
never held no truck with courts.   I'll ride down to Tucson
later.   Packer can't sell my stock without the bill of sale."

" I'll ride up to your camp later, Runyan," Sheriff Boulder
called after the retreating cattlemen.   " I want to have a
talk now with Inspector Green here."

CHAPTER XI

LAW—AND JUSTICE

RAWHIDE RUNYAN rode out of the canyon without answering.
When he was sure that his party could not be seen, he held up
his hand for a halt.   When the cattlemen had gathered round
him, he spoke in a low voice.

" There's something wrong, men.   Packer is trapped unless
he can get back my bill of sale, and Sheriff Boulder is all alone
with those rustling wolves.   Let's put our horses to this hill,
and drop into the canyon from the other side."

Taking the lead, Rawhide put Shadow to the steep slope
and gave the black cow horse its head.   Riding like Indians,
the experienced cowboys went over the top and slid their
horses down the sandy slope, just behind the herd of young
cows.   Leaving their horses in a brush trap, the seven men
began to creep toward Packer's crew, keeping to the shelter of
rock nests.

Runyan held up a hand as the sound of loud voices came

from the mouth of the valley canyon. Peering round a creosote bush, Rawhide could see Dave Packer staring at Sheriff Matt Boulder. The cattle buyer shook his head slowly to signal someone off to the side.

Colt Turner stepped out of the brush with his pistol roaring one shot, ambushing the unsuspecting officer. Matt Boulder was knocked backward over the cantle of his saddle. Dave Packer jumped to the ground, running toward the fallen sheriff.

Before Rawhide could whisper an order, Tad Lacy fired a shot from his rifle. The slug struck the ground in front of Dave Packer and brought him to a sliding stop. The big cattle buyer leaped for his horse as Rawhide leaped into the clear facing Colt Turner.

Runyan landed in the clearing with his boots spaced wide. His right hand ripped down to his moulded holster ; his six-shooter shed leather with gunfire blazing from the end of the long barrel.

Colt Turner triggered a shot into the air as he was battered from the saddle with a boot hung up in the stirrup. The spooked horse shied to the side, showing Patch Watson, who was bringing down his gun for a sneak shot.

Rawhide side-stepped just as Watson pressed the trigger. The bullet tugged at the cowboy's calfskin vest. Rawhide squeezed off a slow shot, and Patch Watson had an extra eye in his forehead from which he would never see.

The Strip cattlemen were firing their Winchester rifles and cutting down the fighting D Bar P crew. A high-pitched voice shouted from behind a clump of prickly pear, the voice of Inspector Green : " I'm neutral ; don't shoot ! "

Rawhide gave an order for his men to hold their fire. The cattle inspector stepped into the clear.

" Hold him so, Rawhide," Slow Joe said cautiously, " while I slip through this herd of she-stuff."

Rawhide motioned for Green to come forward with both hands in the air. He could see Joe going through the herd.

" Did you see Colt Turner shoot the sheriff ? " Rawhide questioned Green.

" It all happened so fast," Green faltered. " I don't know who fired the shot."

" Did you see Dave Packer try to get that bill of sale from the sheriff's vest pocket ? "

" I was hiding," Green admitted, hanging his head.

" Drop that gun, Bull Carter ! " A deep, rasping voice gave the order from behind a nest of rocks. " Walk out with your meat hooks reaching for sky ! "

Bull Carter came from his hiding-place with Slow Joe Hill driving him on the muzzle of his six-shooter. Carter scowled until he saw the bodies of the dead trail drivers who had forted up behind rocks. The ruddy hue drained from his beefy face when he stared at Colt Turner's lifeless body, but he regained some of his composure at seeing Inspector Green under Rawhide's gun.

Slow Joe told Carter to stop. He holstered his gun as he stepped back and said softly : " Turn round, ramrod ! "

The D Bar P foreman turned with both hands high above his head. He lowered them quickly when he discovered that Joe's gun was back in leather. Carter sneered with his thick lips as Joe unbuckled his gun belt and tossed it to Rawhide Runyan.

" I'm going to take you apart, rustler," Slow Joe warned. " I never did like a rustler even when I was riding the owlhoot trail ! "

Bull Carter glanced around. Then, without warning, he whirled back and leaped at Slow Joe.

Joe came in under the lunge and bucked up with his powerful shoulders, spilling Carter in a sprawling heap on the rock-studded ground. Carter rolled over sluggishly. He stiffened as the fingers of his right hand touched the gun which Colt Turner had dropped.

Slow Joe saw the move and made a diving tackle. His shoulder nudged the D Bar P ramrod viciously. His thick arms closed round Bull Carter just under the armpits. The gun flew from Carter's hand as both men crashed to the ground, but Slow Joe had his favourite hold.

Sinking his jaw deep into his opponent's shoulder, Slow Joe pushed up to his feet. His huge hands were locked in the small of Carter's back, squeezing the big rustler until the foreman's lungs strained for air.

Slow Joe raised his victim until Carter's boots dangled in the air. Joe's shirt began to split at the seams as his muscles tightened. Rawhide Runyan and Tom Owens had seen Joe crush a victim in his famous bear trap, but neither would interfere. It was Joe who made his own decision.

" Give up head, ramrod. You buffaloed Tom Owens over the skull with the barrel of your cutter. Come clean before I lower the boom ! "

Bull Carter caught a short breath and began to struggle. Slow Joe tightened his muscles, and Carter stopped struggling. The bull-necked man's ribs were sore from the terrific squeeze, which he knew could break his back like a dry stick.

" I slugged the old mossyhorn," Carter panted. " But Dave Packer had Owens under his gun ! "

Joe loosed his hold a trifle to allow Carter another breath of life-saving air. Rawhide Runyan stared as Joe caught his glance and slowly winked his left eye.

" Talk up, Bull," Joe prompted. " Your boss changed the bills of sales. If you come clean, I might let you live to make hair ropes down at Yuma prison."

Bull Carter talked freely, hanging in Slow Joe's powerful arms. He told of the robberies, how Dave Packer had sent men to bring down the young cows.

Tom Owens came out from behind a cropping of rocks leading a laden horse. Slow Joe grinned and lowered Bull Carter to the ground.

" This is Packer's money horse," Tom Owens explained. He threw off the ties which held the two heavy sacks. " I ought to have three thousand dollars in this cache, all in fifty-dollar bills. If it's my money, every bill will be marked with my T O Connected brand. I used an indelible pencil this time."

Dumping the money on the ground, the old cattleman sorted through the currency. He picked up one sheaf and tossed it aside. A small T O Connected was printed on each bill.

" That's good enough for me," a voice boomed hoarsely, and Sheriff Matt Boulder got slowly to his feet.

" I ain't a ghost," Boulder explained, and pointed to a deep-rolled scar on his silver badge. " Turner's slug hit my badge, and the star belted me over the heart, knocking me out. Now you do some fast talking, Inspector Green ! "

Rawhide Runyan's face hardened while he listened to the frightened inspector's confession. Green told how he had accepted two thousand dollars to pass the rustled cows.

" You and Bull Carter are both under arrest," Sheriff Boulder announced sternly, and he handcuffed the two men together. " Get going, cowboy," Boulder growled at Rawhide Runyan. " You want justice, and I'm the law. Take on out after that rustler boss, Dave Packer ! "

CHAPTER XII

LOBO

SHERIFF MATT BOULDER had remarked that it was a long ride to the old pueblo of Tucson. Rawhide Runyan left the scene of the battle with Shadow in a high lope. He drew the black horse to a walk when he turned a bend in the long valley. His mind was working hard while he read the tracks of a running horse.

Putting himself in Dave Packer's place, Rawhide asked what he would do. The money-laden horse was back at the scene of the fight. The herd of young cows was grazing at the upper end of the grassy valley. The trail herd of bought stock was two days out from the Strip, but Packer didn't know about the stampede. Eight tough cowboys would give the cattle buyer a fighting chance, and Dave Packer was a gambler.

That was the way Rawhide Runyan read the sign. He nodded confirmation of his shrewd reasoning when he came to a fork in the trail where a running horse had turned to swing north. Dave Packer was going back to salvage what he could of his losses.

Rawhide drew his gun and checked the loads in the smoke-grimed weapon. The cattle buyer would be desperate when he discovered that his big trail herd had been stampeded and scattered. Inspector Green had all the bills of sale. His cashier, Colt Turner, was dead.

Runyan came to the place where Packer must have made his decision. Now the hoofprints were deeper and farther apart. Packer had lifted his horse into a run.

The cowboy touched Shadow with a blunted spur, and the big black bellied down in a mile-eating run. Now the cattle trail led through a motte of scrub oak ; it would end in the valley where the herd had stampeded the night before. Daylight would last perhaps an hour longer.

The autumn sun was flanking down behind the western hills when Rawhide left the thick brush and reined to a stop to study the long, broad valley. Cattle were grazing on the bunch grass, except for a little group near the mouth of a sandy wash. These were staring intently at the canyon, a sure sign that they had been disturbed.

While Rawhide watched, a party of mounted men appeared at the lower end of the valley, riding north. He could make out two men riding close together, the handcuffed Bull Carter and Inspector Green. Only one man could be waiting in the little canyon up ahead, and that man would be big Dave Packer.

Rawhide put Shadow to the brush and slanted north-west. What had been cover for Packer would provide him with the same, and the black horse knew every foot of the trail. If he could come in behind Dave Packer before the short twilight settled over the range, Dave Packer would either shoot or give up the gun.

They topped the ridge of a steep slope. Rawhide stopped to blow his horse and dismounted for a look-see. Keeping below the brush tops to avoid being sky-lined, Runyan crawled up to the crest and stared down into the sandy draw.

A tall man was standing just inside the entrance from the valley, staring at something intently. Rawhide knew that Packer had seen the Strip cattlemen, riding with Sheriff Matt Boulder and his prisoners. Packer was gripping a Winchester in his hands. Once or twice he squinted down the long barrel as though he were testing the sights.

Leaving Shadow to graze on mesquite beans in a little clearing, Rawhide loosed his .45 Peacemaker Colt. He moved down the trail with the stealth of an Indian. He was only fifty yards from Dave Packer when the brush thinned out.

If Packer had not been watching the Strip cattlemen so intently, he might have seen Rawhide inching ever closer to him. The big cattle buyer raised the rifle to his shoulder, cuddled the smooth stock against his cheek, and slowly squeezed off a shot. Rawhide rose from his last bit of cover when the rifle barked.

" Drop that long gun, Packer ! "

The cattle buyer was levering a fresh shell into the breech when Rawhide barked the order. Recognizing Runyan's voice, Dave Packer dropped the smoking Winchester to the ground. Turning slowly, he raised both hands.

" Don't shoot ! " Packer muttered hoarsely—his teeth clamping together when he saw Rawhide Runyan facing him with empty hands.

" I'm giving you an outlaw's chance, Packer," Rawhide offered. " I'm not any part of the law, and I'm not riding behind a star. You'll get a fair trial—if you want one ! "

" I want one," Packer accepted instantly. His tone of voice changed as he asked : " Is Colt Turner dead, and Matt Boulder ? "

" Yes and no." Rawhide eyed the cattle buyer steadily. " Turner is ; the sheriff isn't."

" I figured you'd tail me to Tucson," Packer said conversationally. " You must have read my mind."

" When I'm tracking down a wolf, I try to reason out what I'd do if I were the lobo," Rawhide replied tersely.

" If I'm a lobo, it's my night to howl," Packer stated without emotion. " I got Inspector Green with my Winchester, and he won't talk in court."

" What court ? " Rawhide demanded.

Dave Packer shrugged. " So you want it that way ? " he murmured. " You want old Judge Colt to decide between you and me ? "

" Yeah," Rawhide drawled. " I want it that way."

The long shadows of twilight were settling down over the valley behind Packer, leaving a patch of hazy sunshine at the mouth of the canyon. It would be dark soon, but before night came, the law would block off escape.

" I came up here to ruin you, Runyan," Packer stated coldly. " I wanted to toll you down Tucson way, but I didn't know about the stampede. I'm the fastest gun hand in Arizona Territory ! "

Rawhide Runyan experienced the peculiar thrill which always gripped him when a gun-hung owlhooter challenged his speed. " Gun proud," his neighbours said of him, " with powder smoke in his veins."

" I offered you a fair trial," Rawhide said. His voice was thick and harsh. " My offer still goes. Turn slowly, and pitch your cutter to the ground."

" I'm not giving up," Packer refused casually, and there was no trace of fear in his steady blue eyes. " I'll leave it up to old Judge Colt. Make your pass ! "

The racing pulse in Rawhide's fingers had settled down to a tingling vibration. His right hand was hooked in his shell-studded belt just above his open holster.

Dave Packer's hand was shadowing the six-shooter in his buscadero holster. The big cattle buyer was leaning slightly forward.

" After you," Rawhide murmured. " I've got you faded."

The sound of thudding hoofs could be heard out in the valley, closing in at a dead run. Dave Packer's rangy bay was tied to a 'squite bush a few yards away. Packer cocked his head, measuring the distance the riders would have to come, but he showed no haste.

" You're asking for it, cowboy," Packer said to Rawhide. " I'm coming out—with loaded dice ! "

Rawhide Runyan was crouching forward, his tawny eyes watching Packer's big right hand. Little wrinkles splayed out at the corners of the rustler's eyes, telegraphing his intention.

Two right hands plunged down at the same instant. Time hung hesitant in the high desert. A man was about to die !

Rawhide made his draw, bending his knees a trifle to shed leather away from his leaping six-shooter. The gun swivelled in a short arc, exploding with a throaty roar as Rawhide shot from the hip.

Dave Packer was a point shooter. His gun flashed up, levelled off with incredible speed, but the heavy weapon did not explode. A crashing .45 slug bored a tunnel through his treacherous heart before his calloused thumb could ear back the hammer.

The big cattle buyer was dead on his feet ; all movements had stopped except the last convulsive twitch of his reflexes. He unhinged at the knees and pitched face down on the grass.

Rawhide Runyan crouched across his smoking gun with a gun fighter's halo above his head. The thudding kick of his gun butt had stopped the tingle in his sensitive fingers.

He lowered his six-shooter, ejected the spent shell from the grimy cylinder and shoved a fresh cartridge through the loading gate. His gun was back in leather as he turned to face the racing horsemen who were streaming into the canyon with guns held ready for battle.

Old Tom Owens slid his horse to a stop and splattered sand and gravel over the rustler he had almost run down. Sheriff Matt Boulder came in fast and stared at the long figure in the sand.

" You all right, Rawhide ? " Boulder asked hoarsely.

" You heard only one shot," Rawhide answered wearily, now that the long chase was finished. " Is Inspector Green——"

" Yes," Boulder answered in a hushed voice. " Packer got him dead centre with his rifle. Bull Carter is chained to a dead man, but I took those bills of sale from Green's pocket before I came chousing up to lend you a hand."

" We're going to get one of those handwriting sharks to look over these papers, Rawhide," Tad Lacy spoke up. " Even if we have got our young she-stuff back."

" The money ? " Rawhide asked.

" Don't worry about the money," Sheriff Boulder answered with a grim smile. " All the Strip cattlemen will be paid back from the money on the pack-horse. I've an idea that most of the money was stolen. There's close to twenty thousand dollars cash in those bags."

" Dave Packer stood to win himself quite a stake if his plans had worked out," Rawhide Runyan said thoughtfully. " What you might call plunder on the hoof ! "

CHAPTER XIII

RAWHIDE TAKES ORDERS

RAWHIDE RUNYAN rode down through Dark Canyon where the lush grass grew high along the river banks. The young owner of the Diamond Double R was making a rough tally of his shipping beef. He stopped his black saddle horse, Shadow, at the lower end of the canyon and added up his tally as Shadow grazed on the sacaton and bunch grass.

With his grey stetson pushed to the back of his head, Rawhide did his adding. He wore grey pants tucked down inside high-heeled boots, a calfskin vest over his wool shirt, long-barrelled six-shooter holstered on his right leg. Not big as big men go, his five-feet-nine carried the full hundred and fifty-five pounds of whalebone and rawhide.

Suddenly a booming roar blasted out from a thicket where the river made a delta. Two more shots followed in quick succession, as a scared horse with empty saddle fled up the trail from the alder thicket. The spooky horse saw Shadow and came racing up for companionship.

" That's Deputy Dave Jenkins's horse," Rawhide muttered, as he caught the trailing bridle reins to have a look at the riderless roan.

Rawhide's grey eyes narrowed as he saw a trail of fresh crimson across the empty saddle. Dave Jenkins was a good man with a six-shooter, entirely without fear ; he had been Sheriff Jim Blaine's deputy for ten years. If the law was being bush-whacked here in the Arizona Strip, Rawhide Runyan was going to draw cards, with or without an invitation.

Leading the deputy's horse by the reins, Rawhide turned Shadow and followed the trampled trail down through the lush grass. He could hear the faint clop of running hoofs going away, but Rawhide restrained the impulse to take after the runaway. For a weak voice was calling from the shelving river bank :

" Over here, cowboy, and rattle your hocks. I was ridin' up with a message from the sheriff."

Rawhide recognized Dave Jenkins's wind-roughened voice. Runyan left the saddle, and running through the alders jumped down from the shelving bank to land almost beside the wounded deputy.

Dave Jenkins was a tall, raw-boned man with wide shoulders and lean hips. He was propped against a rock, holding his right hand tight against the left side of his chest. From the blood seeping between his fingers, Rawhide knew Jenkins was hit hard.

" Sheriff Blaine wants to see you pronto, Rawhide," the deputy muttered. " He was shot in the back about noon by three bank bandits. He's in bed at Ma Jones's boarding-house ; sent me on the run to get you."

Rawhide Runyan bit his upper lip as he watched the wounded man. He doubted if Dave Jenkins would make the grade, but something had to be done fast. Throwing back his head, Runyan sent a ringing cry up Dark Canyon :

" Slow Joe ! Come down to the delta ! "

" Don't trust that owlhooter too far," Deputy Jenkins murmured hoarsely. " I know you claim he's reformed, but a leopard don't change its spots."

" Who shot you ? " Rawhide demanded grimly.

" I caught a look at the hombre as I spilled from old Gray," Jenkins answered. " It was Shale Pennington, right bower to Bart Heegan. Never mind tryin' to plug this hole. I'm ridin' out, and the trail's gettin' dark."

Rawhide knew that he was working on a dying man, but he fashioned a cloth plug and tried to stop the bleeding. When Jenkins began to cough, a bloody froth flecked his pallid lips. Internal bleeding, which meant the deputy could not be moved.

Sheriff Jim Blaine and his deputy had rodded the law in the Strip for a long time. Blaine was nearing sixty, and he called Rawhide Runyan his unpaid deputy. The law-man had even asked Rawhide to take over his job if anything happened to him.

" You called me, boss ? " a deep voice asked. A big man dropped heavily from the overhanging cut-bank. " Dave Jenkins, eh, and him saddling his hoss for the last ride. Who done for Dave ? "

The wounded man opened his eyes and tried to lift his gun. He glared at Slow Joe Hill with open hostility in his glazing eyes.

" Three shots fired," the deputy mumbled. " Pennington shot once ; I answered. *You triggered* that third shot."

" Yeah, Dave," Slow Joe agreed. His voice boomed even in a whisper. " I heard the shots and saw a gent high-tailing through the brakes. I put a slug through his hat."

Slow Joe Hill was an even six feet of solid bone and muscle. His barn-wide shoulders were incredibly powerful ; two hundred pounds of brawn without fat.

" Owlhooters never change," Jenkins murmured acidly. " Like as not you're in with that bushwhackin' gang ! "

Slow Joe looked up at Rawhide. A slow flush stained Hill's beefy face. True enough, he had been on the dodge until he had met Rawhide. But now Hill was foreman of the Diamond Double R, and proud of his reformation.

" If he was on his feet—" Joe muttered, and then slowly removed his battered black stetson. " Rest his soul in peace," Hill said in a whisper. " He won't find any outlaws to chase up in the Big Pasture where good men head for the Last Round-up. Dave Jenkins was a good man, Rawhide."

Rawhide closed the dead deputy's eyes, covered Jenkins's face with his stetson ; stretched to his feet. Dave would be missed in the Arizona Strip. He had wanted to die in the saddle, with his ball-pointed star pinned to his faded grey vest. Dave had got his wish, but Rawhide Runyan promised silently that his killer would pay in full.

" Blindfold Dave's horse so's it won't spook," Rawhide told Slow Joe. " We're riding in to Rainbow ; we'll take Dave along across his saddle."

Slow Joe removed his jumper, caught Jenkins's horse, and fashioned a blindfold. Rawhide leaned over and unpinned the star from the dead man's vest. Joe came down the bank with the deputy's horse, but Rawhide stopped him from picking up the body.

" You rode on the wrong side of the law trail for a good many years, Joe," Rawhide said, but his voice was mild. " Did you ever ride behind a law star ? "

" Huh ? No, I never, boss," Slow Joe answered in a whisper, out of respect for the dead. " And I ain't never goin' to."

" Hold up your right hand," Rawhide said sternly. " I'm going to swear you in, and you say ' I do ' after I give you the oath."

Slow Joe Hill stared at Rawhide's hard face. He was Rawhide's hired man, and what the boss said was always right. As Rawhide finished, Slow Joe nodded his head and said : " I do ! "

Rawhide stepped beside the big man and pinned the deputy's star on Slow Joe's vest.

" That makes you a special deputy sheriff, Joe," Rawhide said. " Dave Jenkins is dead, and Sheriff Jim Blaine is down with his head under him. He sent for me to come a-running, which means he wants me to hold down his job until he heals his hurts. Jim was shot in the back just this morning, when three bandits stuck up the bank."

" Naw, you don't, Rawhide," Slow Joe argued stubbornly. " Many's the time you and me have helped Jim Blaine, and we never wore any stars. We can help him now, but I don't wear the star ! "

" You'll wear that star and live up to your oath," Rawhide corrected sternly. " Or else——"

" You ain't the sheriff yet," Slow Joe growled, and clenched his ham-sized hands. " Don't hit me, Rawhide. You do, and I'll put you under arrest ! "

For a moment swift anger surged through Rawhide Runyan's veins. He had whipped Slow Joe Hill once ; it had taken a whipping to make Joe see the error of his ways. He could do it again, Rawhide told himself, and he began to move in on the wide-shouldered giant. Then Rawhide smiled wryly, stepped back and dropped his hands. Slow Joe Hill *was* a special deputy sheriff now.

" Any orders, deputy ? " Rawhide asked quietly.

Slow Joe's mouth began to open. He blinked a time or two, shuffled his big boots, grinned sheepishly.

" Quit it, Rawhide," he pleaded. " I don't know what to do, but I sure didn't want you plantin' one in my whiskers. You bend the lead like always, and I'll bring up the drag."

" Come to think of it, we can't work it that way," Rawhide said judiciously. " Seeing as you're the law, *you* bring in the deceased. I'll hit a high lope on into town to lend the sheriff a hand, but you've got to travel slow with that dead law-man."

" Just a minute before you leave, Runyan," Slow Joe barked. " You take Dave's heels ; I'll take his head. Put him face down across his saddle and help me make my ties."

Rawhide frowned, but obeyed orders. He knew that Slow Joe did not want to be left alone with a dead man, but unless Rawhide got to the county seat in a hurry, there might be two dead men, and a new brand of law for the Strip.

They lifted the body of the dead deputy to the saddle, fastened ankles and wrists together. Rawhide stepped back.

" You can go now, Runyan," Joe said casually, turning

his head to hide the grin on his round face. " The law can get along from here on out."

Rawhide glared and jumped his saddle. He nicked Shadow with a blunted spur ; rode down the river trail without a backward glance at Deputy Slow Joe Hill. He promised that there would be another time, and then he smiled.

" What a change in that owlhooter." Rawhide chuckled. " He's riding for the law now, and feeling his oats."

CHAPTER XIV

TOO MUCH LAW

A FEELING of tenseness was in the air as Rawhide Runyan rode down the dusty main street of Rainbow. Men leaning against the tie rails and building fronts nodded silently. Rawhide stared at each man, trying to find out what was wrong. Tom Owens of the T O Connected waved a hand at Runyan, tapped his holster as he brought the hand down to his side.

Rawhide found the answer as he noticed that the old cattleman was gun-naked. He also noted that every other man in town was carrying an empty holster. Nodding his understanding, Rawhide turned down a side street and rode swiftly to a two-storied building where Ma Jones ran a boarding-house.

Ma Jones called softly to Rawhide as he was dismounting at the whittled tie rail.

" Rattle your hocks and come a-running, Rawhide. The sheriff is downright anxious to palaver with you."

Rawhide crossed the board-walk on the run and slipped past Ma Jones, who was standing in her front door with a double-barrelled shot-gun in her toil-worn hands. Ma was Irish, six feet tall, about fifty years old. Her rates were reasonable, her cooking excellent, and Sheriff Jim Blaine was her oldest boarder.

" You'll find Jim in his room upstairs, Rawhide," she said. " I'll be guarding me house until you get some legal authority."

Rawhide's face showed his bewilderment, but he ran lightly up the stairs and knocked at the sheriff's door. A weak voice told him to come in, and the old sheriff sat up as Rawhide entered the bedroom.

" Glad you got here pronto, Rawhide," the wounded man

said with a sigh, and offered his hand. " I sent Dave Jenkins out with a message."

The sheriff had scarcely any strength in his hand-clasp ; his face was grey from pain and loss of blood. His white-clipped moustache seemed to droop, but Jim Blaine's blue eyes were bright with courage.

" Slow Joe's bringing Dave Jenkins back to town," Rawhide said, without meeting the sheriff's watchful eyes. " A bush-whacker shot Dave just above the heart—and Slow Joe saw Shale Pennington riding away from the scene. Dave's dead."

" You say *dead* ? Dave dead, and me down with my head under me ? You've got to wear my star, Rawhide ! Hold up your hand and say your ' I do's ' after me. You'll find my star on the left side of my vest, hangin' there on the bedpost."

" I'll wear the star and carry on for you until you get up off bedground," Rawhide said quietly. " I've already made Slow Joe Hill deputy to take Dave's place."

" If you carry on for me until I heal up those triflin' hurts, the folks will elect you sheriff," Jim Blaine predicted, and recited the oath.

Rawhide said " I do," pinned the five-pointed star on his calfskin vest, drew a deep breath. " Now tell me, Jim," he said. " Every man in town is packing an empty holster. Why ? "

" Because Bart Heegan made himself sheriff until election," Blaine muttered. " Shale Pennington is his deputy. And you want to watch that gambler named Curt Ransom. They made a new law prohibiting the toting of firearms in the city limits. It's a wonder you got here with your hardware."

Rawhide's grey eyes seemed to freeze. His jaw thrust out with determination ; his right hand slipped down to loosen the Peacemaker .45 in his low-slung holster.

" I rode in the back way," he admitted. " Now I know why Ma Jones was guarding her front door with a scatter-gun in her hands."

" Pore Dave," Blaine muttered. " Ma was fond of that lanky deputy. Better not tell her about Shale Pennington."

Rawhide stood by the front window, lost in thought. Bart Heegan and Curt Ransom were partners in the Ace Saloon and Gambling Hall. Heegan also owned the general store, the two livery barns—and the boarding-house. Nearly every storekeeper in Rainbow owed money to Heegan ; most of them were in debt to Curt Ransom, the gambler.

As he thought about Shale Pennington, the expression changed on Rawhide Runyan's face. Pennington was bouncer at the Ace ; a veteran gunman who could call his shots. Pennington had killed Dave Jenkins ; now Pennington was deputy sheriff of Rainbow. Rawhide started for the door, remembering Slow Joe Hill.

" I'll see you later, Jim," Runyan called over his shoulder. " There's two sheriffs and two deputies in town ; that's too much law."

" *Three* sheriffs," Jim Blaine corrected, and leaned back against his pillows. " I'm the law, I appointed you acting sheriff, so don't take any slack from those outlaws. Watch yourself."

Rawhide ran down the flight of stairs three at a time. Ma Jones smiled when she saw the star on his vest. She pointed to a crowd up on the main street.

" Better hurry, Rawhide," she suggested. " Slow Joe Hill just rode into town with a dead man. Shale Pennington stopped Joe, so you better get up there fast ! "

Rawhide vaulted aboard Shadow and raced toward trouble, up the side street. He drew rein at the edge of the crowd in front of the sheriff's office. He could see over the heads of tall men, all wearing empty holsters.

Slow Joe was out of the saddle untying the thongs that bound Dave Jenkins to the big sweating roan horse. Shale Pennington slipped through the crowd, touched Slow Joe on the arm.

" You're under arrest for murder, you flat-footed owl-hooter ! " Pennington accused hoarsely. " Hands high while I take your gun ! "

Rawhide edged back to watch the play. Pennington was taller than Joe by three inches, heavier by thirty pounds. Pennington clicked back the hammer of the gun in his right hand, reached out with his left to empty Slow Joe's holster.

" Look ! men," Pennington said to the crowd. " His gun has been fired recent, and he had the gall to bring in his victim."

Slow Joe slowly lowered his powerful arms as he turned. His little eyes narrowed as he saw the deputy's star on Shale Pennington's vest.

" You shot Dave, you fake deputy," Joe accused in his deep voice.

" You see any powder grime on my cutter ? " And Pennington held out his gun so all could see.

" I saw you runnin' away right after Dave was shot," Joe insisted. " I shot a hole through the killer's hat, and right now he's wearin' same."

" Your hat *is* ventilated, Pennington," old Tom Owens said. " And you had time enough since you rode in to change your gun. Us cowmen don't like this new town law, and we don't aim to stand for it."

" You cowmen'll stand for it and like it," Shale Pennington boasted arrogantly. " I'm arrestin' this owlhooter for murder, and I'll blast him out from under his hat if he resists arrest ! "

Rawhide saw Slow Joe dig in with his heels. Shale Pennington watched with his boots spread wide.

Then Rawhide took down his coiled catch rope, flipped the loop one time. The rope circled out over the heads of the crowd, dropped over Pennington's gun and jerked it from his fingers just as Slow Joe started his charge.

Old Tom Owens caught the gun as he saw Rawhide sitting there in the saddle. Slow Joe rammed into Shale Pennington, caught the big bouncer in his thick arms, and braced his feet.

" Spring the bear trap on that killer, Joe ! Your word's good enough for us ! " Tom Owens shouted.

" Turn Shale loose before I blow you apart," a deep voice interrupted. " Sheriff Bart Heegan speaking ! "

Bart Heegan was a stocky man of medium height, forty-odd years old, dressed in town clothes. He was the head of the town council ; the other members were merely tools who owed him too much money. They either played Heegan's way or he closed them out.

" Drop that six-shooter, Heegan," Rawhide Runyan said sharply. " I don't owe you a cent, I'm the duly appointed sheriff, and my six-shooter's centred on your thieving heart ! "

Bart Heegan glanced up at the cowboy on horseback. Heegan's fingers opened slowly to drop his gun to the red dust. Tad Lancy of the Anchor T caught up the fake sheriff's gun, and snugged it deep in his own holster. He gave Slow Joe the go-ahead :

" Pour it on him, Joe ! He's crippled a dozen men with his hands. Make him fight, Joe."

Slow Joe tightened his arms. Pennington began to struggle. Rawhide knew what would happen if Joe locked his big hands.

" Turn him loose and spoil his good looks, Joe," Rawhide called to his foreman.

Slow Joe's mind moved sluggishly to obey orders. His arms hugged Shale Pennington until the big man's lungs were starved for air. Then Joe loosed his grip, jabbed Pennington in the belly with his left fist, brought his right from his boots in a sweeping uppercut which caught Pennington under the chin and nearly tore the head from his wide shoulders.

5

" Get his badge, Joe ! " Rawhide ordered swiftly.

Slow Joe was getting set to fight with his big boots, but once more he obeyed orders. He reached down, tore the deputy sheriff's badge from Shale Pennington's vest and grinned up at his young boss.

" You and me are the law here in Rainbow now, Rawhide," Joe boasted. " How's old Jim Blaine ? "

" Resting comfortable," Rawhide answered, as he turned to address the crowd. " You men get yourselves fully dressed," he said. " There was too much law in these parts. Shale Pennington and Bart Heegan are just citizens—and I'm holding Pennington for the killing of Deputy Dave Jenkins ! "

CHAPTER XV

A GAMBLER DRAWS CARDS

A SMOOTH voice contradicted quietly : " Your mistake, Runyan. I've just bought chips in this little game, and it's my deal. Drop your gun before I empty your saddle ! "

Rawhide Runyan recognized that smooth, oily voice. He turned his head to face Curt Ransom, who ran the games in the Ace. Ransom wore the broadcloth of his profession, had the usual lack of expression in his dark eyes, and as he said, he was dealing—with a cocked .45 Colt six-shooter in his long-fingered right hand.

" Looks like a draw to me," Rawhide said slowly. " You have a cutter centred on my heart ; mine is centred on your pard's. Touch off your powder and I'll kill Bart Heegan. That's *my* hand ; what're you holding ? "

" Don't anyone move," the tall gambler barked. " Get up, Shale ! "

Shale Pennington started to get to his feet, reaching for his gun. His fingers fumbled and clawed air above his empty holster until Slow Joe Hill began to laugh raucously.

" Stand hitched, killer," Joe growled at Pennington. " You're under arrest, and I've got a gun in your back. Talk some more, Rawhide."

Rawhide Runyan eyed the gambler coolly, estimating his chances for success. Any rash move would start a gun fight in which both sides would suffer losses. The two old cattlemen, Tad Lancy and Tom Owens, would shell the captured guns from their holsters at the first crack of a cap. At last Rawhide found the answer.

" Listen close, gambling man," he told Curt Ransom.
" Between you and me it's a toss-up. But then again, I've got
an ace buried. Slow Joe could kill you before you could
swing your gun, and he'd also kill Heegan and Pennington."

" So we call it a draw all round," Ransom said, in his smooth
low voice.

" You forget the ace I have buried, and I mean Slow Joe,"
Rawhide reminded. " You've passed the deal, and here's
your cards. You don't dare turn your gun away from me.
Tom Owens and Tad Lancy will draw their cutters now. If
you shoot, we'll clean out your crowd. You'll get me, but all
your outfit dies. You heard me, boys ! "

Old Tom Owens clawed his gun loose from leather without
hesitation. He had read the gambler's inscrutable face and
knew Curt Ransom was bluffing. Four sixes beat a full house
every time, and anyway the gambler was playing with Bart
Heegan's chips. Tad Lancy followed the lead of Tom Owens,
lining his sights on Ransom.

" That's better," Rawhide said quietly, a hard smile curling
his lips. " You, Joe ; take your prisoner down to Ma Jones's
boarding-house. Lock him in her storeroom, and stand guard.
Shackle the killing son with those handcuffs we took from
Deputy Dave's body."

Bart Heegan scowled with rage as Slow Joe marched Shale
Pennington down the side street. Heegan had all the keys to
the jail in his pocket—but Ma Jones had changed all the
locks on her doors in the boarding-house, where Pennington
would be locked up.

" I'll evict that old woman," Heegan threatened. " As
sheriff of Rainbow, I can serve the papers myself ! I own her
boarding-house."

Rawhide stared at Heegan with the devils of hate dancing
across his cold grey eyes. Then Runyan smiled slightly.

" Step right down there and evict," he told Heegan quietly,
" but step over here first. I said *step* ! "

Bart Heegan came to Rawhide, who reached out and tore
the new badge from Heegan's vest.

" You're no part of the law," Rawhide said sternly. " Like
as not you've seen that shot-gun Ma keeps close to her hand.
Start your eviction proceedings. If Ma makes a complaint,
I'll come and get you for trespass."

Heegan departed.

" How about this gambler ? " Tad Lancy asked hopefully,
" He's resistin' the law with a deadly weapon."

Curt Ransom knew when his hand was beaten. He smoothly

holstered his six-shooter, turned his back, and walked toward the Ace Saloon.

"Let him go," Rawhide told Lancy. "I'll know where to find him when I want him."

"I'll be waiting," Ransom said, without turning his head. "I seldom buck another man's game, but next time we'll play it my way."

Rawhide Runyan shrugged and jerked his head toward Ma's boarding-house. The two old cattlemen followed without speaking.

Bart Heegan was backing hastily through the front door as they reached the boarding-house. Then Ma Jones appeared with the double-barrelled shot-gun in her capable hands.

"Throw me out, would you?" she sneered at Heegan. "Not while I have me strength, me fine bucko! It takes a court order, served by the sheriff, and you ain't him. On top of that, I've got thirty days to find me a new place."

"I own this property," Heegan blustered. "I want immediate possession!"

"With me rent paid up a month in advance; you've overplayed your hand!" Ma answered triumphantly, without betraying the fact that she saw Rawhide watching with interest.

"I own half of Rainbow," Heegan boasted. "You can't find another place, and we both know it. The town council appointed me sheriff until election, no matter what that cowboy allowed."

Rawhide stepped up softly and tapped Heegan on the shoulder. "You're disturbing the peace," Rawhide said softly. "If you want to back up your eviction, get a court order. I'll serve it according to law!"

A scuffle sounded in the corridor behind Ma Jones. A bellowing voice cried out a warning; the voice of Slow Joe Hill:

"*Tiger on the loose!*"

Prison talk, warning that a prisoner had escaped. Ma Jones leaped lightly down the three stairs with the riot gun swivelling in her hands. Rawhide knew that if Ma found out about the killing of Dave Jenkins, the floor of her hallway would run red with the bushwhacker's blood.

Moving in fast, Rawhide slapped the murderous sawed-off gun down, wrenching it from Ma's hands. He threw the shot-gun to Tom Owens, who caught it with his left hand. A man was running toward the front door; a man with murder in his heart, and a cocked six-gun in his right hand. It was Slow Joe Hill's six-gun, but it wasn't Slow Joe holding it.

Rawhide stood to one side of the door with his scarred boots spread wide.

Shale Pennington slid to a stop. Then he approached the front door cautiously.

" Come out with your hands empty, Pennington ! " Rawhide ordered sternly. " Sheriff Runyan speaking ! "

A roaring shot blasted out through the open door. Before the echo had died away, Rawhide made a leap and chopped a shot from his .45 Peacemaker. A gun clattered to the spur-splintered floor as Rawhide leaped inside.

Shale Pennington was on his knees, gripping his shattered right hand with his left. Slow Joe Hill came running from the rear, wearing a pair of handcuffs. Ma Jones stepped round Tad Lancy with her shot-gun at her hip. She had taken it from Tom Owens without a struggle.

" He ain't dead," she almost whispered, after one look at the grovelling prisoner. " One side, Sheriff Runyan ! He killed Dave Jenkins ! Dave was my friend ! "

Rawhide Runyan stepped directly in front of the shot-gun, his back to the wounded man. His square shoulders blocked the doorway, and Ma Jones, outside on the stoop, began to tremble.

" One side, yearlin' ! " she screamed. " 'Tis me property you're on, and me home's me castle. Step aside or I'll shoot ! "

" You won't shoot, Ma," Rawhide said quietly. " We've got to do this the law way, what with old Jim Blaine lying upstairs and hurt bad."

A foot scraped behind Rawhide, but he made no move. Steel jingled, was followed by a crashing blow and the thud of a heavy body. Slow Joe tapped Rawhide on the shoulder. Joe came out as Rawhide stepped aside.

" I'm thinkin' Shale Pennington is dead," Joe lied brazenly, as he grinned at Ma Jones. " He was goin' to jump Rawhide, a couple of seconds ago, and the boss with his back turned. So I just now did what he did to me when he got away. I hit him on the head with both these blasted handcuffs. You wouldn't shoot a dead man, Ma Jones."

Ma Jones lowered her murderous weapon and advanced upon Slow Joe. Her full face was red with anger as she raised her shot-gun to use as a club.

" I had Pennington marked for me own gun, you big monkey ! " she screamed at Joe. " I should be after knockin' out your brains ! "

Slow Joe bowed his head meekly and held out his manacled hands. " I'm helpless," he said in a booming whisper. " I can't put up a fight, Ma."

Rawhide grinned and turned his attention to the unconscious prisoner. Pennington was bleeding from a deep scalp wound where the handcuffs had struck with all Joe's weight behind the blow. Pennington's shattered right hand was also bleeding. Unless he received medical attention soon, he might bleed to death.

" Ma," Rawhide called, and waited until Ma Jones came to his side, " we've got to have a doctor for the prisoner. I want to use one of your rooms, and you can be his guard. Will you string along with the law, so's we can nurse Shale Pennington back to health ? "

" I will not ! " Ma answered savagely. " I thought that killer was dead. When I kill a sarpint, I kill him all over. One side, cowboy ! "

" Don't raise that gun," Rawhide warned sternly. " I said we'd nurse him back to health, so he can dance on the end of a new rope. That's the way Dave would want it."

Ma Jones was past fifty ; her romance had ended. Tears appeared in her Irish blue eyes ; ran down her weathered cheeks in little rivulets. She was six feet tall, weighed two hundred and ten, but she cried on Rawhide's shoulder like a little girl. Her big shoulders shook with sobs ; then she stiffened.

" I'll play along with the law, Rawhide, laddie," she said in a muffled voice, and raised her head proudly. " I'll nurse that killer until he's as strong as a bull. Providin'——"

" Give it a name," Rawhide prompted gently. " And count it done."

" When he stands on the gallows with the hangman's noose round his neck," Ma answered steadily, her face covered with moisture, " I want to pull the handle that trips the trap-door."

" That's a promise," Rawhide answered. Ma was range-bred stock, stronger than most men, and the law could give or take a point. " Now let's move him upstairs to a room."

CHAPTER XVI

TRAPPED

TWILIGHT settled down upon the dusty town of Rainbow. Slow Joe Hill stood guard outside the room where Shale Pennington was still unconscious. The doctor had finished his work, had declared Pennington would live to die on the gallows.

Ma Jones was busy in her kitchen with two Indian girls helping. Her shot-gun stood behind the door, ready for instant use. Ma's eyes were red with weeping, but only the very young give up entirely to their emotions when romance lies in the grave. Now she lived for one purpose—to drop the trap which would swing Shale Pennington into eternity.

Rawhide Runyan was upstairs talking with Sheriff Jim Blaine. He had told Blaine the whole story ; now he waited for the criticism of experience.

" You'll make a good sheriff, Rawhide," Blaine said thoughtfully. " You've got plenty of what it takes, and you can keep your head. You're not a cold killer ; you don't notch your gun. If it had been me, I think I'd have killed both Heegan and Pennington."

" I've seen you work, old-timer," Rawhide said with a smile. " You wouldn't have killed either of them. I'm going to get my supper, and then take a look around. Rest easy, old Johnny Law."

Rawhide walked downstairs and asked Ma Jones to feed him in the kitchen, explaining that he had reasons of his own. Ma agreed, but asked Rawhide not to play a lone hand.

" Heegan is a lobo," she declared vehemently. " He won't give you a chance, after what happened to Shale Pennington."

Rawhide ate in silence. Law had been restored to Rainbow. When the two wounded men got well, Runyan would return to the Strip up the valley. The doctor had said that both Jim Blaine and Shale Pennington would be up and around within two weeks. Just in time for Rawhide to start round-up of his shipping beef.

He smiled as he pictured what Rainbow town would be like to-morrow. All the cattlemen and cowboys would ride into town with hardware in their holsters. They didn't owe Bart Heegan any money ; they didn't like crooked politics. Rainbow would get a new deal after the coming election.

Finishing his meal, Rawhide stretched to his feet, cat-footed over behind Ma Jones, and kissed her on the cheek. Ma flushed like a girl, but scolded him as the Irish always do when well pleased.

" Go along with you, cowboy. You should be after falling in love with a pretty colleen, and settlin' down. You could have your pick of the whole flock ; but no ; you must stick to your guns."

" Yeah," Rawhide answered, and his tanned face hardened. " Reckon I'm not the marrying kind, Ma. I'll be back shortly."

Ma Jones watched him as he left by the kitchen door. A frown swept over her face. If Rawhide walked up the alley to the main street, he would be opposite the Ace Saloon and Gambling Hall. She started to call to him, changed her mind, and went back to her big wood stove.

Rawhide twitched his gun loose in the holster, tugged his grey stetson down over his eyes, and crossed the dusty street. Stopping just outside the swinging doors, he peered underneath. He saw two men standing in front of the bar. In the card room, at the back, he could see a pair of legs clad in broadcloth over polished hand-made boots. That would be Curt Ransom.

Rawhide shouldered through the batwing doors. He stopped instantly as a gun pressed against the muscles of his broad back. The voice of Bart Heegan spoke softly behind him:

" Keep on walking, Runyan. Curt is waiting in the back room."

Rawhide jerked slightly as a hand emptied his holster. He turned his head to glance into the mirror behind the long bar. Heegan was holding two guns, a cigar in his mouth, a derby hat perched on his bald head. Runyan couldn't fight two guns with his bare hands.

Rawhide continued to the back room. Curt Ransom was dealing himself four hands of poker. He did not glance up, but kept shuffling the cards.

" Get interested, tinhorn," Rawhide said quietly. " You planned this play, and you bet only on a sure thing."

Curt Ransom glanced up, thumbed back the left lapel of his coat. Rawhide stared at Ransom's deputy sheriff's badge, turned his head when Bart Heegan coughed suggestively. Heegan had stuck Rawhide's gun down in his shell-studded belt, was showing a sheriff's badge on his vest.

" Walk into that side room, prisoner," Heegan said roughly. " The law wants to question you, and you better give up head ! "

Curt Ransom got up. Rawhide turned the doorknob and walked into a room lighted by a swinging lamp. The gambler removed his frock-tailed coat without speaking. He stripped to the waist, and flexed his muscles.

Rawhide Runyan could not repress the gleam of admiration which leaped to his startled grey eyes. Curt Ransom was nearly six feet tall, would weigh around a hundred and seventy, and was muscled like a light-heavyweight boxer. Smooth flowing muscles rippled along his shoulders and arms, writhed like snakes as Ransom turned to show his back.

Rawhide knew the answer now. While Bart Heegan held a gun in his hand, Curt Ransom meant to get his revenge with fists. Ransom shadow-boxed like a professional, saying never a word. Bart Heegan finally gave orders.

" Strip down to the waist, Runyan. Let's see you and Curt fight ! "

Rawhide Runyan shrugged out of his calfskin vest, unbuckled his gun belt, and threw his stetson into a corner.

He said carelessly, as he faced Curt Ransom : " Any time you're ready."

Curt Ransom danced in fast, jabbing with a snaky left fist. Rawhide took a hard right cross, going away, but he felt the power behind the gambler's thudding fists. Rawhide knew he must avoid coming to grips with Ransom, to overcome the gambler's advantage in weight and reach. As Ransom stopped his charge, Rawhide crossed with a hard right to the jaw. Curt Ransom smiled derisively. That one-two punch was old stuff, and he parried the blows as he stepped in to counterpunch.

Rawhide Runyan didn't stop with the one-two attack. His left fist whizzed overhead to rock Ransom's black head back. Rawhide stepped in behind a low right-handed punch just over the heart. Curt Ransom was set up for the kill— and then Rawhide heard the hammer of a gun click behind him.

He stopped the driving right which was cocked for the big thing. Curt Ransom recovered ; led with his right. Rawhide turned his head, knocked Ransom's arm aside, and seized the gambler by the wrist. Whipping around like a cat, Rawhide drew Ransom's arm over his shoulder, bucking his back as he pulled down in a swift jerk.

Curt Ransom flew through the air like a sack of spuds, or a rock aimed at a mark. His hurtling body hit Bart Heegan with a crashing thud, and Heegan's gun exploded as both men crashed against the wall.

Runyan rushed in just as Heegan was rolling to his feet. Rawhide caught Heegan under the chin with the heel of his right hand, flipped the boss of Rainbow over like a tumbler, nearly breaking his neck. Curt Ransom was straightening up with a dazed look in his dark eyes.

Rawhide danced lightly across the room, slapped the gambler smartly in the face to clear Ransom's head. Curt Ransom came out of the fog, lashed out with his left, stepped in behind a crushing right-hand blow.

Rawhide knocked it down with his left, twisted aside as

Ransom tried to clinch. Then Rawhide jabbed with his left to the chin to set the gambler up, and lowered the boom. His right fist flashed out straight to Ransom's chin, thudded solidly against bone, and followed through.

Curt Ransom was knocked backward as though a mule had kicked him with both heels. He crashed against the wall, slid to the floor with his eyes closed. Rawhide watched for a moment, blowing on his skinned knuckles.

When Ransom showed no signs of life, Rawhide walked over to Bart Heegan, turned the unconscious man over with his right foot, and retrieved his six-shooter. Taking a pair of handcuffs from his belt, Rawhide dragged Heegan across the floor like a side of beef, and handcuffed him to Ransom's right wrist. After which he shrugged into his vest, replaced his stetson, and opened the door.

" Fetch a bucket of water to wash down a couple of hogs," Rawhide called to the bartender. " And don't reach for that trouble gun under the bar ! "

The bartender brought a bucket of water he had used to rinse glasses. Rawhide jerked his thumb toward the hand-cuffed pair. The bartender smiled grimly ; he had wanted to do this thing for a long time. He threw water all over Curt Ransom, used the remainder on Bart Heegan. Then he ran from the room as both men began to stir.

Ransom was first to sit up. Anger darkened his face, for he felt the tug of metal on his wrist. Bart Heegan tried to surge to his feet, slipped and fell in the water as Ransom jerked him down.

" I'm ready to talk now," Rawhide said ironically. " I can hardly move after the beating you gave me, and I'm ready to give up head. Which one of you hombres is the big augur ? "

" The town council appointed me sheriff until election," Heegan muttered. " What did Dave Jenkins say before he cashed in his chips ? "

Rawhide's face hardened. " Dave named Shale Pennington as his killer," he answered, his voice like chilled steel. " He also said you sent Pennington to kill him, which makes you an accomplice."

" He's a liar," Heegan denied brazenly.

Rawhide leaped across the room and slapped Heegan squarely across the lips. His boots began to jig, the way they do when a cowboy gets mad enough to fight with his feet. Then Rawhide restrained himself, reached down, and jerked the badge from Heegan's vest.

" I'm arresting you for impersonating an officer," he told Heegan. " The town council could have made you town marshal, but not county sheriff."

Curt Ransom leaned toward Heegan, but Rawhide dived between them. He shouldered the gambler down, took a .45 six-shooter from Ransom's belt, and searched the two men. Ransom had a two-shot derringer hide-out gun in the right pocket of his pants. Heegan had a skinning knife in his left boot.

Rawhide went into the room where the roulette wheel and faro layout stood. The wheel was rigged to cheat the players. Rawhide kicked it to pieces with his scarred boots. He returned to the back room, made his talk to Bart Heegan.

" There's not a man in Rainbow owes you a gambling debt, you crooked son ! I'm giving Curt Ransom until daylight to leave town, because he was only working for you. You, Ransom—get out, or get killed ! "

CHAPTER XVII

RAWHIDE'S DEBT

CURT RANSOM veiled his dark eyes to hide a look of triumph he could not conceal. Rawhide Runyan took a key from his pocket, unlocked the gambler's cuff, stepped back with empty hands. Ransom got up, walked over to a chair where he had piled his clothes, and began to dress.

" How about me ? " Heegan asked with a sneer. " I'm a property owner. I own half of Rainbow."

" Shale Pennington'll talk before we hang him," Rawhide answered grimly. " When he talks, you might not own half of Rainbow."

Rawhide picked up a heavy ring of keys he had taken from Heegan's pockets as he had made his search for weapons. Without touching Heegan, Rawhide jerked his head toward the door. When Heegan stared defiantly, Rawhide took the cuff that dangled from Heegan's wrist, used it as a come-along, and marched his prisoner through the saloon.

The regular after-supper drinkers had filled the Ace Saloon as the fight was in progress. Surprise showed on their faces as Rawhide marched through with Bart Heegan. Some were tough hangers-on. Hands dropped slowly to holsters until a loud, suggestive cough from the front door sent shifty eyes slanting to the back-bar mirror for a look. Tom Owens stood at one side of the batwings ; old Tad Lancy was just opposite. Both formed an unofficial guard of honour with six-shooters in gnarled right hands.

Rawhide Runyan nodded his thanks as he herded the boss of Rainbow to the street and down to the jail behind the sheriff's office. Tom Owens fell in behind him ; Tad Lancy stayed to watch the saloon crowd.

" Let's talk some," Heegan suggested. " String along with me. I'll make you sheriff of Rainbow. I'll give you a cut off the profits if you'll look the other way. I run things here in Rainbow ; I'd have owned the place if you hadn't cut the cards the wrong way."

Rawhide fitted a key to the office door, shoved Heegan in ahead of him, and struck a match. He lighted a wall lamp ; turned to stare coldly at Bart Heegan.

" The bank was robbed this morning, Heegan," said Runyan. " Sheriff Jim Blaine was shot in the back as he came up the alley to head off the hold-ups. Three men did that job. They got away with forty thousand. Do you know anything about it ? "

" I know plenty," Heegan blustered. " I was in my office next door to the Ace Saloon when the hold-up was pulled. I recognized two of the bandits, but one got away."

" They all three got away," Rawhide corrected, and the muscles stood out on his cheeks as he locked his jaws to restrain the anger that was pumping the blood madly through his veins. " Get back in that first cell before I kill you ! "

Heegan looked startled, but after one glance at Rawhide's face he walked back to the cell. Rawhide followed, locked the door, and holstered his gun. He blew down the lamp chimney to shroud the office in darkness and spoke softly to Tom Owens.

" Stay here in the dark and stand guard, Tom. I want a talk with Shale Pennington before I see Curt Ransom again. I won't be long."

The fingers of Rawhide's right hand were tingling as he high-heeled down the street toward the boarding-house. Sheriff Jim Blaine had been shot in the back, and Bart Heegan had seen the bank robbery from the window of his office. Dave Jenkins had been killed by Shale Pennington, after which Heegan, Ransom, and Pennington had taken over to run the law.

Ma Jones met Rawhide as he entered the boarding-house, took one look at his stormy face, and gripped his arm.

" Bart Heegan," she whispered hoarsely. " Did he get away ? "

" Heegan's in jail," Rawhide answered tensely. " I want a talk with Shale Pennington. You stay down here."

Ma Jones stared at his broad back as he brushed past her and mounted the stairs. Pennington's room was at the opposite end of the hall from the wounded sheriff's room. Rawhide frowned as he saw that the door to Pennington's room was closed ; then he shrugged. Slow Joe had probably closed the door to guard his back.

Rawhide turned the knob and stepped inside, shutting the door behind him. He jerked around with his right hand slapping for his holster as he saw Slow Joe huddled on the floor along the side wall. His hand stopped instantly when a sneering voice came to him from the bed.

" Reach for the ceiling, cowboy ! "

Rawhide reached, turned slowly to face the bed. Shale Pennington was resting against the pillows with a cocked gun in his left hand. He had managed somehow to get his pants on, but his stockinged feet told that his tight boots had been too much for him. His wounded right hand was in a sling across his chest ; his face was pale under the battered black stetson drawn down to shade his red-rimmed eyes.

" That owlhoot pard of yours went to get me a drink of water," Pennington explained, his rough voice expressive of the contempt he felt for Slow Joe Hill. " I hit him on the skull with a window weight when he came back."

" Curt Ransom talked," Rawhide said evenly. " Bart Heegan is in jail. You three robbed the bank this morning. Heegan shot old Jim in the back."

" So what are you going to do about it ? " Pennington jeered. " After I salivate you, I can go places with my share of the loot ! "

Rawhide shifted his boots, moved away from the door, closer to Slow Joe. Shale Pennington followed him with Joe's gun, lips snarled back in a wolfish grin.

" Stand right there ! " he barked. " When I touch off my powder, your corpse will fall right across that barn-shouldered owlhooter who manhandled me ! "

Rawhide wondered if Shale Pennington had heard that slight sound just outside the door. Runyan also wondered who was on the other side. His face was grim as he made a silent guess.

" If you know any prayers, start reciting," Pennington taunted. " You and that big Irish woman was going to nurse me back to health, and then watch me dance on air. When I count up to three, you better be all prayed out ! "

Rawhide Runyan straightened slowly, squared his shoulders, and smiled grimly. He had lived a lifetime in his twenty-four years ; a man couldn't live forever. Three seconds between life and death !

" *One !* " Shale Pennington whispered hoarsely. " Cave, you cowardly whelp ! Down on your knees ! "

Rawhide licked his lips, took the one chance that was offered him. He started to unhinge his knees. He dived suddenly across the crumpled heap that was Slow Joe Hill.

Bram-m-m !

A terrific explosion roared from out in the hall, to splinter the flimsy door panels. The wick of the lamp on a small table began to gutter in the gusty blast of exploding powder. Buckshot rattled against the headboard of the bed just as the light went out. Then the ghostly rattle of a dying man came from the bed.

" Are ye safe, laddie buck ? " an anxious voice called above the echoes of the sawed-off shot-gun. " Answer me, Rawhide ! "

" Don't shoot again, Ma ! " Rawhide answered quickly, as he came out of the corner where he had made himself thin on the floor. " Lucky for me I heard your foot scrape outside."

" I scraped it a bit for you to hear," Ma Jones said dryly, as she came in and lighted the lamp.

Shale Pennington was slumped against the headboard, eyes staring with jaw agape. His white shirt was spotted red like polka dots, and the red dots were growing larger.

" He cheated the rope," Ma whispered, and crossed herself devoutly. " I had to do it, Rawhide."

" You saved my life, Ma," Rawhide said huskily. " I won't ever forget."

He put his arms round her as Ma Jones began to tremble.

" 'Tis an old fool I am, Rawhide." She sniffled, and then she stiffened. " Rawhide ! Is Slow Joe dead ? Did I get him too when I tripped both triggers ? "

" You can't kill a man with a gun if he was born to be hung," a deep voice muttered gruffly, and Slow Joe sat up. He stared long at Shale Pennington with wonder in his little eyes. " Or can you ? " he whispered.

" Rawhide ! Get in here, sheriff ! " The bellowing tremolo of Jim Blaine's voice roared from the front room.

Rawhide released Ma Jones. He ran down the hall, slid to a stop in front of the sheriff's door as he saw Jim Blaine propped up in bed with a .45 in his steady right hand.

" Hold your fire, shur'ff ! " Rawhide said quickly.

"Who got killed back yonder?" Blaine demanded. "Sounded like the whole house blew up!"

"Shale Pennington knocked Slow Joe out with a window weight, had me under Joe's gun, and Ma tripped both triggers to blast a hole through the door," Rawhide explained. "Saved my life, but Pennington won't ever hang. He's fresh dead."

"I heard part of that palaver," Blaine said sternly. "I think Bart Heegan, Curt Ransom and Pennington robbed the bank this morning. I think it was Heegan who shot me. Now you listen to me, Sheriff Runyan."

"Keep on talking."

"Ma Jones had enough in the bank to pay Heegan the mortgage he's holding against her boarding-house." As Rawhide stood thoughtfully at the foot of the bed, Jim Blaine roared angrily, "Well, what you waiting for, Johnny Law? Are you going to let her lose everything after she saved your worthless life?"

CHAPTER XVIII

BALANCING THE BOOKS

RAWHIDE RUNYAN left the boarding-house and headed straight for the jail. He called softly to old Tom Owens, frowning when he received no reply. A muffled grunt came from the jail office. Rawhide used his key and unlocked the heavy front door.

Before he ran back to look at Heegan's cell he knew that the town boss had escaped. Tom Owens was lying in a corner of the cell, bound hand and foot, a gag in his mouth. The old cattleman started talking as soon as Rawhide removed the bandanna gag.

"I was standing looking out the front window, Rawhide. Curt Ransom snuck in the back door and buffaloed me over the head with the barrel of his gun. They must have had keys made, because Ransom let Heegan out of his cell. They aim to get you when you barge into the Ace Saloon."

Rawhide reached under his arm, brought out a spare gun, handed it to Owens.

"C'mon," Rawhide said gruffly. "I didn't bring Slow Joe."

"But I tagged you nohow," Joe's deep voice whispered softly through the gloom.

Rawhide smiled in the darkness. He had seen Slow Joe keeping to the shadows like a great shambling bear. Runyan talked softly, explaining his plan to Owens and Joe. Then they walked up the alley in silence. When they came to the main street, Tom Owens crossed to the saloon while Rawhide and Joe walked to the corner. There they crossed.

Tom Owens waited until he saw Rawhide and Joe slip up the alley, heading for the side door of the Ace Saloon. Then the old cattleman shouldered through the swinging doors, glanced around for Tad Lancy, and walked up to join his old pard at the bar.

Owens stiffened as he saw Curt Ransom standing at the far end of the bar, drinking with Bart Heegan.

" Where's that fake sheriff ? " Bart Heegan growled at Owens.

" For the fake one, take a good look at yourself in the mirror," a voice answered behind Heegan—and Rawhide Runyan stepped into the card room.

Heegan whipped around with both hands high above his head. Gambler Curt Ransom took a look in the back-bar mirror, saw that Rawhide had both hands hooked in his gun belt. The gambler turned slowly with a sneering smile on his face.

" You keep out of this, Heegan," he said, from the corner of his mouth. " I've always wanted to face this gun hawk on an even break, and he gave me until daylight to leave town. I'm not leaving."

" I said to get out or get killed," Rawhide corrected quietly. " Shale Pennington talked before he died."

Heegan glanced at Ransom, but the gambler stared steadily at Rawhide. There was no emotion on Ransom's features, except for the glitter in his dark eyes.

" Try a new one," Ransom sneered. " That one was old when I was kicking the slats out of my cradle."

" Pennington told about the bank robbery," Rawhide continued. " He admitted killing Deputy Dave Jenkins, but he likewise named the man who shot Sheriff Jim Blaine in the back."

" Who did he name ? "

Rawhide shrugged as Ransom barked the question. Ransom knew the real answer, but he didn't know what Pennington had said. Ransom waited to see if Heegan would speak, but the town boss remained silent.

" You killed Shale Pennington on a law sneak," Ransom accused. " Next to me, he was the fastest gun swift in town."

" Rainbow ain't such a big town," Rawhide drawled. " Besides, he couldn't see through a door."

Ransom knitted his brow and tried to figure that one out. Bart Heegan shuffled his boots, licked his lips, started at Rawhide.

Curt Ransom plunged his hand down like the treacherous strike of a sidewinder. His thumb curled the hammer back as he cleared leather with finger through the trigger guard.

Rawhide Runyan was watching; his finger-tips were tingling. His knees dipped just a trifle as he made his pass. Flame lanced from the muzzle of his leaping gun as it snouted over the tip of his holster.

The hanging lamps began to gutter as the blast of air shattered the stillness of the smoke-filled room. Curt Ransom triggered a shot into the ceiling as paralysis stopped the sweep of his arm. The gun dropped from his hand. Ransom swayed forward. He was dead before he crashed face down across his smoking gun.

Rawhide was standing just inside the back door, blocking the entrance. A hoarse voice shouted behind him :

" Watch Heegan ! "

Rawhide turned sidewise as Slow Joe shouted the warning. Heegan had his arm back for a throw ; a long-bladed knife glittered in the palm of his right hand. Rawhide had eared back the hammer of his gun on the recoil. He fired just as Bart Heegan's hand tilted up for the throw.

Lead crashed against steel as the .45 slug found its mark. The knife shattered and fell in a tinkling shower on the mahogany bar. Bart Heegan went to his knees, screaming like a wounded stallion, clutching his bleeding hand against his chest.

Rawhide holstered his gun. Three strides placed him beside the wounded man. He jerked a rawhide thong from his hip pocket, one of the thongs which had bound old Tom Owens. Shpping the loop over Heegan's hand, he made a tight tourniquet above the wrist, dropped Heegan's hand, and stepped back.

" Start talking, you cowardly son," Rawhide said grimly, barely moving his lips. " Who shot the sheriff ? "

" Ransom did, and he paid," Heegan whined. " Get the croaker to fix my hand. I'm bleeding out ! "

" Bleed out, you lying hold-up," Rawhide muttered. " This makes twice that you figured dead men can't talk."

" I ain't handy with a gun," Heegan moaned. " Me and Curt saw Blaine running down the alley, and Ransom let him have it ! "

" That's not the way Shale Pennington told it," Rawhide

6

said quietly. " Bartender, give this skunk a drink before he faints like a female."

The bartender brought a drink ; the same man who had revived his boss with a bucket of water. Heegan seized the glass with his left hand ; down the hatch at one gulp.

" Gimme another, Al," he pleaded. " Just one more ! "

" I wouldn't give you a drink of *water* if your tongue was on fire," the bartender growled. " You took this saloon away from me with your crooked roulette wheel. Rawhide should have killed you."

" Come in, Joe, and hold this lobo under your gun," Rawhide called over his shoulder.

Slow Joe shuffled in. Rawhide shouldered through a door leading behind the bar. The room was Heegan's private office. There was a locked safe in the office. Rawhide went back out and brusquely persuaded Heegan to give him the combination. Then Rawhide opened the safe.

Rawhide stared at a canvas sack partly covered with a small ledger.

Runyan smiled grimly as he picked up the ledger and read the accounts. Money was owed to Heegan by half the men in town. Rawhide's face twisted as he came to the account of Ma Jones. Six hundred dollars, at twenty per cent. interest.

Rawhide closed the book, pulled out the canvas sack, dumped the contents on the floor. Sheaves of paper money winked up at him. Money with paper bands telling the amount, stamped : DROVERS BANK OF RAINBOW. Rawhide stuffed the money back into the bag and returned to the saloon.

" Heegan," he said, " you and your pards robbed the bank, and here's the evidence."

He dumped the money on the floor, watching the face of Heegan. Tom Owens and Tad Lancy shouldered through the crowd to stare at the currency.

" That saves my spread," old Tom Owens said huskily.

" Mine, too," Tad Lancy echoed. " Every cent I had was in the Drovers Bank."

" This saloon belongs to you, Al," Rawhide told the bartender. " Ransom ran a crooked wheel, and you can tear the pages from this book. Tell every man in Rainbow that he don't owe Boss Heegan a dollar. Get a doctor for Heegan, and Joe, you wrap the jail around him when the doc gets through. Like as not he'll get life for the attempted killing of Sheriff Jim Blaine."

Rawhide walked out, stomped down the boardwalk to the boarding-house. Ma Jones met him at the door with open arms.

" I thought you was dead, laddie buck," she whispered.

" You paid off your mortgage to-night, Ma," Rawhide said. " Heegan marked it ' Paid in full ' ! "

He ran lightly up the stairs and reported to Jim Blaine—shook his head when Blaine asked him to run for office of sheriff.

" Nuh-uh, Jim," he told the grizzled old peace officer. " You're a better man than me for the job, but I'll help out until you get up off bedground. Things are quiet now in Rainbow, the round-up is almost here. I'll just be a part-time sheriff ! "

CHAPTER XIX

THREE SIXES TO BEAT

RAWHIDE RUNYAN was riding his black horse through the rugged mountains of the Virgin Range on the Arizona-Nevada border. His sheep-lined brush coat was buttoned to keep out the evening chill of Iceberg Canyon, and his gloved right hand was never far from the long-barrelled .45 Peace-maker Colt in the cutaway holster on his sturdy right leg.

A brooding silence hung heavy in the twilight shadows which slanted out on the canyon floor from the overhanging cliffs on both sides. Something was in the air, some hint of danger which the Arizona cowboy could feel like a strong omen.

Rawhide Runyan frowned as he rode down the one-way trail through a perfect bushwhack trap. In his early twenties, Runyan was a veteran of the long trails, with powder smoke in his blood. His own Diamond Double R spread was a cowboy's paradise, but Rawhide Runyan had a weakness. When an underdog sent out a call for help, the young boss of the Arizona Strip never failed to answer.

The hastily scrawled letter from Jim Barbee had mentioned mysterious enemies, and Barbee was a fighting man who seldom asked for help. Now Jim Barbee was making a last stand against forces he could not see.

The silence became more oppressive, unbroken except for the swish of the high Jimson weeds against Rawhide's leather-clad legs. Now Rawhide knew why the little town at the mouth of the canyon had been named Jimson. He'd reach there in an hour and get on the outside of a good hot meal.

" Stand your hoss, stranger, and elevate—pronto ! "

Rawhide Runyan instinctively checked his horse as that buzzing voice cut through the brooding silence. Runyan's hands rose slowly. He turned his head to the left.

A tall man stepped from the brush with a cocked six-shooter in his right hand. A blue bandanna covered the lower part of his tanned face.

" Cowboy, eh ? " the stranger said, eyeing Rawhide. " You've straddled that black hoss for quite a spell. If you're packin' a running-iron, you're one dead hombre ! "

Rawhide Runyan felt the hot blood racing through his veins. Only rustlers carried running irons on their saddles.

The masked man held the high hand. He circled Runyan slowly. A grunt came from the man's tight lips as he read the brand on Shadow's sleek black shoulder.

" You wouldn't be Rawhide Runyan ? "

" Wouldn't I ? "

" Then I won't have any competition from you." The masked man grunted. " Hit out for town, but don't prowl the hills if you want to stay healthy. Drift along, cowboy ! "

Rawhide scowled, clucked to his horse and rode on through the Jimson weeds. He wanted to circle back and find out more about the stranger. But Rawhide decided against that. The masked man with the cocked gun was on familiar ground and figuring any stranger might be a rustler.

It was almost dark as Rawhide turned a sharp bend in the trail and raised his eyes to a cluster of distant lights down at the mouth of the canyon. That would be Jimson town not more than a mile away. Rawhide tugged his grey stetson down to shade his eyes against the light. Then :

" Keep that hand up, stranger," a smooth—entirely different—voice purred, from behind a big boulder at the side of the trail. " If you're an owlhooter—well, it's always open season on 'em ! "

Rawhide Runyan gritted his teeth and seethed inwardly. He had been caught twice in the same kind of trap. And now he was accused of being an outlaw. It wasn't his turn to talk, so he held his hands high as he listened.

" Why didn't you come in by the stage road ? " the purring voice asked.

Runyan turned his horse slightly to put the lights of the town at his back. His eyes narrowed as he saw a black mask covering this new stranger's eyes. The blue six-shooter in the masked man's steady right hand was eared back for a shot.

" I figured this was the stage road," Rawhide answered.

" You're a liar, cowboy," the stranger said sharply. " You rode through Jimson weeds all the way down the canyon. What's your business in these parts ? "

" I figured to hunt some white-tailed deer," Rawhide answered shortly. " Any law against it ? "

" If either your six-shooter or rifle have been fired recent, you're a dead stage-coach robber," the tall hold-up man answered.

He came close and stared at Rawhide's holstered gun without touching the weapon. Then he circled and touched the .45-70 Winchester in Rawhide's saddle scabbard. After which the masked man grunted and waved his hand.

" Drift," he said laconically. " If I'm wrong this first time, I can always find you later."

Rawhide Runyan scowled again, wheeled his horse and clattered down the widening trail. He put his right hand on the butt of his six-shooter, and he did not release that hold until he branched into a dusty street. He headed for a lunch-room which was overshadowed by a big false-fronted saloon with glaring yellow coal-oil lamps at each corner. He smiled grimly when the sign informed him that the saloon was the Long Chance.

Rawhide Runyan swung to the ground and hitched his Shadow horse with trailing reins. He dusted the alkali from his worn range clothing with his gloves, high-heeled across the boardwalk and shouldered through the screen door. He took a seat at the counter—and then his wide shoulders jerked back.

A smiling girl waited for his order, but Rawhide was looking beyond her rounded shoulders. There was an open door in the wall into the saloon. Several men were watching him from under the brims of low-drawn hats. Rawhide shrugged. He ordered a thick steak well done, a side of ham and eggs, French fries, and a mug of coffee.

" Give me the coffee first," he told the girl. " I'm choked with trail dust."

" Did you ever try whisky for sluicing ? " a deep voice

asked with a chuckle. " Lay your hackles, cowboy. I'm
Jo-Bob Keene. I run this Long Chance. I'll roll you some
dice for your supper. You're Rawhide Runyan from up in
the Strip, eh ? We might do some business together."

Rawhide turned slowly to stare at Keene—a mountain of
a man who towered six feet four. Keene wore a neat broadcloth suit, its frock-coat of the type worn by frontier gamblers.
He also wore a brace of silvered .45 Colt six-shooters belted
high on his powerful legs. His black eyes matched his hair.

Rawhide was about to reply that he could pay for his own
grub, but a movement in the saloon brought his head up. A
man of forty-odd was staring intently at him, and the man
nodded his head one time. Rawhide recognized him—Jim
Barbee of the J Bar B. Jim was not a stranger in Jimson.

" It's your shake," Rawhide told Keene. " One roll for
the grub. Make it double or nothing ! "

Keene picked up a leather cup and shook the five dice with
his hand over the top. Rawhide Runyan sipped at his hot
coffee as he studied the big gambler's face. Keene was as
straight as a tall pine, and he wasn't fat. Rawhide Runyan
wondered why Keene wore a brace of six-shooters when he
could break a big man in two with his bare hands.

" Size don't count up here, Runyan," Keene said softly,
as though he had read Rawhide's thoughts. " A Colt makes
all men equal, or nearly so. Some are faster than others, and
if they're not, they go gun-naked to keep out of fracases. I
hear you're right rapid with your tools."

Rawhide knew he was facing a deadly gunman. None
other would mention six-shooters as *tools*. And Keene was
the boss of Jimson town.

" I can take care of myself," Rawhide answered coolly.
" Roll the dice."

Keene tipped the leather cup and made his spread. After
studying the cubes, he leaned back with a smile crinkling his
dark eyes.

" Three sixes to beat," he told Rawhide.

Rawhide sipped his coffee as he picked up the dice with his
left hand. After rattling the leather cup, he slapped it lip-
down on the counter and raised it slowly. Keene leaned over,
drew a deep breath.

" You're shot with luck, cowboy," he said softly. " Three
sixes and a pair of aces make a full house. I'll see you later
about the business I mentioned."

CHAPTER XX

WHO ROBBED THE STAGE ?

RAWHIDE RUNYAN left the lunch-room and walked to his horse. He glanced about for Jim Barbee, but the stocky cattleman was nowhere in sight along the dusty main street. Rawhide mounted his scarred saddle when he saw a sign announcing the Jo-Bob Corral and Livery Stable across the street. A small frame hotel stood adjoining the corral.

A gruff voice called softly as Rawhide rode into the darkened livery stable :

" Hold your gun, Rawhide. Better grain your hoss before you ride out to the Bar B with me."

Rawhide slid his gun back into the holster. Somebody was going to get shot if these Nevada gents kept giving him the hold-up order in the dark ! But he grinned now as he recognized the voice of Jim Barbee. He had worked with Jim back in the Arizona Strip when outlaws and rustlers had been as thick as flies in tick time.

Rawhide shook hands with the stocky cattleman, asked where he could find the oat bin, and led Shadow to an empty stall. After giving the black horse a double measure of grain, Rawhide loosed the saddle cinch. Then he told Barbee about the double hold-up during the ride through Iceberg Canyon.

" I couldn't say for sure, but that first gent sounds like Maverick Macey," Barbee answered thoughtfully. " Tall lean gent about thirty, who hunts maverick cattle for a living. That's what he meant when he said you wouldn't give him any competition."

" The second hold-up was also a tall gent, with a low smooth voice," Rawhide volunteered. " He wore a black mask over his eyes, and said something about the stage being robbed."

" Did he talk educated ? " Barbee asked sharply.

Rawhide nodded.

Jim Barbee frowned. " Sounds like Garse Steadman. He owns a quality outfit up the canyon a ways. He gets plenty of money from the outside, and raises hot-blooded horses. Of course, I'm just guessing that it could have been Steadman."

" You don't have to guess about Jo-Bob Keene," Rawhide said confidently. " All three of these gents knew who I was. But Keene said he wanted to talk *business* with me. What kind of business ? "

There was no light in the barn. Rawhide listened carefully while Jim Barbee talked in a low voice just above the crunch of Shadow's grinding teeth. Rawhide grew more puzzled as Barbee droned out what things he knew.

Jo-Bob Keene owned most of Jimson town, and was due to own considerably more. The big gambler was always ready to loan money to small cattlemen at a high rate of interest. If they couldn't repay when the loan was due, Keene took over their ranches, sold off the cattle, and added to his land holdings. According to Barbee, Keene owned forty or fifty sections of land in Iceberg Canyon.

"My ten sections control most of the water in the canyon," Barbee added, interrupting Rawhide's thoughts. "Keene has wanted my place for quite a while, and I owe him two thousand dollars. I was all set to pay him after shipping my beef, but rustlers cleaned me out one night. They drove off a hundred and fifty head. I blamed it on Maverick Macey, but I couldn't find a trace of my stock, so I sent for you. You've got to help me, Rawhide."

"Macey and Keene might be working a squeeze play on you," Rawhide suggested. "Macey gets the cattle, and Keene gets your ten sections of land."

"Except that Maverick Macey hates Keene from the ground on up," Barbee added dryly. "It would be more like Carse Steadman to stand in with Keene, but even that doesn't make sense. Keene has cleaned Steadman out several times at stud poker, so Steadman's not very friendly to Keene."

Rawhide Runyan sat on the feed box and tried to fit the pieces of the puzzle together. A hundred and fifty head of three-year-old steers just didn't disappear into thin air, and the three men he suspected were not over friendly with each other. It was a plain case of dog eat dog, and the devil take the hindmost.

"Let's ride over to see Carse Steadman on the way up to your spread," Rawhide suggested, sliding from the grain box to tighten his latigo. Jim Barbee led out his own horse while Runyan slipped the headstall on Shadow before fitting the bit in place. Rawhide left a silver dollar on the grain box.

The two old friends rode out of the barn and headed for Iceberg Canyon.

It was new country to Rawhide Runyan. Barbee took the lead. He bore to the left until they came to a weedy, deep-rutted road. Barbee explained that Steadman lived close to the stage road.

An hour later the lights from the windows of a big house glowed through the shadowy night.

The two men rode up to a tie-rail in front of the house and swung to the ground. The front door opened to flood the yard with yellow light, and a tall man called a question from behind a cocked six-shooter :

" Your names, gents ? "

" It's Jim Barbee with a friend," the cattleman answered promptly. " We're coming up."

Carse Steadman made no answer as the two men walked into the light and up the stairs to the broad gallery. Steadman stared at Runyan and took a quick step forward to jam his gun against Rawhide's lean-muscled belly.

" Now you talk straight, mister," Steadman whispered, his voice like the angry buzz of a rattlesnake's tail. " I saw you making medicine with Jo-Bob Keene, and if you've got business with him it's bound to be crooked ! "

Rawhide Runyan held his breath for a moment, and gently expelled it. He was staring into Steadman's angry blue eyes, wondering how the tall dandy would look with a black mask covering those light blue eyes. The voice did not sound the same, and it had been too dark to see either hold-up man's clothing.

" I didn't talk business with Keene," Rawhide said evenly. " We wanted to talk to you first."

" *You* talk," Steadman purred.

" I was held up down in the canyon not far from here," Rawhide began. " The stick-up man mentioned something about the stage being robbed. I told him I thought I was on the stage road, but he called my attention to the Jimson weeds growing high. You got any idea who he might be ? "

" He might be Maverick Macey," Steadman answered, but he did not remove the gun from Rawhide's midriff. " Don't touch your gun, Jim ! " Steadman barked at Barbee. " You owe money to Keene, and the stage carried five thousand dollars this afternoon. You might find that money useful to pay your debt."

Jim Barbee stepped back, growling in his throat. His right hand was poised for a strike at his low-slung gun, but Steadman shifted his own weapon to cover the angry cattleman.

Rawhide Runyan moved with the shifting gun, striking like a cat with his right hand. His fist crashed against Steadman's out-thrust jaw, and the cocked gun exploded harmlessly as Steadman sagged to the porch floor under the glaring coal-oil lights. Rawhide Runyan stepped back and slipped inside the door with the same lithe movement—just as the crunch of heavy boots came from the outer darkness.

"Lift 'em, Jim," a deep voice ordered sternly. "I'm what law there is in Jimson, and it looks like you've killed Carse Steadman."

Jim Barbee turned slowly just as big Jo-Bob Keene came up the steps with one of his silvered .45 six-guns in his right hand. Barbee was short on temper but long on courage. His right hand slapped down to his holstered gun.

"Don't draw, Jim," Keene warned softly. "I've never been beaten in a game of draw, and you know it. What became of that wide-shouldered cowboy from the Arizona Strip?"

"Standing right behind you, so unclutch that shooting iron, Keene!"

Keene opened his fingers and dropped his glittering weapon to the planking. He glanced sidewise, saw the open window through which Rawhide had crawled out, and nodded his head. Then Keene made his first proposition:

"Holster up and draw me even, Rawhide. You heard what I said to Jim Barbee, and the same goes for you."

"You said it from behind a full house," Rawhide answered. "That's how I'm talking now, and I don't talk much. You mentioned business between you and me. Such as what?"

"Cattle business," Keene said evenly. "I own sixty sections of grazing land here in Iceberg Canyon, and I need a good man to ramrod the spread after I stock it with cattle. A hundred and fifty a month—cartridges furnished!"

"Pay him no mind, Rawhide," Barbee cut in quickly. "His land ain't worth shucks without my water."

"Which same I mean to get," Keene answered smoothly. "I'll buy out what stock you have left, and you can get a start some other place. Holster yore smoke pole, Rawhide."

Rawhide stepped back as Steadman began to stir. Keene drew in a startled breath as he watched Steadman stagger to his feet.

"I thought he was dead," Keene whispered.

Carse Steadman saw Keene as he was coming out of the daze. Steadman shook his head to clear away the fog, and blurted a savage accusation:

"I had five thousand dollars coming in on that stage, Keene! The stage was held up by a tall road agent before it reached my place."

"That's what I heard," Keene answered. "You owe me five thousand. I know who sent the money, so don't try to run me up a blind trail. You've got a week to get what you owe me, or I'm taking over your Circle S outfit."

Carse Steadman listened with his head turned slightly to the side. He began to tremble with anger as his voice rose to a scream :

" Fit a gun to my hand and draw me even, you killing ape ! The hold-up was a tall gent, which lets Barbee and this Runyan hombre out ! "

" I don't want to kill you, Carse," Keene said softly. " You forget that there's another tall gent prowling the badlands, and Jim Barbee has forgotten the same thing. Lay your hackles and use your brains."

A pistol shot roared out from the murky yard as the Acey-Deucy stetson hat jumped from Keene's black head. Keene smiled with his lips, but showed no emotion.

Then a snarling voice ripped through the darkness, a voice Rawhide Runyan was sure he had heard before.

CHAPTER XXI

DRY-GULCH GUNS

THAT voice said : " You're a snake-tongued liar, Keene ! I don't make mine robbing stages, and you know it. The five thousand bucks on that stage belonged to *me*, and you know how I got the money ! " It was the voice of Maverick Macey.

Rawhide Runyan had stepped behind the corner of the house just as Maverick Macey had shot the hat from Keene's head. The big gambler's body had hidden Rawhide, and now Runyan crept around the big frame house like a stalking Indian. He could hear the murmur of voices as he crept down the opposite side, and Macey was still holding the drop when Runyan came to the corner.

Knowing that Keene would see him when he stepped away from the house, Rawhide wondered if the gambler's eyes would give him away. He stepped out with his gun in his hand, while he watched the gambler's face. Keene's eyes never flickered, but his deep voice began to speak persuasively.

" I wouldn't talk too much, Carse," he said to Steadman. " And I wouldn't get nervous with that gun, Maverick," he added to Macey.

" I either get my money or I'll talk plenty," Maverick growled. " But before I give up head, I'm going to drill you centre ! "

Rawhide Runyan poised on the toes of his boots as he measured the distance. His gun crashed down as he leaped at Maverick Macey's broad back, and Macey triggered a futile shot into the night before he sank to the ground with a smothered groan. Carse Steadman turned just as Rawhide leaped back with his gun covering the two men on the porch.

" I'm gunning you on sight, Runyan," Steadman promised grimly. " And if I know Maverick Macey, he won't rest until he pays his score. You're shot through with luck, but it won't hold out ! "

Jim Barbee drew his old six-shooter, backed down the three steps. Keene was still smiling, but there was a red gleam in his dark eyes. Keene ignored Carse Steadman as he walked down the steps toward his horse.

" Your luck might last if you take up my offer, Runyan," Keene said quietly. " You're not sure which one of the three of us is the worst, but you've put two of us to sleep without firing a shot. When you work your way around to me, it's going to be different."

" I'll think about that offer," Rawhide answered thoughtfully. " I'll also remember your warning. Evening to you, gambling man."

Keene reached down and picked up his gun from the ground. He pouched it with his back turned to Runyan and Barbee, mounted his grey gelding and jingled out of the yard.

Carse Steadman picked up a water bucket and dumped the contents over the porch rail into the upturned face of Maverick Macey.

Macey whooshed and struck out like a swimmer. He struggled to his feet with his hand slapping at his empty holster until the sneering voice of Carse Steadman recalled him to his whereabouts :

" Stop clawing air, you dry-gulching swine ! Rawhide Runyan dehorned you just as you were finding your sights on Keene ! "

Maverick Macey slowly turned his rawboned frame to face Runyan. Water dripped from Macey's sandy hair and from the tip of his long nose, but he dug his boot heels into the slop as he hunched his shoulders.

" I'm coming, gun hawk," he warned hoarsely. " The man don't live and keep on living who buffaloes me from the rear with his cutter ! "

" Don't jump," Rawhide warned quietly. " You can't fight a .45 slug, and I've got one ready. You mentioned something about giving up head. I'm listening if you still want to talk ! "

Maverick Macey dug deeper and glared ; there were yellow flecks in his greenish eyes. Then he slowly came out of his fighting crouch.

" There were three of us on the prod, Runyan," he said gruffly. " Who do you think robbed the stage ? "

" Who rustled Jim Barbee's shipping steers ? " Rawhide countered.

" Macey did," Jim Barbee accused hotly. " That owlhooting son twirls a wide loop and packs a careless running-iron. He got my cattle, and Keene gets my land ! "

" I'll pass that for now, Barbee," Macey said just above his breath. " I'm accused because I trap wild mavericks back in the tangles. Well, a herd like yours can't be run off without leaving a sign. Steadman's the gent who did the job, and he had five thousand on the stage when it was robbed, or so he says ! "

" Look, Macey," Carse Steadman answered in a low, venomous tone. " I'll shoot it out to-night, or the next time we meet. I'm coming out smoking when I make my pass, you lop-eared horse thief. I just noticed that's one of my quarter horses under your saddle. I've hunted that dappled colt for more than a year ! "

Rawhide Runyan knew cowboys, and Maverick Macey was a good one. Macey was set again for a fight. But Rawhide stepped between the two men and spoke over his cocked six-shooter.

" You gents better make it the next time you meet," he suggested firmly. " I rode down here to help my old saddle pard, Jim Barbee—and if you three gun rummies are mixed up in his trouble, just count me in. Get your horse, Macey ; you can ride with Jim and me."

" You've got trouble with me regardless, Runyan," Carse Steadman announced grimly. " You hit me with your fist, and what I said to Macey goes for you. I'll smoke you down or give up the gun ! "

" You called the turn, dude," Rawhide answered carelessly, but the angry blood was pumping through his veins. He told himself that men would have been shot in the Strip with less than half the gun-play that had occurred since he rode down Iceberg Canyon in the twilight. He climbed his black horse while Jim Barbee held the drop, and he did the honours while Jim mounted his brush-scarred saddle.

Carse Steadman, with a scowl on his dark face, watched

the three men ride out of the yard. He was too well dressed for cattle and mining country, but no one in Jimson knew the source of his income. That is, unless Jo-Bob Keene was in on the secret. And Keene wasn't the kind to talk.

Maverick Macey rode between Runyan and Barbee as they trotted up Iceberg Canyon in the faint light from a sickle moon. Macey was strangely silent after his truculence. But when the tall cowman began to chuckle, Rawhide turned quickly.

" I know where a bunch of cattle are hidden," Macey said, looking straight ahead. " There's going to be a war in these parts, and I might talk—for a price."

Jim Barbee glanced at Rawhide and nodded. " Let's light down," Barbee suggested. " I'd like to hear some plain talk."

" A dog that will fetch a bone will carry one back," Rawhide said coldly. " I don't compromise with rustlers or horse thieves—and Maverick Macey is both."

" Easy there, cowboy," Macey said thinly. " I offered to fight your gun with my bare hands once before, and the same goes now. Unsay them words ! "

" You stuck me up when I rode down the canyon this evening," Rawhide accused bluntly, " after reading my brands and earmarkings. And you talked out loud that I wouldn't give you competition."

" I should have let you have a slug then," Macey snarled. " Am I still a rustler ? "

" It's not legal to carry a running-iron on your saddle, even back here in the tangles," Rawhide answered, as he pointed to the iron by Macey's left leg.

" My brand is the M Bar M," Macey said hoarsely. " I take out mebbe twenty head a year, and a maverick hunter gets his beef the hard way ! "

" About that five thousand dollars you claimed you had on the stage," Rawhide said quietly. " That's just about what a man would net from a hundred and fifty head of steers."

" Or he might have run on to a rich vein of silver somewhere back in the hills," Macey answered slyly. " Now what would a cowboy do with a silver mine—especially if it was on another hombre's land ? "

Rawhide Runyan stopped his horse to block the trail. Jim Barbee closed in from the other side to put Maverick Macey in a squeeze trap. Barbee's features were quivering with excitement as he jerked his six-shooter from the holster and jammed the muzzle against Macey's lean ribs.

" Talk, you rustlin' son ! " he growled hoarsely.

Suddenly, then, a rifle barked from a timbered ridge on the right canyon wall.

Jim Barbee, hit by the bullet, grunted as he slid from his saddle.

Maverick Macey dug under his left arm with his right hand. Rawhide Runyan clawed for his holster when he saw the sheen of metal in the moonlight—the sheen of Macey's hide-out gun.

Rawhide nicked Shadow with the spurs just as the snub-nosed gun roared in Macey's freckled fist. Rawhide flipped a shot at Macey from his hip just as his horse lunged forward. A Macey slug tore at the edge of Rawhide's calfskin vest. Then he heard Macey's body thud. Rawhide necked Shadow into a turn to ride back in a crouch above his smoking .45 Colt.

Maverick Macey was down on his face, with the hide-out gun still gripped in his hand. He was dead.

Rawhide picked up the battered black stetson to cover the dead man's partly visible face. Then he growled in his throat, turned to Jim Barbee.

" Hunt cover, Rawhide ! " Barbee said from the shadow of a rock. " That dry-gulcher with the rifle only nicked me in the shoulder. Now you know why I sent for help ! "

CHAPTER XXII

JIM BARBEE REMEMBERS

RAWHIDE RUNYAN had not seen the flash of the rifle, and he had no way of determining the hiding-place of the hidden marksman. He crouched between rocks across the stage road from Jim Barbee, watching the waving Jimson weed on the canyon floor as he tried to reason just where Maverick Macey fitted into the picture.

Jo-Bob Keene was the undisputed boss of Jimson town, and it was evident that the big gambler entertained dreams of empire. Recalling Macey's remark about a rich silver vein, Rawhide wondered how much Keene knew about Macey's discovery. Rawhide also remembered the group of men in the Long Chance Saloon who had watched him as he was rolling dice with Keene. Gunmen all, probably working for the gambler.

He pondered the puzzle for a time, shrugged, and shifted his thoughts to Carse Steadman. Steadman operated a gentleman's ranch, raising thoroughbred horses. The source of his income was unknown, but he had lost five thousand dollars to Keene at poker.

Rawhide stirred restlessly and called softly to Jim Barbee telling the cattleman that they would discover nothing if they remained guarding the trail. They both needed sleep, and Barbee suggested that they ride on to his ranch which was just a mile up the canyon.

The three horses had taken cover in the high, flowering weeds. The two men worked away from the trail. Rawhide Runyan whistled softly and caught the split reins when Shadow came to him with the other two horses following. Jim Barbee caught his own horse and asked what they would do about Maverick Macey.

Rawhide stared for a moment at Macey's empty saddle. He spoke softly to Barbee and led Macey's horse toward the body of its master. They picked Macey up and placed him face down across the saddle. They mounted their own horses and Jim Barbee led the funeral horse by the bridle.

" Macey's M Bar M spread is just over the ridge," the rancher told Rawhide. " We can leave the body there, while we take a look inside his shack."

The shack was littered with discarded clothing, and con- sisted of a small sleeping-room with a lean-to kitchen. They placed Macey on his cot, pulled a blanket over the corpse, and Jim Barbee said he was glad that part of it was over. Rawhide Runyan was poking around the room, but he stooped suddenly to pick something from a half-filled gunny sack.

" Look here, Jim," he called sharply. " I don't know much about metals, but this sample looks like silver to me."

Jim Barbee hurried to Runyan's side and took the heavy piece of quartz. The rancher held it close to the smoky lantern, turned it over in his hands, and whispered low in his throat.

" Say ! I've seen that kind of quartz somewhere around here. That's high-grade ore, Rawhide ! There's a dozen or more silver mines south of Jimson, but they don't handle ore like this piece."

Rawhide Runyan was continuing his search as Jim Barbee talked excitedly. There was a war sack under the cot, the kind which serves a cowboy for a trunk. Rawhide reached under the cot, pulled the sack into view, and Barbee watched as he dumped the contents on the dirty plank floor.

Several bills of sale for small jags of shipping beef were clipped together. Rawhide thumbed through the papers. He remarked that Macey had been telling the truth about the maverick cattle he had trapped and sold, and the pickings *had* been slim. Twenty-two steers for one year ; twenty-three the year before. Rawhide leaned forward to study a signature on the bills of sale.

"Macey sold his catch to Keene," he said softly. "This one calls for thirty dollars a head, delivered at Jimson. How much land did Macey own here ? "

"One section," Jim Barbee answered. His roughened hands caressed the piece of high-grade ore. "All Macey had was a small barn and several holding corrals. He used a pair of big oxen to bring in the wild steers. He'd fasten a steer to one of those big oxen with a neck yoke, and the ox would always come to its own pen for the grain Macey fed it. Year in and year out, Macey never could have saved five thousand dollars."

Rawhide grunted, reached for another piece of paper and read it. "Look, Jim," he said, and his voice rose with the excitement of his discovery. "Macey somehow sent out a shipment of ore to the smelter at Red Wing. If Macey had five thousand dollars coming in on the stage, it must have been payment for his shipment of silver ore."

Jim Barbee nodded slowly, but his eyes were bright with excitement. Maverick Macey had kept a tally book, using four straight lines up and down with a cross bar to make a tally of five steers. Any cowman could read his crude figures, and Rawhide Runyan frowned as he studied the old tally book.

"Maverick Macey didn't run off your shipping steers, Jim," he said positively. "He would have kept a record for his own protection, and none of these pages adds up more than twenty-five head. But Macey did say he knew where a hundred and fifty head of beef were hidden. Hm-m-m. Let's get on over to your place and sleep on it."

Jim Barbee turned up the lantern chimney and blew out the light. Rawhide stuffed the tally book and bills of sale into his hip pocket as he followed Barbee outside. They reached the Bar B Ranch as the moon was waning. After stabling their horses, Barbee led the way to his comfortable log house. He indicated a bunk in the front room where Rawhide was to spread his blankets.

Rawhide Runyan came out of a sound sleep with a start. A hand clutched his shoulder ! His thumb cocked the hammer of his six-shooter as he raised his right arm in the dark. Then he held his shot—for the husky whisper of Jim Barbee identified the hand on his arm.

7

"Rouse around, Rawhide," Barbee murmured. "I just remembered where I've seen that kind of rock. It lacks only an hour till sun-up. I've got fresh horses in the barn. Breakfast can wait! Let's go!"

Rawhide yawned as he reached for his boots. He had already started the day by putting on his hat, and his shell-studded gun belt was hanging on a peg at the head of his bunk. Jim Barbee told Rawhide not to be finicky; said they could wash their faces and hands in the spring at Wolf Hole. The two men left the house by the kitchen door and walked out to the long, low barn.

Shadow whickered at Rawhide, and the cowboy glanced sidewise at Barbee as he gave the tired black horse a half gallon of white oats. Barbee jerked his thumb at a big grey gelding in a box stall, and Rawhide carried his riding gear to the stall. He would ride the grey on this jaunt.

There was a grey smudge in the eastern sky as the two men quit the ranch and headed for a high ridge at a brisk lope, with Barbee in the lead. The smudge brightened over toward Squaw Peak, and the sun broke through as the two riders stopped on a timber-fringed mesa.

Rawhide sat his saddle and filled his lungs with the rarefied air. A clear spring was gurgling out of the rocky soil, and a deep hole had been formed about a dozen feet below the spring.

"I dunno why, but the natives and Injuns have always called it Wolf Hole," Barbee explained. "You're looking at the main water supply for Iceberg Canyon, so now you know why Keene wants my land."

Rawhide Runyan dismounted and tethered his grey horse to a springy branch. He walked over to the pool, doused his head under the icy water and lathered his brown hands with a small bar of soap. Jim Barbee looked on and called him a dude, but Rawhide completed his ablutions with a smile on his rugged bronze face. After drying on his neckerchief, he settled his hat and turned to Barbee.

"Don't stand there like a fortune-teller," Rawhide said casually, knowing that Barbee would be disappointed at his apparent lack of interest. "You mentioned something about that silver ore. It certainly didn't take long to spend the night on your four-bit outfit!"

"Ten sections ain't a feed lot," Barbee snapped, and then he grinned. "Leave the horse and follow me afoot," he said.

Rawhide Runyan followed Barbee down a twisting trail to the base of a towering cliff. Part of the peak had broken off to leave a rubble of glittering rock at the bottom. Barbee picked up a chunk and passed it to Rawhide.

" Heft it ! "

Rawhide hefted the fragment and grunted his surprise. He turned the rock over and exposed a dull leaden surface which he tried to scratch with a thumbnail. Then he balanced the chunk in his left hand as he stared at Jim Barbee.

" You're plumb rich, Jim ! " Rawhide said, with a ring of awe in his deep voice. " You ought to make a million out of this ore on the mesa ! "

" My note is due day after to-morrow," Barbee said in a hollow voice. " Keene'll foreclose. It'd take a month to freight out enough ore to pay what I owe."

" Mebbe not," Rawhide contradicted stubbornly. " Let's ride back to your spread for a bait of hot grub. After we get some vittles under our belts, you and me are riding over to the Circle S to make medicine with Carse Steadman. I just now remembered something."

CHAPTER XXIII

THE RED WING STAGE

RAWHIDE RUNYAN and Jim Barbee might have been two cattle rustlers as they kept to the heavy brush, riding the deer trails on the horse ranch of Carse Steadman. Part of the Circle S was under stake-and rider fence, and Rawhide stopped his grey to stare at a section of crossed rails.

The weathered poles made an unusual pattern to a man who has been trained to read sign from early childhood. Jim Barbee rode over when he saw Rawhide stop. Barbee stared his unbelief for a long moment. Then his face hardened as he turned to Runyan.

" That section has been moved recent, Rawhide," he said hoarsely. " Moss always grows on the north side, and it's growing thataway on those other sections. Whoever let down these bars didn't put them back so's they'd show the moss— and Maverick Macey said he knew where my stolen herd was hidden."

He and Runyan reached for their ropes at the same time, and each caught an upright in his dinky loop. The horses were turned for a pull, and the tampered section spilled to the ground when the trained cow horses went to work.

Rawhide flipped his noose free, coiled his twine, and sent his horse across the tumbled rails.

Jim Barbee followed with his eyes watching the ground. They rode for several minutes during which they crossed a small stream three times. At each crossing they noted marks of the cloven hoofs.

Jim Barbee reached for the rifle under his saddle fender as he jerked his head toward a brushy horse trap.

" That's a blind valley over yonder, Rawhide. She's brush and cactus all around, with walls making a saucer. There's only one opening. That's it on the yon side of Coyote Creek. Carse Steadman uses it for a horse trap to hold his brood mares, but those tracks in the mud weren't made by horses. C'mon ! "

Rawhide Runyan nodded grimly as he followed Barbee across the shallow creek. He knew what they would find in the trap, but his mind was busy with another problem. A hundred and fifty head of shipping steers were as good as money in the bank, but they merely represented money until they were sold. A man either sold his beef to Jo-Bob Keene or shipped it out—and Barbee's note was due the day after to-morrow.

Runyan knew that Keene would not buy the steers. To do so would give Jim Barbee the two thousand he owed Keene, and Keene wanted Barbee's ten sections of land which controlled the water supply of Iceberg Canyon. Barbee would recover his stolen cattle, but he would lose his land and, with it, the rich silver deposit.

A shout from Barbee brought Runyan back to realities, and he sent his horse at a high lope to join the rancher. Barbee had snaked down a stake-and-rider, had ridden through the opening, and was staring at a small herd of grass-fattened steers scattered over the blind valley. Every steer was branded with the Bar B iron. Jim Barbee was staring at his stolen money-on-the-hoof with fight in his eyes. He gripped the handle of his belt gun until his knuckles showed white.

" Carse Steadman is the rustler, and we called poor old Maverick Macey it," he muttered savagely. " I'm taking powder smoke to that rustler, and I ain't lingerin'."

" Wait ! "

Rawhide clipped the one word viciously. Jim Barbee faced him sullenly, weathered face black with rage.

" Wait is what broke the wagon," Barbee blurted. " I waited myself out of the years it took me to build up this spread since I left the Arizona Strip. I'm taking show-down to Carse Steadman ! "

" You ain't," Rawhide contradicted inelegantly. " You forget that nick in your right shoulder, and your gun arm is stiff. You likewise forget that Macey stole a shipment of your high-grade ore, and that Macey and Steadman claimed to have had five thousand each on the Red Wing stage."

" Money ! " Barbee muttered savagely. " I need money. If you wasn't here, I'd stick up that stage myself."

" And either get yourself shot or a long stretch in prison," Rawhide said. " Let's put that fence back to keep in your beef, and then you and me are taking a ride. I just got me another hunch."

Jim Barbee grumbled as he fiddled with his six-shooter. Rawhide Runyan rode away, dismounted by the break in the fence. He replaced the bars after Barbee had ridden through. Then he mounted his borrowed horse and led the way through the brush at a gallop.

It was easy to back-track the trail through the brush and Jimson weeds. Rawhide Runyan had learned to track in more difficult country—the badlands of high Arizona. He did not speak to Barbee until they came to a hairpin turn in the stage road, where they stopped to blow the horses. Rawhide stood up in the stirrups and pointed without speaking.

Far below in the valley, they could see the Red Wing stage-coach with its four-horse hitch. The driver had stopped his teams, and he was holding the ribbons in his upraised hands. A tall bandit stood in the road, with the sun glinting on a pistol in his right hand.

" It's a stick-up ! " Barbee gasped. " The road agent has a black mask over his eyes ! "

" He's one of the gents who stopped me last night," Rawhide said. " Too far for rifle range, so don't spoil our play with a wild shot."

Jim Barbee lowered his Winchester reluctantly. He and Rawhide watched while the driver kicked the strong box from under the seat. The bandit stepped aside, waved the driver ahead. After the stage had rattled away in a cloud of red dust, the robber shot the lock from the strong box, fumbled for a moment in the box, and disappeared in the brush. Not until then did Rawhide give the word to ride.

" Let's take the short-cut to the Circle S ranch-house," he said to Barbee. " We can talk to him about that herd of yours, and find out if he lost any more money on the stage."

Jim Barbee nodded with a little smile of anticipation curling his lips.

Barbee asked no questions, and Runyan volunteered no information on the long ride down Iceberg Canyon.

They raced into the Circle S yard, rode behind a long log barn where they dismounted and tied their horses. Then Rawhide led the way to the house.

Just as they reached the broad gallery which ran the full length of the front of the house, Carse Steadman raced into the yard and slid his lathered horse to a stop. He was dressed in an expensive riding suit with tight-legged pants tucked down in polished English boots. His light-blue eyes widened as he saw his visitors, but he recovered himself instantly.

"It's happened again!" he shouted. "The Red Wing stage was held up and robbed!"

"Looks like you'd have hightailed into Red Wing to notify the law down there," Runyan said. "Did you lose some more money?"

Carse Steadman dismounted slowly before answering. He wore a belted .45 six-shooter around his lean hips under the tight riding-coat. His voice was low and deadly as he leaned forward, staring at Rawhide Runyan.

"Are you the law?" he asked in his smooth voice. "Deputy marshal, or Wells Fargo detective?"

"Neither," Rawhide answered with a shrug that put his right hand above his holstered gun. "Which was you expecting?"

"Maverick Macey had you tagged for a stock detective," Steadman answered, his voice more composed. "We knew Barbee had sent out for help."

"Maverick never stole Jim's beef herd," Rawhide said quietly. "We found the herd in a horse trap back in the brushy hills. We just rode in to ask you about it."

"Meaning you think I rustled that shipping herd?" Steadman asked, and once more that deadly note crept into his humming voice.

"Call yourself names," Rawhide answered with a careless shrug, but his grey eyes were steady and watchful. "Me and Jim saw that stage hold-up a little earlier to-day, and I recognised the road agent."

A deathlike silence seemed to creep across the big yard. Jim Barbee was holding his right shoulder with his left hand, while Rawhide and Steadman faced each other in a duel of nerves. The distance between them was not more than five paces, and neither man could miss if powder began to burn.

The fastest man would win the show-down, and both knew it was coming.

"You slugged me last night, Runyan," Steadman buzzed just above his breath, and the sound mingled with the hum of bottle flies.

"You bushwhacked Maverick Macey last night," Rawhide retaliated, speaking softly so as not to set off taut muscles. "Macey was just getting ready to talk."

"Macey packed a hide-out gun, and he swore to get you," Steadman answered, but his voice was husky. "Jo-Bob Keene said he'd match your six—but after me, he's first. How do you want it, Johnny Law?"

"After you, *I'm* first," Rawhide Runyan said. "Make your pass, you rustling stick-up!"

Carse Steadman dropped his right hand and started his draw. Rawhide Runyan drove his hand down and side-stepped at the same time. He never underestimated an opponent, and he knew that a tie was the same thing as a defeat when old Judge Colt sat on the gun fighters' bench.

Rawhide's gun snouted over the lip of his holster and exploded at his hip in a perfect point shot. Carse Steadman was bringing his gun up to catch the sight with his squinting eyes, and the report of his gun was like a stuttering echo to Runyan's shot. It was that lingering stutter which marked the difference between life and death.

Carse Steadman spun sidewise and unhinged his long legs. A bit of black cloth fluttered from his vest pocket as he fell across the smoking gun—a silk mask like the one the road agent had worn to cover his eyes.

CHAPTER XXIV

PAID IN FULL

WHEN Steadman's polished boots had stopped rattling, Rawhide walked over to Steadman's sweating thoroughbred and lifted a pair of saddlebags from behind the cantle. Jim Barbee watched while Rawhide emptied the pouches. The rancher's mouth flew open as Runyan flipped a flat package to him.

"But this is addressed to Jo-Bob Keene," Barbee argued. "Five thousand in currency, mailed by the Red Wing smelter."

"Yeah," Rawhide grunted. "For a shipment of *your*

silver. Keene was the hold-up who robbed the stage *yesterday*.
Carse Steadman stuck up the stage to-day, but this money
belongs to you. Now you can pay Keene what you owe him."

Jim Barbee skinned the heavy wrapping from the money
and shoved the new currency down into his hip pocket. He
didn't like the set-up. His right arm was inflamed from the
bullet nick in his shoulder—and he was remembering that
Jo-Bob Keene always kept his promises. Keene had promised
to shoot Rawhide Runyan on sight, and Barbee wanted to be
in good shape for his own show-down with Keene.

Jim Barbee argued back and forth in his mind without
finding the answer. He told himself that he'd get the drop
on Keene, pay off his note, and save a shoot-out between
Keene and Runyan. Rawhide turned slowly in the saddle,
shaking his head.

" You won't take cards in it, Jim," he said quietly. " I
knew Keene was rated a fast gun-swift before I got your letter.
Mebbe I was just looking for a good excuse to come down and
match his cutter. In any case, I made a promise of my own."

Jim Barbee felt like a small boy who has been whipped by
a big bully—even though his land and cattle had been saved
and he owned a rich silver deposit he hadn't known was on
his land.

" I've got to dress this scratch, Rawhide," he said in a
hollow voice. " It hurts like the devil ! "

Rawhide Runyan smiled grimly with his face turned away.
His blood was tingling as he thought of a meeting with big
Jo-Bob Keene, but his voice was quiet and steady as he
agreed :

" Sure, Jim. Keene won't run away. And that wound
might give you trouble. We'll hit out for the Bar B because
I want to stop at Macey's place on the way back."

Jim Barbee looked surprised at Runyan's prompt acceptance
of his request. What he didn't see were the tracks of a big
horse in the red loam. Those prints were deep, as though
the horse was ridden by a heavy man—tracks with a scarred
frog in the right front hoof, like the tracks that had been made
in front of Carse Steadman's house the night before.

Rawhide Runyan swung his horse and checked the loads
in his .45 Peacemaker Colt. Five loads, with the hammer
riding on an empty for safety. If a man couldn't hit what he
was shooting at with five shots, he'd better throw the gun
away and run like a coyote.

Jim Barbee rode beside Rawhide with an expression of
relief on his tanned face. His arm was hurting like a sore

tooth, and like as not he had some fever. Dizzy spells swept over him from time to time, and his tongue was dry and thick from thirst.

Barbee swayed in the saddle when the two horses stopped in front of Maverick Macey's shack. Rawhide dismounted, went inside. His eyes narrowed when he saw that Macey's body had been removed. A pair of town pants hung from a peg, and Rawhide searched the pockets, removing some papers. After studying them for a moment, he tucked them inside his shirt and went out to rejoin Barbee.

" We'll ride past the mesa and stop at Wolf Hole," Rawhide said casually. " The cold water'll do you good, and we can look at your wound again."

Jim Barbee nodded dully as he swung his horse to follow Rawhide Runyan. A man could ride when he couldn't walk. Rawhide noticed that Barbee's eyes were almost closed, and that the fever was getting worse. Barbee was riding by instinct, gripping his right shoulder with his left hand.

Rawhide was studying the ground as they climbed the steep trail leading to the springs. His eyes shifted across a little valley to the glittering rubble at the base of Squaw Peak. He dismounted, caught Jim Barbee, who was swaying in his saddle. Rawhide helped the feverish man to the ground near the waterhole.

Barbee flattened out, stuck his head under the cold water. The shock revived him almost instantly. Drawing his frogging knife, Rawhide cut the right sleeve from Barbee's shirt. He frowned when he saw the deep gash was rimmed with red alkali dust. After washing the wound, he took a small bottle of permanganate from his saddlebags to cauterize the bullet scrape.

Jim Barbee bit down hard on his teeth and drew in a deep breath. Taking the makings from his shirt pocket, he rolled a corn-husk quirly and flicked a match to flame with a thumbnail. He inhaled deeply, blew a cloud of pungent smoke over his head. As he was lifting the cigarette to his lips again, he stopped abruptly and spoke in a low, jerky tone :

" We've got company, Rawhide. Jo-Bob Keene's ridin' up the trail from that silver ledge ! "

" Yeah, I saw him," Rawhide answered, as he turned slowly to face the oncoming horseman.

Keene stopped his big dappled grey and swung leisurely to the ground. His black eyes were watching Rawhide Runyan, and he elbowed the tails of his long black coat away from the silvered guns on his powerful thighs.

" You look kinda peaked," the gambler said to Jim Barbee. " You've got until to-morrow to pay off your note."

" I'll pay it off now," Barbee answered. He reached slowly to his hip pocket.

Keene poised his right hand above his holster until Barbee's hand came into sight, gripping a sheaf of new bills. After counting out the correct amount, Barbee shoved the stack down into his pocket and tendered the counted money to the gambler.

" Just give me back my note, Keene," Barbee said quietly. " I collected some dinero, and I found that shipping herd of mine. Not only that, but my pardner found a rich silver mine right here on my own land."

Keene straightened slowly, but only his piercing black eyes showed any emotion. Now they glowed like rubies while the gambler smiled with his lips.

" Did you rob the stage this morning? " he asked.

" Carse Steadman robbed it, and Steadman's dead," Rawhide Runyan answered for Barbee. " He figured it was his turn because you did the same thing yesterday."

" Prove it ! " Keene rasped. " I figured Macey did that job yesterday—and then you killed Macey to get the money to pay off your note, Barbee ! "

Jim Barbee was sitting by the pool, paying no attention to Keene or Runyan. His eyes were closed.

Keene flicked his black eyes to the face of Rawhide Runyan.

" It was *you* killed Macey," Keene said. " You also killed Carse Steadman, and they were both fast with a six-shooter. You and me rolled dice not long ago, and I made you a promise. Remember ? "

" I remember," Rawhide answered. " I saw your horse's tracks pointing this way, which saved me the trouble of riding to town—where you might have too much help."

" I don't need help," Keene stated arrogantly. " I've never been beaten on the draw. You rode in here and ruined my plans just as I was about to strike it rich. With you out of the way, Jim Barbee'll be a cinch."

" Uh-huh," Rawhide grunted. " But you forget that I did beat your hand once before."

" Lightning never strikes twice in the same place," Keene said positively. " You had three sixes to beat, but that was with the dice."

Rawhide shrugged carelessly. " I was thinking about you and your two business associates. Both of them were fast with a six-shooter, and they both tried to kill me. Both of them are dead."

"They would have died anyway," Keene said, as he imitated Rawhide's shrug. "You saved me the trouble. I made you a promise ; now I'm giving you a chance."

Keene telegraphed his intention when he elbowed his coat tails away from his brace of silvered six-shooters. His long-fingered hands struck down in perfect unison. But Rawhide Runyan was already in motion.

Rawhide dipped his right hand down and up, with flame lancing from the muzzle of his .45 Peacemaker. He was concentrating on *one* gun while Keene was drawing *two*. The big gambler took a slug in the left side of his chest just as his weapons cleared leather with the muzzles pointing down.

Keene blasted a pair of holes in the ground just before he crashed down on his face, dead.

Rawhide Runyan jacked the spent shell from his smoking gun and thumbed a fresh cartridge through the loading gate. He turned with a ring of smoke making a gun fighter's halo above his head. Then he heard Jim Barbee chuckle grimly.

"Look at that packet sticking out of his pocket," Barbee whispered. "It's as much like mine as two peas in a pod."

Rawhide reached down into Keene's pocket. The packet was addressed to Maverick Macey from the Red Wing smelter. The seals had been broken, but the bank band round the currency was marked : FIVE THOUSAND DOLLARS. Rawhide handed the money to Barbee without comment.

"Macey, Steadman, and Keene," Barbee said in a hushed voice. "You did it, Rawhide—even if you had three sixes to beat ! "

CHAPTER XXV

RUNYAN RIDES GUN SIGN

RAWHIDE RUNYAN was riding fast, with surging anger in his heart, and a Winchester in the saddle boot under his left leg. The big black horse under him was running easily in a mile-eating lope, following a plain trail where a herd of cattle had stampeded under expert driving. One look at Runyan's stern, tanned face gave definite evidence that the boss of the Diamond Double R was riding gun sign.

In his early twenties, Rawhide Runyan was a veteran of the cow-country wars. Although not a tall figure, his frame was powerfully built and he carried himself with dignity. His neighbours in the Arizona Strip called him a cowboy's cowboy, looked to him for leadership, and followed him without question.

Rawhide passed the upper end of Dark Canyon with blazing tawny eyes. Three hundred head of his Diamond Double R cattle had been rustled, but he wasn't asking for help. They were headed for the badlands where the only law that men recognized was carried in gun leather.

The grass played out below an abandoned dam, relic of another battle with outlaws. Rawhide Runyan pulled Shadow to a sliding stop, loosed his six-shooter against crimp, swung to the ground. An unfamiliar scuffling sound came from the sandy rubble which marked the beginning of the badlands.

Rawhide leaned over in a crouch, his right hand on his six-shooter. He keened his ears. The scuffling noise grew louder. The .45 Peacemaker Colt jumped to his hand as a long, slanting shadow announced the coming of a tall stranger.

Rawhide waited with his thumb curling back the hammer of his gun. He was on the prod, taking fight to the enemy. His deep voice cracked like a whiplash as the tall stranger rounded a rock and stepped into the clear.

" Grab a handful of sky, hombre ! " Runyan snapped.

The tall stranger stopped in his tracks, turned his head to see his captor, and held up his hand in the sign of peace. Long brown hair hung to his spare shoulders, a wisp of it stuck out through a hole in his battered old black stetson. His greenish suit had once been black broadcloth ; long tails hung down from his clerical coat.

" I bring you greetings, Rawhide Runyan," the stranger said in a deep, solemn voice. " I am Sam Judas, a man of peace, a giver of light."

" Sky pilot ? " Rawhide asked suspiciously. " With that brace of hoglegs hiding under your coat tails. How come ? "

" I am not an ordained minister," Judas hastened to explain. " But it is true that I preach the Word, and bring solace to the dying. You are on the trail of rustlers. I like what I read in your face. There will be work for Sam Judas to do."

A big man galloped up on a deep-chested horse ; a man fashioned like a great shaggy bear. He was Slow Joe Hill and he had been an outlaw until Rawhide Runyan had reformed him—starting the reformation with a terrific beating. Now Slow Joe was Rawhide's trusted foreman.

" Sam Judas, or I'm a liar ! " Slow Joe bellowed. " Long time no see you, parson."

" Well, I never," Judas said slowly, offering a bony hand to Slow Joe. " I heard you were riding the straight-and-narrow, Joe, old friend. But like myself, you are girded for war."

" Now look, Sam," Slow Joe said gruffly. " Me and Rawhide don't have time right now to listen to a sermon. We're trailin' cow thieves, and we're ridin' fast."

" Pause a spell, my impetuous contemporary," Sam Judas said quickly. " I come with a plea for help."

" You call me names like that and yo're going to need help," Joe growled. " I ain't nothin' of the kind."

" You ever hear of Simon Tolliver ? " Judas asked, showing no fear of Slow Joe.

" Hear of him ? I know him as well as I know you," Joe answered. " Him and Idaho Crim used to run the biggest gang of cut-throats in the badlands."

" Not *used* to," Sam Judas corrected. " They still *do*, and they passed about two hours ago with a bunch of Diamond Double R steers. They went that way." He waved a skinny arm toward the vast waste land. " You can't find them unless I help you."

" We don't need help," Rawhide answered crisply, as he started to climb his saddle. " Let's go, Joe."

Sam Judas flipped his coat tails back with his elbows and his skinny hands flashed down. Then he was crouching behind a pair of long-barrelled .45s. The chips were down, and he had won first hand in the game of draw.

" Wait up a spell," Sam Judas rumbled. " Your herd has disappeared into thin air. I know where they are, but you hotheads would never find same ! "

Slow Joe stared at Judas and clenched his big fists. He began to move slowly toward the tall, gaunt man—who calmly cocked both hammers of his heavy guns.

" I'm goin' to bust you apart with my hands," Slow Joe growled, shuffling slowly forward.

" Stop where you are, Joe ! " Sam Judas said sternly. " I will not waste either words or powder on you. Take one more step and I'll shoot your boss out of the saddle ! "

Rawhide remained perfectly still. The hands of Sam Judas were steady as rocks—and the lust to kill was changing Slow Joe's little greenish eyes to a glowing red. Rawhide spoke sharply :

"Back, Joe! Dead men can't catch rustlers!"

Slow Joe stopped instantly with one big boot poised in the air. He came out of his crouch, shook his head jerkily, spoke gruffly to Sam Judas.

"You win, Judas. I could take all your slugs and still tear you apart. I'll do it some day, but right now it's your turn to talk. Turn them guns away from Rawhide."

"Greater love hath no man," Sam Judas murmured with a frosty smile, as he quickly holstered his weapons. "I ask your pardon, Runyan," he continued humbly. "You seek the men who stole your cattle ; I ask your help against these same men."

"Yeah? Keep on talking, man of peace," Rawhide said evenly. "Joe and I'll listen. Fly at it!"

"You've heard of the Canyon of the Damned?" Judas asked.

Rawhide Runyan jerked in the saddle. The Canyon of the Damned was a deep valley in the badlands. It had neither inlet nor outlet, and many were the legends told about it. A band of Apaches was said to have been trapped in the Canyon, but that had been sixty years before Rawhide had come to the Arizona Strip.

"I know the place," Rawhide answered with a shrug. "I've seen little horses down there through my glasses. What about it?"

"There is a hidden secret trail to the valley floor," Judas answered. "My friends are in trouble."

Slow Joe made a sound with his lips, touched his forehead with a big finger as Rawhide looked his way. Sam Judas also saw the gesture. He smiled.

"I am *not* touched in the head, my sinful friend," he told Slow Joe. "My friends are the little people in the Canyon of the Damned."

"Watch him, Rawhide," Slow Joe warned. "Now he's talkin' about the little people."

Rawhide Runyan turned partly to one side. His right hand flashed down and came out filled with blued steel. His voice low and soothing, he talked to Sam Judas :

"Joe and I'll help you, so don't be afraid of the little people."

The gaunt man's brown eyes flashed with sudden anger. His right hand poised above the grips of his gun, then he relaxed.

"I was a sinful man until I learned the error of my ways," Judas said. "Now I try to help where I can, using what comes to my hands."

" Like those two guns," Rawhide prompted, as Judas
stopped talking. " You execute the sinners, after which you
say a prayer over the grave."

" It has happened as you say," Sam Judas admitted with
a slow shake of his head. " Listen to me, Runyan." His deep
voice was strong with sincerity. " The little people I mentioned
are descendants of the Apache Indians who were trapped in
the Canyon of the Damned ! "

Slow Joe was inching his way toward Judas, who was
preoccupied with his own thoughts. But Rawhide spoke
sternly as Joe dug his heels in for a leap.

" Circle off there, Joe ! I believe Sam is right."

" Must be the heat," Slow Joe grumbled, as he loosened
his mighty muscles. " Let's all go down and play with those
little people."

" Where there is no sense, there is no feeling," Sam Judas
quoted, staring at Joe with disgust etched on his weathered
features. " If the little people didn't kill you, those owlhooters would. Now you keep your big mouth shut while I
make medicine with your boss." And Sam Judas turned back
to Rawhide Runyan.

" You saw the little horses, Runyan," Judas began quietly.
" They are small and stunted because of interbreeding. The
same thing happened to the Indians who were trapped in the
canyon by a landslide. Even though the little redskins can
now get out by the secret trail, they've stayed in the canyon
for safety. There are twenty of these little Indians in the
canyon. There were thirty, but that was before Simon Tolliver
and Idaho Crim found the secret entrance."

" You mean the outlaws killed ten little Indians ? " Rawhide asked in a whisper.

" In cold blood," Sam Judas answered, and there were
unshed tears in his solemn brown eyes. " That is why I came
to you for help. I want to save the little people."

Slow Joe squared his shoulders, stomped up to Sam Judas,
gravely offered his hand.

" Sorry I spoke out of turn, parson. You're more of a man
than I am, and you always was. Bend the way to this secret
entrance ; me and Rawhide'll help you save those runty
Apaches."

Sam Judas gripped Joe's big hand, smiled gravely behind
his silky brown beard.

" You never can tell where you'll find gold," Sam said.
" It's hidden mighty deep under your skin, Slow Joe, but the
metal is there just the same. Follow me."

CHAPTER XXVI

CHIEF BLUE STONE

SLOW JOE asked Judas: "Where's your hoss? Me and Rawhide travel mighty fast."

"I travel by shank's mare," Sam Judas answered with a smile. "Which means I take my foot in my hand when I travel. Don't worry about me, Joe. You and Rawhide won't be able to keep up with me unless I slow down my usual gait."

Rawhide Runyan narrowed his eyes as he studied the gaunt speaker. Sam Judas was somewhere around forty, give or take a year. He was built for speed in spite of his drawling speech and slow mannerisms, tough as whang leather, and possessed of unusual strength. Patterned after the swamp men down in the Louisiana bayou country where the natives take their religion seriously.

"Light a shuck, Sam," Rawhide said quietly. "Joe and I'll try to keep up with you if you don't take too many short-cuts where a horse can't travel up."

A gleam of appreciation glowed briefly in the brown eyes of Sam Judas. He nodded his head, turned on his heel, and started through the badlands at a shuffling dogtrot. Leaping over boulders where the horses had to go round, Sam Judas would wait patiently until the horsebackers had caught up, after which he would again lead out with tireless gait.

Once he disappeared in a patch of prickly pear. When Rawhide and Joe rode up to the thicket, Sam Judas was not in sight. Slow Joe scratched his head while Rawhide made a careful search of the ground. A drawling voice called from a point behind them:

"Thisaway, men. Just wanted to show you how easy it would be for Tolliver and Crim to bush you back here in the lavas. Better blow the hosses a spell; it gets a mite rough from here on."

Rawhide Runyan smiled wryly. Sam Judas had the stealth and craftiness of an Indian, and like a red man, he never got lost. Slow Joe was trying to get his bearings in the waste land, where one tall boulder looked like a thousand others.

"Know where we are?" he asked Rawhide.

"About six miles from the old dam," Rawhide answered positively. "Back yonder is Castle Rock atop Rainbow Mountain. I don't see any trace of our cattle."

" Your critters are down in the upper canyon by now,"
Judas said slowly. " Good feed in there after the rains, but
when the summer winds blow hot, the feed and water dry up
fast. Let's be on the move."

Not much to go on, but Rawhide Runyan was finding a
solution. The rustlers would feed the cattle in the canyon
while the feed held out, during which time they could blot
out and change brands. This means that they would make a
drive before the drought set in, probably to some Utah market.

Sam Judas picked his unerring way through the rubble,
his long brown hair waving in the breeze. Now the brush was
growing in profusion ; creosote bush, sage, and tough mesquite.
The tall guide parted the brush and beckoned for Rawhide to
follow, motioning the two men to the ground as they rode into
a little clearing.

" Leave the hosses here for a spell," he said. " We can't go
down the trail now, but I want to show you something few
white men have ever seen."

Rawhide tied Shadow with trailing reins, and the black
cow horse began to graze on mesquite beans. Sam Judas
turned on Slow Joe with a scowl as Joe lumbered through the
brush like a bear.

" You make more noise than a brush ox," he growled at
Joe. " Pick 'em up and put 'em down easy, unless you want
to stop owlhoot lead ! "

Joe nodded, with a guilty expression on his full round face.
He promised to make less noise, trying to imitate Rawhide's
noiseless tread through the loamy sand. Sam Judas walked
away scowling, held up a hand for silence as he reached the
far end of the brush-fringed clearing.

" Not a sound," he cautioned in a whisper. " Those
Apaches can hear a leaf in the wind and they can see even
better than that. Watch where you put your big feet, and
take a look down yonder."

Rawhide Runyan peered between the parted branches,
drew in a deep breath. He knew that he was looking down
into the Canyon of the Damned, which had been the prison
of the lost tribe for nearly seventy years.

A tiny rivulet of water caught the sun down on the valley
floor, two thousand feet below. Several animals were
drinking—tiny spots which might have been wild dogs. One
of them threw back its head to scent the wind ; then the band
scampered for the rocks with the unmistakable gait of horses.

" Those critters are pygmy hosses now," Sam Judas
whispered. " They don't weigh much over two hundred

8

pounds even when the grass is lush. Now look half-way up that cliff wall and tell me what you see."

Rawhide Runyan looked, clicked his teeth, a frown furrowing his brow. He could see cattle grazing along wide shelves, and the cattle weren't runts. Undoubtedly full-sized steers from his Diamond Double R herd.

"They can't get down any farther," Judas whispered. "Move back now, and don't shoot. I hear the chief coming."

Rawhide strained his ears and could detect no sound but the humming of insects and the occasional cry of a bluejay. Then his head jerked up. A deep guttural voice spoke from down below the rim.

"How, Long Hair. You bring the great white braves."

"Heap mighty fighters," Sam Judas answered. "They come in peace; mebbe so bring some help to your people. We make strong medicine with you, my red brother."

A black head appeared at the edge of the mesa rim while Rawhide and Slow Joe stared. Two feathers were woven into the scalp lock; Rawhide noticed that they were taken from a hawk, denoting that the wearer was a chief. Two copper-coloured hands reached for a hold on a twisted root to pull the chief's small lithe body over the rocky edge.

"Rawhide Runyan, Chief Blue Stone. Other white man is my friend, Slow Joe." Sam Judas nodded slowly.

Rawhide studied the little Apache chief, reading his points, liking what he saw. Chief Blue Stone was five feet tall in his beaded moccasins, but his deep chest and wide shoulders spoke of unusual strength. Black beady eyes set deep in a face of sculptured copper, straight nose, high forehead, square fighting jaw. His age might have been anywhere between thirty and fifty; Indians change slowly after reaching maturity.

"How, white brave," the Indian spoke to Runyan. "My medicine is strong, but medicine of white men is stronger. Me born here; my father chief when we fight the braves who wear this," and he pointed to a turquoise ring on his left forefinger.

"That's a Navaho ring," Rawhide said. "Navahos at peace now."

Sam Judas spoke rapidly to Chief Blue Stone in the Apache tongue. Rawhide Runyan could read some of the sign language. Judas was telling the Indian that the cattle on the far hill had been rustled; that Rawhide and Joe were at war with the white men who had invaded the canyon.

"They shot three of the little people this morning," Judas

told Rawhide. " The redskins killed one rustler with arrows·
Little people afraid of thunder-sticks of the white men."

" Tell him we will help his people," Rawhide said to Judas.
" We will come again in the dark of the moon."

A horse whinnied softly back in the brush-fringed park.
Sam Judas and Chief Blue Stone disappeared instantly,
stepping back into the brush. Rawhide took two steps and
slipped through an opening.

Slow Joe Hill was staring across the brush with his head
cocked to one side. A gun slipped into his big right hand
just as a hurtling figure leaped from the brush and bore Slow
Joe to the ground. A clubbed gun rose and fell to put Slow
Joe out of the fight.

Rawhide Runyan crouched in the brush, careful not to make
the tops wave to betray his hiding-place. The attacker of
Slow Joe Hill was a big man, six feet four in his high-heeled
boots. The stranger cocked the heavy six-shooter in his hand
as he faced the brush where Chief Blue Stone was hiding.
The stranger rasped :

" Come out of that bresh, you sneakin' redskin ! I heard you
palaverin' with this barn-shouldered hombre."

Rawhide Runyan started to draw his gun, changed his
mind, and waited. Chief Blue Stone stepped into the clearing,
a hunting knife in his right hand. His voice was calm as he
spoke.

" What you want ? "

" I want you, yuh runty root eater. The Big White Chief
wants to talk to you. You do what he say, mebbe no kill.
You savvy ? "

" Blue Stone savvy," the Indian answered gravely. " Blue
Stone no go with you."

" Drop that knife before I dot yore eyes," the outlaw
barked, as he raised his long-barrelled six-shooter.

Rawhide Runyan slid from the brush without making a
sound. The Indian saw him, but his features did not betray
his emotions. The young white brave had said that his
medicine was strong ; the young white brave spoke with the
single tongue.

" What you want with Blue Stone ? " questioned the
Indian.

" That's better, redskin," the outlaw said, as he lowered
his gun. " Tolliver wants to rescue your folks, and he wants
to trap some of those little horses. Anything to turn an honest
dollar, that's Simon Tolliver. Turn around while I hobble
your hands with a piggin' string."

Blue stone turned without a word.   The burly outlaw reached for a piggin' string caught in his belt.   He slipped the noose over Blue Stone's right wrist, but he never finished his ties.

Rawhide Runyan made his jump with all his weight behind the fist that struck the outlaw on the side of the jaw.   Blue Stone turned just as the outlaw crumpled in a heap.   The Indian's long hunting knife rose for a fatal thrust, but Rawhide caught his wrist in a grip of steel.

CHAPTER XXVII

SLOW JOE MAKES A FRIEND

RAWHIDE said slowly : " He is asleep. A brave man does not kill his enemies while they sleep."

Blue Stone shifted the knife to his left hand, whipped into a turn to bring Rawhide's arm over his shoulder and pulled down with all his strength.   Rawhide was taken by surprise, but he went with the pull to throw Blue Stone off balance.   Rawhide landed on the back of his shoulders, looped over into a roll and came to his feet.

Chief Blue Stone was after Rawhide like a cat, his knife held for an upthrust.   His black eyes were shining like polished ebony as he closed in for the kill.

Rawhide Runyan was tempted to slap for the gun in his holster.   He quickly changed his mind as he realized that he would have to shoot if his gun cleared leather.   Rawhide threw himself backward to the ground just as the Indian charged.

Blue Stone tried to stop his rush, but Rawhide caught the Indian's left leg between his boots.   After tripping his catch, Rawhide jumped the Indian, caught the knife hand between his strong fingers and vised down with all his strength.

Blue Stone gasped and dropped the knife.   He made no attempt to struggle, but a slow smile curled the corners of his mouth.   Rawhide followed the Indian's gaze.   Then he too was watching with silent fascination.

The tall outlaw was stretching his hand out along the ground in an effort to retrieve his fallen gun.   Slow Joe Hill was creeping up on the unsuspecting rustler.   Joe dug his spurs in for a leap just as the outlaw's fingers touched the gun. Joe made his jump as the outlaw came out of his crouch.

Slow Joe hit the outlaw all spraddled out, forcing him to the ground.   Slow Joe stood an even six feet, weighed two hundred pounds of hard bone and solid muscle. Both men came up at the same time, locked in each other's arms.

" Burly Jackson, eh ! " Slow Joe grunted. " It's you or me ! "

Burly Jackson leaned back and smashed a solid right at Slow Joe's beefy face. The blow sounded like the handle of a bullwhip on a pile of soggy hides. It brought a spurt of crimson from Joe's flat nose. His head rocked back under the impact, then he buried his face in Jackson's shoulder.

Rawhide Runyan watched the battle, but this time he did not interfere. Gunfire would attract Simon Tolliver and his gang, spoil the plans Rawhide had made, and besides, Burly Jackson was a killer.

Slow Joe caught his hold behind the outlaw's broad back. His fingers locked just above the hips as Jackson tried vainly to punch himself loose. Slow Joe began to squeeze slowly, increasing the pressure as the outlaw's lungs began to starve for air.

Rawhide had forgotten all about Sam Judas until a drawling voice spoke sternly and told Slow Joe to turn his victim loose. If Joe heard, he gave no heed. The red haze of madness was upon him, the bear trap was waiting to be sprung.

" Don't spring it, Joe ! " Sam Judas said. " Thou shalt not kill ! "

Slow Joe bent his knees and lifted just enough to bring the outlaw's feet from the ground. The tremendous muscles in his shoulders began to writhe and twist under his heavy wool shirt. Again the voice of Sam Judas spoke with a peculiar penetrating quality :

" I'll shoot if you lower the boom ! "

Slow Joe hesitated, raised his head to listen, his face covered with blood from his streaming nose. His locked hands shifted and he leaned back against his boot heels.

Sam Judas had stepped out of the brush with one of his six-shooters in his bony right hand. His bearded face was stern and uncompromising ; a fanatical light blazed in his deep-set brown eyes.

Rawhide Runyan palmed his own gun to cover Judas. He wondered if he could shoot the gun from the gaunt man's hand, but as he struggled for a decision, Slow Joe took the play away from them both.

Slow Joe leaned back and began to turn to the right. Burly Jackson's feet slipped from the ground. Joe began to whirl like a top. Sam Judas could not shoot without hitting both men, and he was a disciple of his own doctrine. Rawhide heard him murmur again : " *Thou shalt not kill !* "

Slow Joe was leaning back as he worked up a giant swing. Burly Jackson's body was whipping the air with his feet far above the ground. Joe's boot heels had dug a deep round hole in the ground ; little puffs of dust plumed up at every turn.

Now Slow Joe leaned back to bring the outlaw to a level with his shoulders. Joe suddenly unlocked his grip. A muffled breathless scream died on Burly Jackson's lips as the rushing air tore the last remaining breath from his straining lungs.

The outlaw flew far out into space like a great wingless bird—far out above the Canyon of the Damned like a buzzard brought down in flight.

Rawhide Runyan pulled back and turned away. Chief Blue Stone leaned forward to watch, while Sam Judas dropped to his knees to say a prayer for the doomed. Judas sighed as a thudding crash came from the depths far below.

" Have mercy on his soul," Judas muttered weakly.

Blue Stone stretched to his full height and walked over to Slow Joe Hill. Joe was breathing heavily, eyes closed, head sunk on his massive heaving chest as though he were waiting for something.

" You my brother," Blue Stone said quietly, as he gripped Slow Joe's hand. " You hold still, white man. We be blood brothers."

Slow Joe opened his eyes, felt the point of a knife on the little finger of his right hand. He watched without emotion as Blue Stone made a slight cut on his own right hand. Then the Indian took Joe's hand, pressed the two slightly bleeding fingers together, spoke in his soft guttural voice :

" You my blood brother now, Shaggy Bear," he muttered.

Slow Joe took a deep breath, turned to see where Rawhide was. He had expected the usual clout on the chin which always brought him out of the madness. Rawhide was smiling, nodding his head.

" Me Shaggy Bear," Slow Joe said with pride. " Me and the chief is brothers. How, my runty pard."

" How," Blue Stone said solemnly. " Any time you get in trouble, Blue Stone and his little people come help. You help ? "

" Spell it out and count 'er done," Slow Joe answered, and there was no doubting his sincerity. " I ain't never had any kind of a brother before."

" Me go now," Blue Stone said quietly as he prepared to lower himself over the edge of the mesa. " You go ? " he asked Sam Judas.

Sam Judas shook his head slowly. His fingers moved rapidly as he talked to Chief Blue Stone in the sign language. Judas turned to Rawhide Runyan to offer an explanation.

" Told him I'd stay up here a while to scout around."

Slow Joe Hill had walked into the brush ; he came back with rifles taken from the saddle scabbards. Handing Rawhide a Winchester, Slow Joe levered a shell into the breech of a heavy Sharps and pointed to a distant wall with his chin.

" There's a couple of white men yonder, Rawhide. They mean to use Blue Stone for a target as he climbs down to the lower trail. Let's me and you drive 'em to cover."

Rawhide looked over the edge to satisfy his curiosity. Chief Blue Stone was lowering himself like an agile monkey, using stout roots and jutting boulders for hand and footholds. The flat bark of a rifle came from the distant canyon wall, followed by the whining drone of a speeding bullet.

Rawhide jumped back into the brush for cover as he saw Blue Stone make himself thin in a small pocket behind a huge boulder. Slow Joe Hill was sighting down the long barrel of his old Sharps buffalo gun ; it roared like a cannon as he squeezed off a slow shot. A man on the far trail pitched forward, his hands high, and threw his rifle into the canyon. The outlaw followed his gun in a sliding tumble, bouncing from ledge to ledge.

" That's one thunder-stick for Blue Stone, if the gun don't bust," Joe said grimly.

Rawhide Runyan was lining his sights on a second figure over on the upper trail. His first shot was drowned by the roar of Slow Joe's Sharps. The two men spaced their shots in a slow barrage until their magazines were empty, giving Chief Blue Stone time to scramble down his dangerous ladder.

Rawhide crawled to the edge of the mesa and craned his neck. Blue Stone had made his descent ; now he was racing down a steep trail which twisted through the brush which covered the sloping canyon wall. Rawhide turned quickly, his eyes searching for Sam Judas.

" Where did Judas go ? " Rawhide asked Slow Joe. " I forgot all about him when that owlhooter sniped at Blue Stone."

" He went thataway," and Slow Joe jerked his head to the west.

" Say," Rawhide whispered hoarsely. " You reckon that man of peace is fool enough to scout the hide-out of Simon Tolliver by himself ? "

" He don't lack for grit," Joe muttered. " And he's bull-headed as a Missouri mule. Carries a Bible in the tails of his coat ; it would be just like Sam to hoof it down there to preach a sermon to Simon Tolliver and Idaho Crim."

" I'd hate to have that Judas hombre against me," Rawhide said softly. " Now you see him, now you don't. He could slip into a man's camp and cut his throat without making a sound."

" You know me and my big feet, boss," Slow Joe muttered. " I ain't worth shucks on a sneak, but we ought to try to give Sam some help."

" You stay here with the horses," Rawhide answered grimly. " Sam Judas might need some help, if I can follow his trail."

" Take 'er easy, Rawhide," Joe cautioned anxiously. " If you don't get back by sundown, I'm comin' after you. Accordin' to my tally, there ought to be six of them down there, and one of them is wounded."

Rawhide waved a hand and disappeared into the brush. Slow Joe watched the brush tops, smiled with satisfaction when he could discover no movement.

Rawhide Runyan had watched Sam Judas and had noted how the gaunt scout had marked some distant point which he followed like a homing pigeon. Sam Judas had pointed out where the secret trail began ; it led to a big cave uncovered by a landslide.

A broken twig caught Rawhide's attention. The print of a big moccasin was plain at the root of the cresote bush. Rawhide stopped to reload the magazine of his rifle. Then he disappeared into the brush.

CHAPTER XXVIII

THE CHALLENGE

Rawhide Runyan halted in a brushy pocket near an alder thicket. The alders meant a water-hole was close by, and near the rim of the canyon where Sam Judas had pointed out the secret entrance. On hands and knees, Rawhide parted the brush slowly to peer in all directions.

A battered old stetson rose suddenly above the brush tops. It disappeared quickly, but Rawhide recognized the headgear of Sam Judas. Rawhide made a crouching run until he reached the alders. He flattened out on his belly as he glimpsed Sam Judas across the deep water-hole, which was worn in solid rock.

Sam Judas was walking down a deep gash where a landslide had gouged a trail. He made no effort to conceal himself and showed no surprise as a squat, wire-shouldered outlaw stepped from a fringe of brush with a cocked six-shooter in his right hand.

" You reach for one of them cutters under your coat an' I'll blow you out from under your hat," the outlaw warned. " What you want, Judas ? "

" I come in peace, Idaho Crim," Judas answered quietly. " You have killed some of my little people, but you suffered losses. I warn you and Simon Tolliver to go while there is time."

" Up them flippers, parson," Crim ordered harshly. " I'm taking your hardware, after which you and me'll take a pasear through the cave to see Tolliver. We're having a funeral pretty soon, and we needed a sky pilot to do the honours."

Rawhide Runyan slowly raised his rifle to cover Idaho Crim. Then he lowered it slowly ; bushwhacking was not one of his faults. Perhaps Sam Judas had a plan ; the long-haired scout was a man of mystery.

Idaho Crim advanced slowly, reached under the long coat tails, and disarmed Sam Judas. He jerked his head for Judas to precede him, motioning toward the screened opening of the cave.

As they parted the brush, Rawhide was on his feet.

He reached the brush just in time to see Idaho Crim say something to another outlaw who was evidently guarding the cave. Rawhide knew that the guard would turn to watch the two men for a moment. Runyan used that precious time to race across the clearing. As the guard turned back, Rawhide was flattened along the wall in a little crevice.

The guard was a tall, lathy outlaw in his late twenties. He placed his rifle on the ground with the barrel leaning against the wall. Taking tobacco and papers from a shirt pocket, the guard began to roll a smoke.

Rawhide Runyan slipped out of his hiding-place, gun in hand. As the outlaw was licking the edge of the brown paper, Rawhide leaped behind his swinging gun. He caught the falling outlaw, pulled the limp form to the brush, tied the guard's wrists with the piggin' string which Burly Jackson had used on Chief Blue Stone. After binding the unconscious man's ankles with the guard's own belt, Rawhide fashioned a bandanna gag which he tied tightly between the gaping jaws of his prisoner.

Keeping to the brush, Rawhide slipped inside the cave. He stopped a while until his eyes had shed the bright sunlight. When he opened his eyes, he could see a point of light far down the slope. The floor of the cave was covered with moist sand which made no sound as Rawhide raced toward the lower opening. This was the canyon's secret entrance.

Idaho Crim was herding Sam Judas into a large grassy park as Rawhide reached the lower opening, staying well inside. Several men were lolling on the grass, staring at the prisoner with hostile eyes. A tall man stretched to his feet, stroking a small moustache with his left hand. He wore expensive whipcord pants pushed down into polished hand-made boots. A fifty-dollar stetson rode jauntily on his black head ; crossed gun belts fitted his lean hips with the holsters tied low.

" Caught me a visitor, Tolliver," Idaho Crim announced. " You know Sam Judas ; he knows you. Wants to palaver some about his little people."

" Howdy, parson," Tolliver greeted in a deep voice. " You see anything of Rawhide Runyan ? "

" Saw him and Slow Joe Hill," Judas answered honestly, and Rawhide bit his lower lip. " I stopped Joe from killing Burly Jackson."

" Where *is* Jackson ? "

" Down there in the Canyon of the Damned," Judas answered soberly. " He wasn't hurt much ; it was the fall that killed him."

" Tally two against Slow Joe," Tolliver murmured carelessly. " I recognized the roar of his buffalo gun just before Slim Brown pitched over the edge. The fall didn't kill Slim."

" They who live by the sword shall die by the sword," Sam Judas quoted solemnly. " Shall we proceed with the funeral Brother Crim mentioned ? "

Rawhide saw Tolliver crouch as Sam Judas reached into his long coat tails. A gun leaped to the outlaw's hand ; then the hammer lowered—for Judas produced a worn Bible.

" I was within one inch of killing you," Tolliver snarled. " I knew you when you had eight notches whittled on your gun. You used to carry a hide-out in your coat tails."

" I have put away sinful ways," Judas answered with dignity. " We will proceed to the graveside."

" Not me," Idaho Crim refused bluntly. " I'll stay right here to guard the camp. I've got to figure out a way to trap some of those runty Apaches and their ponies. The circus shows will pay us plenty."

The reclining outlaws stretched to their feet, pulling hats low over their eyes against the glare of the sun. Simon Tolliver jerked his head at Sam Judas, led the way to an open grave round a bend in the steep trail.

Rawhide Runyan moved forward a few steps in an effort to see the grave. Idaho Crim whipped around like a cat ; his voice came to Rawhide like the lash of a whip :

" Knew you was there all the time, Runyan ! Saw your shadow once as you crossed to the water-hole. Knew you wouldn't shoot me in the back, and right now you're outlined against the sky from the upper end ! "

Rawhide Runyan caught his breath. He had the sensation of a sleepwalker who suddenly awakes in strange surroundings. He could feel the damp darkness around him, could see the bright warm sunshine out in the clearing. He wanted to turn his head to see the mouth of the cave's entrance, but caught himself just in time.

Idaho Crim had his right hand poised above the heavy .45 six-shooter on his short right leg. The outlaw laughed softly.

" I've wanted to match sixes with you for quite a while, Rawhide," he said quietly. " With you out of the way, it'll be a cinch to clean out every cattleman in the Strip."

Runyan waited, knowing that his silence would get on the outlaw's nerves. He also had a distinct advantage. Crim would not see his hand move in the darkness.

Rawhide shook his shoulders angrily. He told himself that he was not a cold killer, admitted that he was gun-proud. Escape was impossible, for Idaho Crim could pick him off if he attempted to race back up the long cave.

" I'm coming out," he told Idaho.

" Welcome to the Canyon of the Damned," Crim answered mockingly.

Rawhide Runyan watched warily as he began his slow advance. He knew that he would be blinded if he stepped suddenly into the glare of the sun. Idaho Crim also knew it as he went into a crouch facing the mouth of the cave.

Rawhide stopped a few feet inside the entrance. His eyes gradually absorbed the light as he took a slow step forward. Idaho Crim faced him like a giant spider—feet wide apart, both elbows spread out.

" Take your time," the outlaw sneered. " After the smoke clears off, I'll kick you over the rim."

Rawhide Runyan took the last step which placed him squarely in the sun. With shoulders stooped slightly, he faced Idaho Crim for show-down.

" Make your pass ; I've got you faded," Crim sneered.

Rawhide Runyan did not break his silence. If a go-ahead was needed, he would give it. His left hand moved out as though he were throwing a pair of dice.

Idaho Crim rapped down for his gun with the movement of Rawhide's left hand. Rawhide's right hand made a circling stab downward, which caught his gun and shucked it from the holster at the same time. His shot roared out and was answered by a flash of orange flame from Idaho Crim's six-shooter.

Rawhide felt the tug of lead against the edge of his calfskin vest. Idaho Crim took three backward steps as he tried to catch his balance. The last step was in thin air as he reached the canyon rim—and stepped into space.

Turning on his heel, Rawhide Runyan sped back up the sloping floor of the cave like a deer. He knew that the sounds of battle would bring the outlaws rushing round the bend from the grave of their dead companion. If they stopped to look for Idaho Crim, he might have a chance to reach the upper entrance.

He could hear the shouts of excited men behind as he raced through the long cave. Rawhide began to zigzag as a shot blasted after him. He knew he was silhouetted against the sky, but a few more yards would take him to safety.

Rawhide gasped as a bullet scraped his ribs. The lead burn was like a hot iron. Rawhide threw himself low against the left side of the cave, knowing that he would blend with the wall. Guns continued to roar. Rawhide crept toward the entrance. A few feet more and he crawled round a protecting wall.

Not until then did he turn. He could see several men outlined at the lower opening ; now he was conscious of the target he must have made. Sighting carefully, he picked a target and pressed trigger. A howl answered his shot.

Rawhide triggered his gun until it ran dry.

CHAPTER XXIX

TWO STRIPES FOR RAWHIDE

RAWHIDE RUNYAN slid deep into the brush which screened the upper entrance to the long cave. His fingers plucked fresh shells from his cartridge belt while he tried to devise a plan of attack. His eyes roved over the gouged trail where the landslide had broken the prison-like walls of the Canyon of the Damned.

Ejecting the spent shells from his six-shooter, Rawhide thumbed bright cartridges through the loading gate. Sam Judas had made himself a voluntary prisoner for reasons of his own. Rawhide remembered the guard he had captured at the mouth of the tunnel ; he had hidden his rifle near the prisoner.

Rawhide smiled grimly as he realized that he was creeping through the brush without a sound. It seemed that every living thing about the deep canyon was either hunted or a hunter. The trail was plain where he had dragged the unconscious outlaw across the grass.

Rawhide Runyan stopped with a jerk as he came to the pocket where he had left his prisoner.

The man was lying flat on his back, staring up at the turquoise sky with sightless eyes. The feathered haft of a hunting arrow fitted snugly against the dead man's corded throat, showing how he had met his death.

Rawhide growled softly as he found the prints of hand-sewn moccasins in the short grass. An Indian evidently had stalked the outlaw ; one of the little Apaches from the deep canyon, no doubt.

The angry scowl fled from Rawhide's bronzed features as he read what had happened. The outlaw had somehow managed to free his hands. The little Indian had made his kill from the brush without warning. The story might have been different if the outlaw had escaped with Rawhide's rifle while Rawhide had been in the cave. Runyan would have been caught between a cross fire from which escape would have been impossible.

Rawhide Runyan crouched low with the feeling that he was being watched. He could feel eyes staring at the back of his neck, but when he slowly turned his head, the dense brush was devoid of movement.

" Joe," he called softly. " Come out of that brush ! "

The rattle of galloping hoofs was his only answer, and Rawhide upbraided himself for carelessness. That horse had roared out of the cave while he was reading sign near the dead outlaw ; his own Shadow horse was waiting in the mesquite thicket almost a quarter of a mile away.

" Me friend," a guttural voice said softly. " Blue Stone help white brave."

Rawhide jerked round, slapping for his gun belt. Chief Blue Stone, with a fresh scalp tied to his beaded belt, was

standing close to the dead outlaw. The dead man had not
been mutilated, but his shell-studded belt had been removed.
Now it hung awkwardly from Blue Stone's lean hips.

" Hair come from man who fly down into canyon like a
bird," the Indian explained, touching the scalp on his belt.
" Squaw she fix um and give to chief."

Rawhide recognized the coarse black hair of Burly Jackson.
So even these Apaches scalped their victims, although the
only white man they had seen before the slide had been Sam
Judas.

" How you make thunder-stick go loud noise ? " Blue Stone
asked with childlike curiosity.

" You give me long gun," Rawhide said sternly. " You
keep the little thunder-stick."

He stooped quickly and retrieved his Winchester, pointing
to the six-shooter which dangled from the Indian's right hip.
Rawhide took the tie-backs and fastened them round the
Apache's sturdy leg. After which Rawhide drew the .45 Colt
and showed Blue Stone how to thumb the hammer back and
press the trigger.

" Be very careful," he warned. " Thunder-stick go off,
mebbe so shoot Indian in foot. Point it like this." And he
illustrated his instructions.

" When the moon grow dark, Blue Stone led his braves to
the attack," the Indian said gravely. " This many left," and
he held up both hands with fingers extended, repeated the
gesture with six fingers.

" Sixteen braves," Rawhide murmured. " With bows and
arrows."

" Chief Blue Stone have thunder-stick," the Indian
corrected. " Mebbe so get more."

Rawhide knew that in some way the Indian had learned of
the death of Idaho Crim, who had gone over the cliff with one
six-shooter in his holster. Then there was the rustler Slow
Joe had killed. Rawhide turned swiftly.

" We go to your white brother now, chief," he said.

" Black horse there," the Indian said, pointing to a patch of
alders. " I give him drink."

Rawhide stared with amazement. No other man could get
close to Shadow. The Indian must be trying to fool him.
Rawhide whistled softly. He shook his head gravely as
Shadow came loping from the thicket near the water-hole.

" Wonder you didn't get killed," was all Rawhide had to
say. " Shadow one-man hoss."

Blue Stone walked aside and spoke softly. The black

horse whinnied and minced over to rub against Blue Stone's shoulder.

"Injun magic," the Indian said solemnly. "Me likeum horse; horse likeum me. We go now to white brother."

Rawhide jumped his saddle without a word. If Shadow trusted the redskin, that was good enough for the boss of the Diamond Double R. He put the horse to a running walk, with Blue Stone trotting tirelessly just ahead.

The Indian halted suddenly with one hand raised for silence. Then he motioned for Rawhide to dismount, after which the Indian circled through the brush like a hunting dog. Several times Blue Stone stopped to sniff the air. Rawhide Runyan watched as the chief ran to a thicket of prickly pear. A moment later the chief led a saddled horse from the thicket and motioned for Rawhide to come to him.

"White man near," Blue Stone muttered softly, "I smell his horse; we hideum now."

Rawhide walked into the thicket with his eyes studying the ground. High-heeled boots had made little holes in the firmer ground; the tracks led toward the cliff where Slow Joe waited. Rawhide turned to tell the Indian of his discovery, but Blue Stone had disappeared.

Rawhide Runyan shrugged, knowing that the Apache had read the sign as a white man would read the printed page. Runyan loosed the gun in his holster, pulled his grey stetson low to shield his eyes, and followed the boot tracks in a crouch. He stopped abruptly, for the growling voice of a white man broke the silence:

"Stand hitched, redskin. I came to get *you*, but I found this barn-shouldered cowhand. I aim to kill him unless you come with me!"

Rawhide parted the brush without making a sound. Slow Joe was on the ground, bound hand and foot. Chief Blue Stone held his hunting bow in his right hand. The outlaw was pointing a cocked six-shooter at the Indian's heart. The outlaw leaned forward to stare at the scalp on Blue Stone's beaded belt.

"So that's what happened to Burly Jackson," the outlaw muttered hoarsely. "And you're packin' Jim Deming's six-shooter!"

"I go with you," Blue Stone said with quiet dignity. "Shaggy Bear my brother."

"You'll go with me all right," the outlaw grated savagely. "After I put a slug through your sneaking heart!"

"Don't press that trigger!" Rawhide Runyan warned,

suddenly. " I'm offering you an even break. I killed Idaho Crim. He thought he was fast. Holster your gun before you turn. Stay out of this, chief ! "

The outlaw holstered his gun with a grin on his pock-marked face. Slow Joe Hill spoke in his wind-roughened voice:

" Watch that sidewinder, Rawhide. He's almighty rapid with his tools."

" White brother not dead," Blue Stone murmured. "Apache get more thunder-sticks."

" I'm Pock Kelly," the outlaw introduced himself. " So you're Rawhide Runyan, the hombre who uses outlaws up fast."

" The same," Rawhide admitted. " If I could trust a cow thief, I'd give you a chance to ride out of the country."

" Who, me ? " Kelly asked. " Why, you sun-baked yearlin', I wouldn't light a shuck for the devil himself. I'm Pock Kelly, the fastest gun-hawk in the Strip ! "

" No you ain't," Slow Joe contradicted bluntly. " You did beat me to the draw, and you threw down on the redskins. But it beats me how you owlhooters ride back here to gun-auger with Rawhide. He ain't got a bullet burn on him."

" Mebbe he tore his shirt on the brush," Kelly sneered. " Like as not the buckthorn drew that blood on him."

Rawhide had forgotten the bullet slash he had received in his gun duel with Idaho Crim. He acknowledged it now with a grim smile on his hard fighting face.

" Mebbe Idaho Crim nicked me. Are you faster on the draw-and-shoot than he was ? "

" I beat him one time to the gun," Kelly boasted. " Tolliver saved Crim when he stepped between us."

Without warning the outlaw's right hand slapped sidewise for his holstered .45 Colt. Rawhide made the peculiar circling pass which seemed to throw his gun into his hand.

Two bursts of flame preceded the double roar which blasted the thin mountain air. Two fighting men faced each other through the acrid smoke.

But Pock Kelly was the first to stagger. He went back a step, broke at the knees, and pitched forward.

Rawhide Runyan took a deep breath, holstered his .45 Peacemaker, pulled his wool shirt from his grey pants. Two vivid slashes stood out on his white skin ; the lower one was bleeding some.

" Close," he muttered with a grin, as he tucked his shirt back into place. " I wonder how fast Simon Tolliver can clear leather ? "

" Mebbe so we know when the moon get dark," Blue Stone said soberly. " You save my life ; Blue Stone not forget. No shoot now, white brave," he cautioned Rawhide. " My people bring food up trail.

CHAPTER XXX

STAMPEDE

A SICKLE moon rode high and faded out in the dark western sky. Rawhide Runyan and Slow Joe Hill were guarding the upper entrance to the long cave. Chief Blue Stone had returned to the Valley floor, but he had given instructions to the six Apache braves who had brought food and had remained to help guard the trail.

Little men who wore breach clouts and thick buckskin moccasins. Only one of the Apache braves was as tall as Blue Stone ; the rest were like small, muscular boys. They carried hunting bows, long lances tipped with flint heads, and skinning knives grown thin from long usage.

" White medicine man, he smart," Blue Stone had said.

Rawhide waited in the darkness, busy with his thoughts. So Sam Judas was a white medicine man, eh ? He had taught the Apaches the white man's tongue. Sam Judas who had once been a notorious outlaw and killer.

An Indian brave near Rawhide whispered a warning :

" Get thunder-sticks ready. They come."

Rawhide heard a muffled sound which gradually grew louder. Only running cattle could create such a roar—stampeding cattle which were seeking escape from some unseen terror.

Rawhide Runyan knew what was happening. Chief Blue Stone and his braves had promised to slip behind the herd with dry coyote skins. Now the roaring boom of guns began to echo through the cave, to tell that the rustlers were trying to mill the stampeding steers down there.

Rawhide Runyan called to Joe above the muffled roar of trampling hoofs. Three Apache braves came over to Rawhide's side ; three more went across to side Slow Joe. The cattle would trample anything that stood in their path ; they would scatter through the waste land after they crossed the water-hole.

The rumble grew louder as the maddened herd entered the tunnel from the lower end. Rawhide Runyan drew his gun and crouched behind the protecting wall. Slow Joe was on

9

the opposite side ; if they could turn the herd to the south, the cattle would stampede back to their old range.

A big roan steer shot suddenly out of the cave, well ahead of the herd. Rawhide fired a shot over the big leader's head. He fired twice more in rapid succession. The big steer veered sharply to the south, crashing through the brush.

Rawhide emptied his gun to force the onrushing herd after the racing leader. The din was terrific as the cattle reached the rocky rubble of the badlands. Clashing horns and rattling hooks mingled with the bellowing thunder of the maddened steers. The dust rose high to choke the silent watchers.

Rawhide ejected the spent shells from his hot gun, reloaded with feverish haste, pulled his bandanna neckerchief high above his nose. The last of the cattle lunged out of the cave, but Rawhide detected a new note above the bellowing roar. Horses were following the drag, and guns began to blaze from the cave.

Rawhide held his shot as a horse raced into the clear, its rider firing six-shooters with both hands. Slow Joe fired and the outlaw rider yelled as he toppled sidewise from the saddle. Another horse came plunging out, bellied low to the ground. Slow Joe's gun roared twice to spill the gunman from the saddle.

The terrified horses followed the stampeding cattle. The rumbling roar grew less and finally died away. After listening at the mouth of the cave, Rawhide called softly :

" You hurt, Joe ? "

" Just a scratch across the left arm," Slow Joe answered hoarsely. " One of the Apaches is down."

Rawhide crossed the trail as the Indians came out of their hiding-places. They gathered silently about their dead comrade. Then they turned and walked slowly toward the water-hole. Rawhide took one look and sped after them.

The Indians were staring at the body of a rustler, mumbling in their own tongue. One of them stepped out with a scalping knife in his hand. Rawhide stopped him with a sharp command :

" Medicine man say not raise hair. Bad medicine ! "

The little Indian sheathed his knife ; pointed to three arrows protruding from the dead rustler's body. Slow Joe pointed to the second rustler.

" Got him twice in the same place," he said gruffly.

" He got what was coming to him," Rawhide agreed. " Let's get back there to guard that cave."

" White man come," one of the Indians said softly. " Mebbe so medicine man."

"I come in peace, Runyan," a deep voice called. "Hold your fire."

Sam Judas stalked from the cave with his left hand up in the sign of peace. The Indians gathered round him, but Judas came straight to Rawhide.

"Just one white man alive down there," Judas said. "Will you risk your life for my little people?"

"You mean Simon Tolliver's down there?"

Judas nodded. "Tolliver was sleeping on high ground. Two men riding herd were killed in the stampede. The little Apaches got the other one. Tolliver wants to bargain."

"Keep on talking," Rawhide said.

"It says in the Book that greater love hath no man than to lay down his life for a friend," Sam Judas quoted solemnly. "Chief Blue Stone is your friend."

"He's *my* blood brother," Slow Joe interrupted. "Give up head, you long-haired sin buster. What about Blue Stone?"

"Prisoner," Sam Judas answered. "Simon Tolliver is holding Blue Stone and four of his squaws. Says he'll bet them all agin' his chance to beat you to the gun. If he wins, he rides out free with the five Apaches. He's faster than Idaho Crim."

"Lay your hackles, Joe," Rawhide said. "If Tolliver killed you, and he would, I'd still have him to fight. Get on down the trail, Sam. Tell Tolliver I'll be there come daylight. Tell him you'll give the go-ahead by dropping your hat."

"Spoke like a man, and speed to your hand," Sam Judas answered. He stalked into the cave like a messenger of doom.

"Daylight come soon," one of the Indians muttered, as he glanced at the leaden sky. "White chief go alone?"

"I go alone," Rawhide answered soberly. "Simon Tolliver will kill Chief Blue Stone if you follow me. If Tolliver's medicine is stronger than mine, do not harm him. I have spoken!"

Silence for a time, which was broken as one of the Indians spoke softly to Rawhide:

"You go now, White Chief."

Slow Joe gripped Rawhide's hand. Joe tried to find words. The big man was breathing heavily; finally his voice came in a hoarse whisper:

"There's a curse down there in the Canyon of the Damned, pard. You've got to break that curse. Good luck!"

Rawhide answered Slow Joe's grip, tugged his stetson low, and walked into the long cave. He shrugged irritably as he recalled the gloomy uncertainty in the voice of Sam Judas.

Idaho Crim had been fast ; Pock Kelly had been faster. Both had marked him with their lead—and Tolliver was the kingpin of the trio.

There was no sound except for the muffled tread of his high-heeled boots. The grey blur grew larger down the dark passageway. Rawhide loosed his gun against crimp by instinct. The slightest sticking of the gun might mark the difference between life and death.

Now he was at the lower opening of the cave. He stopped to shed the gloom from his dilated eyes. It was light out in the wide, grassy park ; the sun would be slanting over the tall peaks if he waited long. Rawhide touched his gun again, stalked from the cave, stopped to get his bearings.

Blue Stone was tied hand and foot, hanging over the edge of the cliff. Four little Indian squaws were huddled against the side of a huge rock, hands bound behind their backs. Sam Judas stood off to one side, his head uncovered.

Rawhide Runyan glanced at them but briefly. Then his eyes swept to a tall man facing him across the park—a man with brilliant black eyes, a tiny moustache, and a sardonic smile on his darkly handsome face.

" You're either a brave man or a foolish one, Rawhide Runyan," Simon Tolliver said. " I came back here into the Strip for just one purpose. Of course I had expected to combine business with pleasure, but a man can always find new business."

Rawhide Runyan raised his eyebrows without answering. He had stopped whistling in the dark when he was a boy. He had accepted Tolliver's terms ; there was nothing more to say.

" You've recovered your cattle," the tall outlaw continued. " That leaves me no choice except to take my pleasure.

Rawhide stared at the smiling, confident face ten paces across the grassy park. He could also see the deep floor of the canyon behind Tolliver—the Canyon of the Damned. Rawhide took a deep breath and nodded his head toward Sam Judas.

" Get ready, gentlemen," Judas said in his deep, resonant voice. " I will hold my hat above my unshorn head. When I drop it——"

" At your pleasure," Simon Tolliver said with a smile.

Sam Judas fingered his battered old stetson and glanced at the faces of both men. Rawhide Runyan was in a slight crouch. Simon Tolliver had both elbows spread, palms above the ivory handles of his twin guns. Two guns to one !

Sam Judas raised his hat to the level of his head. For a moment the hat poised. Then his hand opened.

Tolliver made a swooping stab with both hands, palming his balanced weapons in perfect unison. Rawhide Runyan drove his right hand down, swivelled to the right against his hip—and tripped the trigger.

He had beaten Simon Tolliver to the shot !

Tolliver triggered his guns just as he was staggering back. His right hand was flung aside by Rawhide's bullet, which smashed his clutching fingers. Tolliver caught himself as he thumbed back the hammer of his left-hand gun against the recoil.

Rawhide Runyan chopped another shot, caught his smoking gun on the recoil. Tolliver dropped his second gun. The outlaw stood for a moment like a bird with broken pinions, blood streaming from his mangled hands. Then like an untamed hawk, Tolliver rushed to the canyon rim and leaped into space.

Sam Judas showed no emotion as he walked over and pulled Chief Blue Stone to safety. After cutting the thongs which bound the four squaws, Sam Judas came to Rawhide Runyan.

" You have saved my little people," Judas said humbly.

Rawhide turned as Blue Stone touched his arm. Runyan's gun was back in leather.

" You and your people are free now, Chief Blue Stone," Rawhide said. " The Evil Spirit has left your home. It is no longer the Canyon of the Damned ! "

CHAPTER XXXI

DEPUTY MARSHAL RUNYAN

RAWHIDE RUNYAN was riding the stage road which led to Boothill, Arizona. He spoke softly to his black horse, Shadow, as a mule deer leaped from the road into the trail-side brush, a hundred yards down the steep grade. Something had frightened the big deer ; no living thing was safe from Scar Costigan and his gang of owlhooters. Maybe the gang was nearby.

There were those who said that Rawhide Runyan was gun boss of the Arizona Strip. He had worked hard for his Diamond Double R outfit ; had been forced to fight many times to keep what he had earned. Outlaws found no haven in the Strip or its environs ; but most of them were gun-proud and insisted they were faster than the man who had sworn to keep them and their kind at a respectful distance.

Rawhide Runyan wasn't a big man, but he seemed made of rawhide and whalebone. His rigging and gear were the best that money could buy—plain top-hand equipment.

Screened by the heavy brush, Shadow stood motionless, not more than ten yards from the dusty road. Down where the mule deer had sought cover, a wide-shouldered man stepped into the clear. His floppy stetson was pinned up in front ; long cow-horn moustaches drooped at each side of his loose mouth. His flat face was completely devoid of expression. Now he spoke over his shoulder to someone back in the brush.

" The stage-coach is comin', Cowhide. I'll stick up the driver ! "

Rawhide Runyan frowned. Maybe this was Blue-nose Smith, an outlaw who killed his victims every time he was recognized.

The bandit pulled a blue neckerchief up over his nose, drew a heavy six-shooter, and waited for his prey.

Rawhide Runyan could hear the singing steel tires on a heavy vehicle ; the driver of the west-bound stage would be certain to stop at the top of the grade to blow his four-horse hitch.

Then Runyan did a strange thing, for him. He, also, wore a blue neckerchief. And he now pulled it up over his nose and mouth. His right hand dropped down to loosen the .45 Peacemaker Colt in his holster and his eyes began to smoulder like smoky agates.

Rawhide's left arm pressed against a badge pinned inside his heavy wool shirt, and he frowned. He had always helped the law, but seldom as a peace officer. Now he was a United States deputy marshal, making an attempt to do what older men had given their lives to do without success.

As Rawhide Runyan watched the bandit, he was remembering the three sheriffs who had been killed in the tough little town of Boothill. The town was controlled by Scar Costigan and his outlaw gang ; even the acting sheriff was an owlhooter. Rawhide had told himself that it was none of his business, but Sheriff Jim Blaine of Rainbow had asked him to help United States Marshal Charley Snow.

Rawhide stepped down from his saddle, made his way to the edge of the brush, watching the bandit who waited at the top of the rise. He could hear the driver swearing at his teams as the leaders topped the crest. The heavy brake brought the Concord stage to a stop, to rest the horses.

Then the bandit shouted the stick-up command :

" Stand and deliver ! "

The driver was a tall, lathy skinner who had grown old in his chosen profession. His boot set the brakes. He rolled a cud of Prairie Twist to the left side of his cheek, spat over the front wheel—and raised both hands shoulder-high.

" I ain't a-carryin' no bullion this here trip," he announced loudly, as he stared into the muzzle of the bandit's six-shooter.

" Pitch that canvas sack to the ground ! " The robber's voice was humming with menace.

" Just like you say, Smith," Stage Driver Matt Price agreed. He started to wrap the leather ribbons round the whipstock.

Smith's little close-set eyes began to glow with a strange red light. The masked bandit knew that he was recognized—and Price realized his mistake too late.

" Here's the gold ! " Matt Price shouted. He pushed the heavy canvas sack from the seat.

Then Matt Price took the only choice he had. He made a dive over the left side of the wide seat just as Smith glanced up and triggered a shot.

Matt Price landed near the brush all spraddled out on hands and knees. Smith started around to circle the lead team.

But a barking command from down the grade brought the bandit to a sliding stop :

" Drop that gun, Smith ! " Rawhide was talking from behind his cocked gun.

Smith had a slug ready for Matt Price. But now Smith whirled like a cat, chopping his shot at Rawhide Runyan.

Rawhide pulled away to the right ; his six-shooter roared gustily as the outlaw's bullet whined past his head. Rawhide had learned to fight fire with fire—and he knew that Blue-nose Smith was playing for keeps.

The outlaw went back a step under the thudding impact of Rawhide's .45 slug. Then Smith recovered his balance and swayed forward ; he took a running step, and another. Still running, he broke at the knees and made a diving headlong fall on the steep down grade.

Matt Price was on his knees, firing under the body of his Concord stage.

A mounted second bandit was rattling away in the brush ; this one lurched in the saddle as Rawhide Runyan caught his sights and slowly squeezed off a shot. Then the second bandit was swallowed up in the high brush.

Rawhide pulled his bandanna down and walked up to join the old long-line skinner. Matt Price was staring at two gaping holes in the knees of his wool pants.

" Lost a lot of skin, stranger," he told Rawhide ruefully. " Hadn't been for you, I'd be where Blue-nose Smith is, and I ain't fitten to die. I've led a misspent and wuthless life, but thankee kindly for saving what's left of it."

" Better load Smith's corpse in the coach and deliver it to Sheriff Blaine at Rainbow," Rawhide suggested. " He's worth a thousand dollars, dead or alive, and the money'll help the widows and orphans of those three sheriffs the Costigan gang killed."

" Shuckin, cowboy," Price said slowly. " You're Rawhide Runyan, eh ? But you're out of your county. You taken up to roddin' the law ? "

" You almost lost your job five minutes ago," Rawhide answered sternly. " Talking too much with your mouth wide open. You knew Smith always killed his victims if they recognized him. You allow I saved your life ; remember mine won't be worth much if you go shooting off your head."

" Sorry, Rawhide," Matt Price answered in a subdued voice. " I won't talk, but you want to watch that crowd in Boothill. The bandit who got away was Cowhide Jackson, and you broke his left wing, unless I'm wrong. Help me load the deceased in my coach, but I ain't going to like his company."

After the body of Blue-nose Smith was placed inside the coach, Matt Price walked around the horses, kicked around in the brush. Presently he turned to Runyan with a grin on his weathered face.

" Cowhide Jackson got the gold," the stage driver said cheerfully. " It weighed fifty pounds, and was worth a dollar and a half." Seeing the question in Rawhide's eyes, Price explained with a chuckle : " That sack was filled with iron washers ; I'd like to see Scar Costigan's face when he starts to divide the loot ! "

" You were carrying gold, weren't you ? " Rawhide asked. " Not that it's any of my business."

" The real gold is safe enough," Price answered. The smile fled from his seamed face. " It's under the back seat of the coach ; Smith's corpse is guarding it. Well, I got to be getting along, and time's a-wastin'."

Rawhide watched as Matt Price climbed to his high seat. Price wrapped the heavy leather ribbons about his gnarled hands, cracked his blacksnake whip and kicked off his brakes.

" Mind you don't spit agin' the wind ! " he yelled. His teams started down the grade at a trot.

Rawhide waved his hand, jacked the spent shell from his six-shooter, reloaded as he walked back to the place where he had left Shadow. Cowhide Jackson would carry the news to Costigan, the outlaw leader who ran the town of Boothill. Marshal Charley Snow had given him descriptions of most of the gang, had emphasized that all were killers.

There was Hoop Daniels, so called because of his saddle-warped legs. Judge Bisley Blair, who served as justice of the peace, used his .41 Bisley Colt for a gavel. Sheriff Faro Powers ran the games in the saloon known as Robbers' Roost ; he was a brawny outlaw who had built his own gallows, and always tripped the trapdoor himself.

Rawhide checked off the list until he came to Scar Costigan. Costigan carried a scar on the left side of his swarthy face, running from temple to jaw. A whisky-crazed Apache had nearly finished the outlaw ; the Apache had died with three bullets through his heart.

If rumour was half right, Costigan was double fast with the twin six-shooters he wore tied down on his long powerful legs. Costigan had black piercing eyes to match the colour of his greasy hair. He was a mixture of many breeds, most of them bad. Only a fool would underestimate the outlaw leader ; Costigan was the brains of his gang.

Rawhide Runyan's eyes began to smoulder as he rubbed the handle of his six-shooter. He admitted to himself that he had powder smoke in his veins. He too was gun-proud ; had never walked away from a show-down. Because of this, he was marked, just as the bull's-eye is marked on a target.

Rawhide shrugged his wide shoulders, mounted his black horse and continued his interrupted ride to Boothill. His left arm again touched the law badge pinned inside his shirt ; it brought a frown to Runyan's tanned rugged face.

That badge had been none of his own choosing, but he had accepted it, and the responsibilities that went with the ball-pointed star. Back in the Arizona Strip his neighbours called him a cowboy's cowboy. Now he was a United States deputy marshal.

CHAPTER XXXII

BOOTHILL LAW

RAWHIDE RUNYAN rode down the one street of Boothill, conscious of many eyes which scrutinized him with veiled indifference. In most cases he could pick the honest men from those who ran with the Costigan gang, or who at least paid tribute to the outlaw chief.

There was something about each man which told a plain story to anyone trained to read sign. The outlaws were a swaggering type who wore their six-shooters tied low, with handles pitched out for a fast draw. Cattlemen and cowboys in town to spend their pay were either carelessly indifferent or sullenly resentful.

Rawhide stopped his horse in front of a small lunch-room ; he had made a dry and fireless camp the night before, knowing that he could get breakfast in Boothill. True to his calling, he ordered ham and eggs, a side of hot cakes with black-strap syrup, strong black coffee made without too much water.

Rawhide glanced up as a squat, powerful man entered the lunch-room. The stranger was deep-chested, wide between the shoulders. A low flat-crowned hat rode on the back of his curly black hair and the stranger wore a necktie, the only one in Boothill. He also wore a long-tailed black coat with a sheriff's badge pinned on the left lapel.

" Mornin', stranger," he greeted Rawhide Runyan. " I'm Sheriff Faro Powers, and I make a point of getting acquainted with folks who ride into the up-and-coming town of Boothill, Arizona. I can't seem to remember your face."

" They say the law never forgets a face, once it's seen the face," Rawhide answered carelessly. " You run the games up at the Robbers' Roost, eh ? What's in a name ? "

" What might yours be ? " Powers asked.

" You've heard of Billy the Kid ? " Rawhide asked in return.

" You ain't him," Powers answered, a gleam of anger in his slitted grey eyes. " Quit trying to cloud the sign, cowboy. Are you lookin' for trouble, or a chance to lose your summer's wages ? "

" Is there any difference ? "

" I stood outside and sized you up," Powers admitted. " You're gun-swift from the way you wear your hardware. Mebbe you're lookin' for someone special."

" If I am, I don't need any help," Rawhide said in a low

voice. He finished his hot coffee. " I'll be seeing you around."

Pushing back his stool, Rawhide paid his check and left the lunch-room. Powers followed him outside with a scowl on his smooth-shaven face. He reached out a heavy hand and gripped Rawhide by the left shoulder.

Rawhide whirled with the turn. His right fist drove a blow to the sheriff's jaw, with all Runyan's weight behind his Sunday punch.

Faro Powers grunted, unhinged his knees, slid face-forward under the tie-rail. Shadow was ground-tied with trailing reins; the black horse did not move a muscle until Rawhide spoke softly. Then Shadow minced to the side. Rawhide fitted his foot to the stirrup and climbed into his saddle.

" You looking for a job, cowboy ? " a drawling voice asked.

Rawhide turned to stare at a lean Texan who wore his wool pants tucked down into hand-made boots—boots with heavy tabs on the outside.

" I'm Joe Houston ; I own the Circle H," the Texan explained. " Welcome to Boothill, Rawhide, but you can't stay in town. Better bed down out on my spread to make it look good. Had a letter from Sheriff Jim Blaine over Rainbow way."

" Howdy," Rawhide answered. A warm smile relieved the hardness of his fighting face. " I was going to look you up, but that gambling sheriff tried to spoil my breakfast. You ready to ride now ? "

" I've got a wagon down at the store," Houston answered. " Taking a load of grub out home ; the store is right next to the jail. You can sit your hoss behind my wagon ; might hear something interesting when Powers rouses up."

The two men rode down the street at a walk. Joe Houston nodded at a few men, stared at others with cold disdain. A heavy wagon was loading supplies from a platform at the side of the general store. Houston jerked his head for Runyan to ride behind the wagon.

Rawhide nodded and neck-reined Shadow behind the wagon. His eyes studied a long low building across the valley from the store. Barred windows marked the building as the jail ; the sheriff's office was out in front.

A dust-coated bay horse came clattering up the street at a dead run. The rider carried his left arm in a bandanna sling ; the sling was coated with dried blood. This wounded man slid his horse to a stop just as a tall, swarthy man stepped from the sheriff's office.

" I've been shot, Scar ! " the wounded man shouted, as he swung awkwardly to the ground. " Got hit with a lucky shot, but the same gunslinger killed Blue-nosed Smith ! "

Rawhide Runyan looked around the tail gate of the freight wagon. He recognized the wounded man as Cowhide Jackson. He carried a heavy canvas sack just behind the pommel of his scarred saddle. It chinked as Jackson pulled it to the ground.

" *You* should have been killed instead of Smith," the swarthy man said thickly. " Riding into town shooting off your big mouth, and dumping that stuff right here in front of the jail ! "

" I'm weak from losing blood, Scar," Jackson tried to excuse himself. " Let's get inside the office."

Rawhide recognized the outlaw leader from his first name. Scar Costigan was wanted in Texas for murder ; wanted two thousand dollars' worth. Six feet tall, built on the lean side for speed ; a hundred and eighty pounds would be a close guess as to the tall outlaw's weight.

The two men walked into the sheriff's office ; Costigan threw the canvas sack onto a scarred oak table.

The side window was open ; Rawhide Runyan watched as Costigan picked up a knife and cut a small hole in the sack.

A gun leaped to Costigan's right hand. His left rested on the sack with his fingers open. Several iron washers covered his palm. A second later the washers struck Cowhide Jackson in the face, flung there by Costigan's viciously swung arm.

" Blue-nose Smith's dead, and you bring me iron washers ! " Costigan said, with a deadly hum in his deep voice. " Either old Matt Price or you made the switch ; one of you is as good as dead ! "

Cowhide Jackson wiped his bleeding face with his right hand. One of the washers had struck him on the nose, from which a trickle of blood was dripping down onto the floor. But whatever else he might be, Cowhide Jackson was not a physical coward.

" If you think I made the switch you better use your gun, Scar," he said in a low whisper. " I'm in as deep as you are, but a man can't die but one time. You might get me with your cutter already in your hand, but you can't beat that man who winged me on the fly ! "

Scar Costigan eared back the hammer of his .45 Colt. His black eyes stared at Jackson without winking, like the eyes of a snake. Scar's finger trembled on the trigger. However, Jackson's final statement saved his life. Costigan held his fire ; he leaned forward with sudden interest.

" Mebbe I was wrong, Cowhide. Tell me some more about that hombre who did for Smith."

" Holster your smoke pole," Jackson growled sullenly. " If you're going to throw down on me again, I want a chance for my taw."

Rawhide sat saddle with every muscle relaxed. Cowhide Jackson was an outlaw and a killer, but he was a man. He wasn't afraid to die ; he would take a long-odds chance to live.

Scar Costigan holstered his six-shooter with a gleam of admiration in his dark eyes.

" We'll draw even if I don't like your palaver," he told Jackson. " This hombre who shot Blue-nose Smith. Anyone we know ? "

" I don't know about you, but I don't want any part of Rawhide Runyan," Jackson answered sullenly. " He's the top gun boss over in the Strip. He gave Smith first shot—and drilled Blue-nose centre when Smith's own shot missed ! "

" Rawhide Runyan, eh ? " Costigan murmured. " I've heard a lot about that gun-swift gent." His dark face changed suddenly. " Me and Blue-nose Smith was different that-away," he boasted. " I put my shots where I call them ; I don't ever miss ! "

" Yeah ; well, I got to see the croaker about this arm," Cowhide Jackson said. " Mebbe he can do something about my nose, which you busted with the gold I brought in. I'll fight you or any of the gang, but count me out when you tangle with Rawhide Runyan."

" Just a minute," Costigan barked. " Yonder comes Sheriff Faro Powers ; looks like he tangled with a buzz saw. You wait until we hear what happened to the sheriff."

Rawhide Runyan edged his horse out of sight behind the big Circle H wagon. He could see by tilting his head ; a smile twisted his lips as Faro Powers staggered into his office. His eyes still held a dazed look of bewilderment ; the sheriff had been the best skull-and-knuckle fighter in Boothill, until to-day.

" What happened to you ? " Costigan demanded.

Powers sat down heavily in a chair. " Stranger rode into town a while back," the sheriff answered in a thick voice. " He wouldn't talk when I asked his name ; cowboy from his brand and earmarkings. About five feet nine ; won't weigh much more than a hundred and a half, but he's a heap tough. He hit me when I wasn't lookin' ; I just now roused around."

" That's him," Cowhide said, just above his breath. " That's

Rawhide Runyan to a T. Was he wearing a calfskin vest and a blue neckerchief ? "

" That's the jigger," Powers answered. He recovered some as he stared at Jackson. " Did *you* meet up with that hombre ? "

" Nuh-uh," Jackson admitted honestly. " He got me going away ; I must have been all of a hundred yards from him. His slug busted my left arm ; then I ducked low in the brush."

" Rawhide Runyan," Scar Costigan purred softly. " I've wanted to meet up with him for three years. He's the fastest gun-slinger in Arizona—excepting myself."

The long fingers of his right hand caressed the ivory grips of his six-shooter. Scar Costigan found pleasure in anticipation. His black eyes happened to glance at Jackson's face ; and Scar's own face darkened with anger as he saw the doubt in Jackson's veiled eyes.

" You don't think I'm faster, Jackson ? " Costigan asked softly.

" A man never won a bet by thinking," Jackson said bluntly. " I'm on my way down to see Doc Bedford. You and the sheriff can make medicine about Rawhide Runyan, and it better be strong. I'll be down on bed-ground for three or four days, but you won't be needing any help from me."

" On your way, yellerbelly," Costigan sneered. " I'll talk to you some more when you heal up your hurts."

CHAPTER XXXIII

STRONG MEDICINE

DEPUTY MARSHAL RUNYAN might have been carved from stone. He sat motionless in the saddle. He felt no twinge of conscience because he had wounded Cowhide Jackson, but he could not repress the admiration he felt for the outlaw's courage. Jackson had declared himself honestly and openly ; he would have no part in the trouble Scar Costigan had concocted for Runyan.

Rawhide was conscious of the bustle on the platform above him. Old Joe Houston was giving orders for loading the big wagon, which was beginning to bend at the heavy springs.

Then Rawhide stiffened suddenly as something hard pressed against his spine.

" Up them flippers, or I'll let daylight through you ! " The man behind the gun spoke in a low, hoarse whisper.

Rawhide raised his hands before he turned his head for a look. A slender man of medium height was watching him over the sights of a cocked .45 six-shooter. A man with sandy hair hanging down over mean little eyes which changed colour from green to amber.

Rawhide lowered his eyes ; his lips curled in a slight smile as he stared at the hold-up's legs—legs shaped like Hoop Daniels, afoot or on horseback, ending up with scarred boots on which the heels were run over on the outsides. There was no mistaking Hoop Daniels afoot or on horseback.

" Hey, Faro ! " Daniels yelled. " Look what I found in the grab bag ! "

Sheriff Faro Powers whipped round with both hands streaking toward his twin guns. Killer light flared in his slitted eyes under the flat-topped hat. He started to cock both hammers with his thumbs.

Rawhide Runyan knew that Powers meant to kill him without giving him the slightest chance. Rawhide also knew that Hoop Daniels would shoot him in the back if he tried to match his draw against the outlaw sheriff's drop. Runyan was in the middle of a cross fire, with no way out.

" Gut-shoot him ! " Hoop Daniels yelled.

" Hold yore fire, Faro ! " a deep voice boomed softly from up on the platform. " Me and Long Tom Jordan have you and your sneakin' pard covered. Drop your hardware before we drop our hammers ! "

Hoop Daniels obeyed instantly. His trembling hands betrayed the cowardice which is inherent in every bushwhacker.

Faro Powers was made of sterner metal. His thumbs rested on the lowered hammers of his twin guns, and he refused to drop the heavy weapons.

Another voice interrupted to break the stalemate :

" You and Long Tom are covered like a tent," the deep purring voice of Scar Costigan stated smoothly. " Rawhide Runyan's under arrest, but he'll get a fair trial. If he's found guilty, I'll give him a chance to ask for a new trial by a higher court. Judge Colt will carry out the sentence ! "

Rawhide Runyan stared at Scar Costigan, who stood in the doorway of the jail. Costigan's ivory-handled six-shooter was on full cock, covering Joe Houston and the cowboy known as Long Tom Jordan. A pulse began to beat in Rawhide's wrists ; a tingle ran through his saddle-toughened frame.

" Lower your guns, boys," he said to Houston and Jordan. " All I'm asking for is a fair trial, and I always get one from old Judge Colt ! "

Houston and Jordan holstered their guns reluctantly. Faro Powers waved his left-hand gun, ordered Rawhide to dismount. The sheriff holstered his left-hand gun, jabbing his right gun deep into Rawhide's lean belly.

"You resist arrest, I'll blow you apart," Powers warned. "I'm takin' your hardware!"

Anger darkened Runyan's face. His muscles tensed. Then he submitted to the law, and the cocked gun pressed against his vitals. Powers lifted the balanced six-shooter from Runyan's holster, stuck it down in his belt—and jerked his head toward the jail.

Joe Houston followed the sheriff into the office. Houston scowled as Rawhide walked into a cell, and went into a crouch when Powers clicked a key in the heavy lock.

"Lay your hackles, Houston," Costigan warned softly. "We're going to have law and order here in Boothill—*our* kind of law."

"How much is his bail?" Houston demanded hoarsely. "I'll pay it, and get him a lawyer!"

"Come in here, judge," Costigan called to a man in an adjoining building. "We have a legal question to decide."

Judge Bisley Blair left his desk in the justice's court, crossed the narrow alley, ducked his head as he entered the sheriff's office. The judge stood six feet six, wore a pair of nose glasses fastened to a silk ribbon, and carried a .41 Bisley Colt in a holster on his right leg. He smoothed back his grey hair and stared at Joe Houston with fishy blue eyes.

"The question, gentlemen," he said importantly. "Blackstone and I have been intimates for years."

"The sheriff just caught a gunman from over in the Arizona Strip," Costigan explained briefly. "Gunman's name is Rawhide Runyan; he murdered Blue-nose Smith. On top of that, he resisted arrest, assaulted the sheriff, and wounded Cowhide Jackson."

"I cannot accept bail for a murder charge," Judge Blair stated emphatically. "Hold the prisoner for trial, without bail. That is the law, gentlemen."

Judge Bisley Blair turned abruptly and walked back to his office. Joe Houston stared at Costigan and Powers. When Houston could control his anger enough to speak, he made war talk with one gnarled hand on his six-shooter:

"Boothill got its name from that skull orchard up on the west hill, Costigan. You and your gang are a pack of outlaws; I've heard you remark that Boothill was for your kind of trash. In a way you're right, and Rawhide Runyan has made a fairly good start. Boothill *is* for outlaws, and Blue-nose Smith is only the beginning ! "

Rawhide Runyan listened with a cold smile on his tanned face. He knew what a fair trial meant in the language of men like Costigan and Powers. Even if found guilty, he had been promised a new trial in a higher court—one from which there could be no reprieve.

" Don't worry about me, Houston," Rawhide called to the boss of the Circle H. " I drew chips in this game ; I'll take my chances. Scar Costigan only thinks he's fast."

The ruse worked, and drew the wrath away from Joe Houston. Scar Costigan whirled like a cat, his hand streaking for his gun. He recovered his control with his six-shooter half out of leather.

" I ain't much on waiting, or on long-drawn-out trials," Costigan said, his voice humming like a taut fiddle string. " You'll come up before Judge Bisley Blair at two o'clock this afternoon."

" A man after my own heart, in some respects," Rawhide answered with a grin. " I'll see you later, Joe."

Joe Houston walked from the sheriff's office with a puzzled gleam in his grey eyes. He knew he was beaten any way he turned, but the confidence in Runyan's voice suggested that the Strip cowboy had something in his mind.

" Trial is at two o'clock sharp," Costigan called tauntingly. " All you cowhands check your hardware at the court-room door ! "

Joe Houston walked dejectedly back to his wagon, tugging thoughtfully on his cow-horn moustache. Then his eyes brightened with anger. Hoop Daniels was studying the big black horse, Shadow. Daniels boasted that he could ride anything on four legs ; it was evident that he was going to attempt to make good his boast.

Houston climbed the platform and nudged Long Tom Jordan. Jordan was nearly as tall as Judge Bisley Blair, with a protruding Adam's apple which he was continually trying to swallow.

" Watch Daniels, but don't interfere," Houston whispered.

Rawhide Runyan was also watching from the window of his cell. Daniels came up alongside Shadow, but instead of fitting his left boot to the stirrup, he made a leaping vault.

The horse flattened its ears and stepped back instead of forward. Daniels missed the saddle completely, and thudded head-on against the heavy platform. When he did not get up, the black horse lowered its head and nodded drowsily.

Rawhide Runyan smiled grimly and turned back to the cell door. Costigan was leaving the office ; he spoke to Faro Powers over his shoulder :

" I'll have a boy bring the prisoner some grub. Don't let anyone take it into the cell to him ; that's *your* job. And remember, sheriff—Rawhide Runyan is marked for *my* meat gun ! "

CHAPTER XXXIV

ACE IN THE HOLE

LAWMAN RUNYAN rested on the wooden bunk in his six-by-eight cell. Like most men who spend their lives in the saddle, Runyan had learned the art of perfect relaxation. He could hear the jangle of dishes over in the lunch-room as he dozed lazily.

Rawhide sat up suddenly. A strange voice spoke from the outside office door. A boy from the lunch-room had brought a tray laden with food ; Runyan could smell the aroma of sizzling steak and strong coffee.

Sheriff Faro Powers took the tray and brought it back to Runyan's cell. He drew his right-hand gun, fitted a key to the heavy cell lock with his left hand. He passed the tray through the door warily, slammed and locked the iron door before he holstered his gun.

" Wasn't for Scar, I'd let you have it now," he muttered hoarsely.

" You did, and thanks for the grub," Runyan said with a grin. " You being a public servant, I've got you working for me."

Ignoring the scowling sheriff, Rawhide attacked his food angrily. A cowboy ate when he could, and whenever food was offered. Powers returned to the front office, muttering under his breath.

After finishing his dinner with apple pie and coffee, all the laziness had left Runyan. He pressed against the cell door to see Faro Powers.

Sheriff Powers was sitting in a big chair with his polished boots on the scarred oak table. He was smoking a black cigar, blowing perfect smoke rings over his head, blowing smaller rings through the larger ones.

Rawhide Runyan slipped his right hand under his left arm. He was not a two-gun man ; he had never seen one who could shoot accurately with both hands. The six-shooter in the Wes Hardin holster under his shirt was a spare. It saved time if reloading was necessary ; sometimes it was an ace in the hole.

Rawhide hefted the gun for balance ; it was a twin to the one Faro Powers had taken from him. He holstered the six-shooter and twitched it a time or two before he moved back to the wall.

" That was right good grub, sheriff ! " he called to Powers. " I'm through with the dishes."

Faro Powers grunted and removed his boots from the table. He came back to the cell door, glaring at the prisoner who had called him a " servant."

" Remove the crocks," Rawhide said lazily. " I'm taking a siesta until court convenes."

Faro Powers muttered a curse and his hand streaked for his gun. He slogged the weapon deep into leather promptly— and stared into the muzzle of the gun which had leaped into Rawhide's right hand.

" Unlock this door," Rawhide said, " or I'll drill you through both hands ! "

Faro Powers glanced at the office door, hoping that Costigan would return to relieve him. Rawhide saw the hopeful expression ; he sighted at the sheriff's heart.

" Open up, or I'll take the keys when you fall," he threatened. His voice was low and deadly.

Faro Powers was a gambler ; he knew when a man wasn't bluffing. He reached carefully for the ring of keys at his belt, fitted one to the lock, and stepped back.

Rawhide Runyan walked through the door, stepping across the tray of dishes. He side-stepped like a cat as Powers slammed the door, which missed Runyan's left leg by inches.

Faro Powers took a gambler's chance, slapping for the gun under his long-tailed coat. Rawhide leaped forward, clubbing down with the barrel of his gun. The blow caught Powers on the side of the head, knocking the lobo sheriff down like a shot steer.

Rawhide wiped his gun on the sheriff's broadcloth coat, reached behind the unconscious man's belt, and retrieved his captured six-shooter. Then he returned the spare to the holster under his left arm.

Hooking his fingers in the sheriff's coat collar, Rawhide dragged Powers into the cell. He took a large silk handkerchief from the sheriff's pocket, fashioned a gag which he inserted between his victim's jaws. After tying the gag behind the sheriff's neck, Rawhide walked out, turned the key in the lock and left the jail by the back door.

A low whistle brought Shadow mincing to him. Joe Houston and Long Tom Jordan were staring from the high wagon seat ; Rawhide placed a finger to his lips for silence. He swung aboard Shadow, walked the black horse up the alley, tossing the jail keys into a clump of jimson weeds.

Rawhide nicked Shadow with a blunted spur to mend his pace. Turning in the saddle, he told himself that the town of Boothill wasn't so much of a town. Perhaps three dozen sprawling buildings, mostly false-fronted shacks.

Rawhide stopped Shadow abruptly and stared at a cross-studded hillside. A dozen fresh graves attested to the accuracy of Scar Costigan and his owlhoot gang. An Indian was digging a grave on the west side of the cemetery, apart from the other graves, and nearest to town. He stopped digging to eye Runyan impassively.

" Caliche very hard," he volunteered, to make conversation.

Rawhide nodded. Sometimes it was necessary to use blasting powder to hollow a grave in the rocky caliche soil, which was composed of petrified clay and volcanic rock. Runyan knew without asking that the grave was being prepared to receive the mortal remains of Blue-nose Smith.

" How far to Circle H Ranch ? " he asked the Indian.

" Three-four miles that way." The Indian pointed toward the foothills to the north. " White man rancher Houston lose much beef. Take um to Siwash Canyon."

Rawhide had heard about Siwash Canyon, a long narrow valley with only one entrance. It was on the Circle H range ; Joe Houston used it to shelter his she-stuff cattle when the winter snows banked high on the open range. He would have to pass the canyon on his way to the Circle H.

The Indian began to wield his pick with his back to Runyan. Rawhide sighted the V-shaped notch which marked the entrance to Siwash Canyon. He told himself that tracking rustlers wasn't a one-man job, especially against a crowd of killers like the Costigan gang.

A quizzical smile tugged at the corners of Rawhide's mouth as he rode across the bunch grass. He had worked alone in the Arizona Strip when he was first getting his start, building up his own Diamond Double R spread. He also wondered why he didn't stay home and mind his own business. Somehow something always stirred within him at the thought of outlaws.

He could hear the bawling of steers as he neared the entrance to Siwash Canyon. Riding slowly through the narrow pass, Rawhide stopped his horse abruptly. A man was standing just inside the valley with his back to the entrance ; a man with bowed legs which resembled a hoop.

Suspecting a trap Rawhide's right hand slapped for his gun.

Then the noose of a rawhide rope circled his head just after he heard the whirring warning. The .45 Colt Peacemaker spilled from his hand and the rope tightened about his arms with a jerk. Hoop Daniels, he of the bowed legs, turned slowly with a cocked six-shooter in his right hand.

"Walked right into it, didn't you, Runyan ? " the bow-legged outlaw jeered. " That Injun pointed the way, so you decided to play your hand solo. Throw off your loop, Monty. Me and Rawhide are takin' a little ride back to Boothill town."

Rawhide loosened the noose and dropped it to the ground. He turned in the saddle to get a look at the roper named Monty. The latter was a tall cowhand, coiling his rope and sitting his horse back in a little brush pocket. A cigarette hung loosely from one corner of his mouth ; a long-barrelled six-shooter was on his right leg.

Hoop Daniels climbed into his saddle, holstered his gun, and jerked his head for Rawhide to lead the way through the entrance. As Rawhide turned Shadow, his right hand slipped under his left arm. Monty saw the move and made a stab at his holstered six-gun, clearing leather just as Rawhide's spare gun flashed in the afternoon sun.

Two shots rang out with a stuttering roar. That stutter meant that one of the gun fighters had shot second. Rawhide's grey stetson flew from his head. Then he turned to cover Hoop Daniels with his smoking spare gun.

Daniels was caught flat-footed with his gun in the holster. He jerked up both hands. Monty flopped over the right side of his saddle. Daniels whispered a question :

"Is Monty done for ? "

Rawhide dismounted without losing the drop. He walked slowly to Daniels and took the outlaw's gun. Then he picked up his own regular .45 gun, which had dropped in a patch of grama grass. Seating it in his holster, he slowly shook his head.

"Bullet shock," he told Daniels. " I throwed off my shot ; he took it below the left shoulder."

"I'll ride clear out of the country," Daniels offered eagerly. "Give me a chance, Runyan ! "

Rawhide Runyan shifted his gun to his left hand, fumbled for a moment inside his shirt. He unfastened the badge, pinned it over his heart outside his shirt, watching the face of Hoop Daniels.

" Deputy Marshal," Daniels whispered hoarsely. " I suspected you was the law all along."

" We're riding to Boothill," Rawhide said grimly. " I want to see how an outlaw judge handles a case—and it won't be me on trial."

He smiled. An expression of relief swept over the face of Hoop Daniels. A worried frown creased Rawhide's forehead and he glanced at the wounded Monty, who was still unconscious.

" Better tie your pard up so he don't bleed out when he rouses around," Rawhide told Daniels. " I'll send a doctor out to patch him up, and a wagon to haul him to town."

Hoop Daniels took a piggin' string from his saddle and obeyed orders. He used Monty's rawhide rope to bind the unconscious man's ankles. Then his right hand reached swiftly inside Monty's left boot as he fingered his ties.

The wicked bark of a derringer shattered the stillness. Rawhide spurred his horse. The .32 slug nicked Shadow's left ear, making him rear high just as Rawhide chopped a shot from his holster gun. When Rawhide had quieted the black horse, he stared at Hoop Daniels, who was lying face-down across the legs of his pard, with the derringer still in Daniels' hand.

" You killed a man, Shadow," Rawhide whispered to his horse. " I meant only to wing him, but you spoiled my aim."

Rawhide turned Shadow and rode slowly from Siwash Canyon. When he passed the rocky cemetery, he held up two fingers. The Indian nodded his understanding ; he had heard the shots echoing from the canyon. The young white brave made strong medicine ; the Boothill he was working in was reserved for outlaws—and there were now two more graves to dig.

CHAPTER XXXV

JUDGE BLAIR'S COURT

AT the edge of Boothill, Rawhide glanced toward a sign hanging in front of a white house, and rode round to the back. A motherly-looking woman answered his knock, and said she would call the doctor at once.

Dr. Bedford was in his middle fifties, small and plump,

with a merry twinkle in his blue eyes. Rawhide told him where to find the outlaw named Monty, and the doctor said he would drive out in his buckboard.

"Where does Cowhide Jackson live?" Rawhide asked casually.

"Keep it under your stetson, but he's right here with me, healing up his hurts," the genial medico whispered.

"He ain't a bed case," Rawhide grunted. "Put Monty in bed, and bring Cowhide up to Judge Blair's court."

The doctor nodded.

Runyan rode up the street, turned down an alley, and walked his horse to the rear of the jail.

As though expecting him, Joe Houston climbed down from his big wagon, bringing a double-barrelled shot-gun with him. He motioned for Long Tom Jordan to stay on the wagon to act as look-out, came close to Rawhide, and whispered behind his hand :

"Scar Costigan found Sheriff Faro Powers in your cell, Rawhide, and let him out. Powers made a run for my wagon, but me and Tom was tongue-tied. Where in tarnation you been?"

"Out to Siwash Canyon," Rawhide answered, and told the old cattleman his story.

"Hm-m-m," Houston hawed thoughtfully. "Stealing my cattle, was they? What you aim to do, deputy?"

Rawhide had forgotten about the ball-pointed star pinned to his shirt under his calfskin vest. He fingered the badge with a frown creasing his forehead.

"I'm cleaning house here, Houston," he answered finally. "I might as well start with the sheriff. You take a back seat in the court-room ; watch old Judge Bisley Blair."

Rawhide turned and pushed the back door open. He tiptoed down the corridor between the cell blocks and stopped at the cell where he had been imprisoned. The aroma of a strong cigar came to his flaring nostrils from the front office. Only Sheriff Faro Powers smoked cigars in Boothill town. Cowboys and loafers alike smoked brown-paper quirlies.

Rawhide took a step forward, and paused as he saw Powers with his polished boots on the office table.

"Don't move, Powers," Rawhide warned softly. "I've got a gun behind your ear, and it's just about two o'clock. You're under arrest, and I'm arraigning you for trial. Stand up, and reach high."

Faro Powers sat like a man who has been stricken with paralysis. Having the superstitions of most gamblers, he was afraid to crowd his luck, and besides, his kind of gambling man bet only on a sure thing.

Rawhide repeated : " Get up ! "

Faro Powers lowered his boots, raised his hands high, and stretched to his feet. Not until then did he turn to face his captor. His face changed upon discovery that Rawhide was empty-handed. Then Powers saw the ball-pointed law star.

" United States deputy marshal, eh ? " he said, and his voice was a thin whisper of sound. " What's the charge ? "

" Rustling, robbery, and murder," Rawhide tolled off the charges. " You killed Sheriff Carl Brady. You can keep your guns. We're going over to see Judge Blair."

Faro Powers went out the room without argument. He turned to the right, crossed the alley, stepped inside the court-room.

Judge Bisley Blair glanced up with a frown at Rawhide Runyan. The judge started to pick up his .41 Bisley Colt which he used as a gavel.

Rawhide covered the judge and spoke sternly :

" Don't get careless with that hog-leg, your honour. Wasn't you expecting me ? "

" Harummmph ! " the judge hedged. " I heard you broke jail. You are charged with the murder of one Blue-nose Smith ! "

" Mebbe your eyesight is impaired, judge," Rawhide said. " I'm wearing a law star on my vest. I killed Blue-nose Smith when I caught him in the act of robbing the stage. I've got a witness I can produce. What's the verdict ? "

Judge Blair was in a legal tight, and he knew it. He picked up his Bisley—by the *barrel*—and rapped on his desk.

" Charge is dismissed," he announced, refusing to meet the glance of Faro Powers. " Next case ! "

Rawhide Runyan reached down into his right boot, produced a stiff paper which he handed to the judge.

" Murder warrant for one Faro Powers, self-appointed sheriff here in Boothill. Charged with the killing of Sheriff Carl Brady, the deceased incumbent."

Rawhide watched the face of Judge Blair as the old impostor read the Federal warrant. Faro Powers stood at one side in the prisoner's dock. Both thumbs were hooked in his belts above his twin six-shooters.

" This is a trifle irregular," Bisley Blair murmured. " Powers will have to be tried before a Federal court. Take your prisoner, Deputy Marshal Runyan."

Rawhide Runyan stiffened until a shadow darkened the

court-room door. It was old Joe Houston. Joe took a chair in the back, with his scatter-gun across his bony knees. Neither Blair nor Powers removed their glances from the face of Rawhide Runyan.

" I arrest you in the name of the law, Powers," Runyan said sternly. " I'm coming to take your guns ! "

Faro Powers went into a crouch with both hands shadowing the grips of his twin six-shooters. Judge Bisley Blair was crouching above his bench, the tips of his fingers touching the barrel of his gun. Rawhide Runyan stood with feet apart for balance, waiting for the lightning to strike.

" You'll get *both* guns ! " Powers snarled.

He struck down with both hands at the same time.

Rawhide watched like a hawk until the twin six-shooters started up. Then his own right hand swept down and up with blinding speed, with thumb curling back the hammer.

Orange flame tipped the muzzle of his gun just as Faro Powers cleared leather. Powers triggered a pair of slugs into the planking even as death overtook his flagging muscles.

Rawhide went to one knee, for he saw Judge Blair swivel his Bisley Colt for a shot. Knowing that he could not beat Blair to the shot, Rawhide made a sprawling dive just as Faro Powers crashed headlong.

Rawhide heard the Bisley roar while he looped over the body of Powers. Like a shuddering echo, a bellowing roar followed the pistol shot. Long-suffering Joe Houston had tripped both hammers of his scatter-gun !

For a moment Rawhide hugged the floor. Buckshot splattered against the back wall. He could see the high swivel chair on which the judge sat ; the legs were rocking back and forth. Then the front legs tipped up suddenly. Judge Bisley Blair lost his balance and thudded to the floor.

Rawhide Runyan came to his knees with a dazed expression in his tawny eyes. His ears throbbed from sound of the double explosion of Houston's shot-gun—a sound like ocean waves breaking against high rocky shores.

" I had it to do, Rawhide," he heard Joe Houston saying, and he heard the words in the way they come from the mouth of a deaf man. Soft and far-away, with a faintly hollow echo after each word.

Rawhide held his nose tightly, blew hard with his lips closed. This cleared his ears some, but he made no attempt to speak until he had reloaded his smoke-grimed six-shooter. He could see a dozen splotches of red on Bisley Blair's vest.

" You salivated him like a sieve," Runyan told Joe Houston.

" Huh ? What'd you say ? "

Rawhide shook his head as he pointed to the dead judge. He held up both hands with fingers extended.

" Old Betsy runs nine shot to the barrel," Houston boasted grimly. " That old scalawag won't hold water."

Rawhide turned to stare down at Faro Powers. He turned the dead sheriff over, unpinned the emblem of the law, placed it up on the high desk.

" He wasn't no sheriff, any more than Bisley Blair was a judge," Houston bellowed, still fighting the foggy stuffiness that clogged his ear-drums. " He was a crooked gambler ; *segundo* to Scar Costigan. You got him plumb centre through the heart."

Rawhide flushed, and heard himself repeating Joe Houston's excuse. " I had it to do, Joe. But I gave him a chance to surrender."

" Shore you did, deputy marshal ! " Houston roared back. " But you knew he wouldn't give up his guns."

Rawhide admitted to himself that he knew ; he felt no regret. Three honest sheriffs had been killed in cold blood ; two of them had been his personal friends.

He turned slowly. Wagon wheels were grinding to a stop in front of the court-room.

Doc Bedford was helping Cowhide Jackson out over the wheel of his buckboard. Rawhide motioned for them to come inside. Rawhide stepped aside.

Cowhide Jackson moaned softly and slumped down on a chair.

" Don't draw on me, Rawhide," he pleaded. " I'll talk. I helped Blue-nose Smith rob the stage, but Scar Costigan gave the orders. We either carried them out or they carried us up to that Boothill graveyard out near Siwash Canyon."

" I'm the coroner," Doc Bedford said. He walked toward the bodies on the floor. " Both dead by gunshot wounds," he declared solemnly. " Did they resist arrest ? "

Rawhide Runyan nodded. He wanted to get out in the air, wanted to ride with the high desert wind in his face.

" Justifiable homicide," he heard Doc Bedford state professionally.

" Scar Costigan said that Boothill was for outlaws," Cowhide Jackson muttered. " I reckon he was right—both the town and the graveyard."

Joe Houston was standing in the front door, looking toward his big wagon. Long Tom Jordan was making motions with his left hand, pointing toward the Robbers' Roost Saloon.

Joe Houston glanced up the street and side-stepped inside
the court-room.

"Loose yore cutter, deputy," he whispered hoarsely to
Rawhide. "Scar Costigan is coming down to keep his
promise ! "

"Which means the rest of you gents stay out of it," Rawhide
said grimly. "If he cuts me down, he rides out free ! "

CHAPTER XXXVI

OLD JUDGE COLT

DR. BEDFORD pulled loose a drapery which hung over the
archway leading to the jurors' room. After covering the bodies
of the dead, the medico righted the high stool from which
Judge Bisley Blair had fallen, and climbed upon it.

"I always preside at a coroner's inquest." He thus declared
his legal position. "This will be the first time the papers
will be properly filled out when the smoke clears away."

"Thanks for your confidence, Doc," Rawhide Runyan said
with a grim smile. "Boothill town was giving Arizona a bad
name. The only honest men here in town were the postmaster
and Bill Blanton, who runs the general store. None of the
cattlemen lived in town ; the real law didn't have a chance
without some help."

"Here comes Costigan," Joe Houston warned. "Three
men with him, and every one of 'em loaded for bear. I
passed the sign for Long Tom Jordan to bring up the drag
after those outlaw mavericks have stepped inside."

The boardwalk echoed to the heavy tread of spur-dragging
boots. A cowboy invariably drags his spurs when he is on the
prod and looking for war.

Rawhide Runyan stood at the east end of the big room
with his back against the wall. Joe Houston stood at the
opposite side ; he broke his shot-gun at the hinge and slipped
two shells into the barrels. Doc Bedford perched on the high
stool behind the long bench.

Scar Costigan walked right into the court-room and took
two steps forward. His three henchmen stepped just inside
the door, hands on their belt guns. For a moment no one
spoke as Costigan sized up the arrangement.

"Where's Sheriff Faro Powers ? " he barked at Doc Bedford.

"Remove your hat when you address this court, and in the
presence of the dead," the little medico said quietly, but his

voice was stern. " Faro Powers, the gambler, lies under that drape before the bar of justice."

Scar Costigan glanced down at the drapery. " I see *two* bodies," he corrected slowly, in a booming whisper. " Who's the other corpse ? "

" An outlaw by the name of Bisley Blair," Doc Bedford answered. " He tried a sneak with that .41 Bisley Colt he made out to use as a gavel. The deceased met their deaths from gunshot wounds at the hands of the Federal law ! "

Scar Costigan swung his eyes to stare at Rawhide Runyan. When he saw the badge of a United States deputy marshal, a change swept over the brawny outlaw chief. The hands of the clock pointed at twenty minutes past two ; Costigan had been too late for the trial.

" Faro Powers should have shook you down when he arrested you, Runyan," Costigan said. " He paid for his mistakes, and I'm appointing Hoop Daniels as acting sheriff in his place."

" Hoop Daniels is dead," Rawhide answered. " I caught him rustling Circle H cattle out in Siwash Canyon. I gave that Indian in the graveyard the sign to dig another grave."

" I told him to add one more," Doc Bedford interrupted. " Monty died as I was bringing him in."

Scar Costigan's swarthy face showed no emotion. He stood immovable, his left hand rubbing the livid scar on his cheek. Then he barked a sharp order over his shoulder :

" You three get the drop on this court ! "

The three outlaws just inside the door jerked into sudden activity, slapping the grips of their six-shooters.

But all motion stopped quickly as a drawling Texas voice spoke from the boardwalk just behind them.

" Reach for sky, you wide-loopin' rustlers. Long Tom doin' the talkin', holdin' aces full ! "

Long Tom Jordan had made no sound while making his way from the wagon through the ankle-deep dust. Like his boss, he held a shot-gun in his capable hands ; the barrels were sawed off short.

One of the trio of outlaws glanced over his shoulder, spoke from the corner of his twisted mouth :

" Start reachin', boys. He's lined up behind a sawed-off scatter-gun ! "

" As acting justice *pro tem*, this court is now in session," Doc Bedford announced solemnly. " Hear ye ; hear ye ! Deputy Runyan, what is the charge against the accused defendant ? "

Scar Costigan swelled up like a giant toad. His word had been law in Boothill; he alone had given the orders.

"Who's a defendant?" he roared at Doc Bedford. "I came down here to prosecute Rawhide Runyan for murder!"

"You came, you saw, but you haven't conquered—yet," the doctor quoted. "As Deputy Marshal Runyan told Bisley Blair, Runyan was riding behind a law star when he killed Blue-nose Smith while the aforementioned outlaw was holding up the stage."

Joe Houston coughed and called attention to the shot-gun in his rope-burned hands.

"You three long-riders behind the accused," he said harshly. "Dehorn yoreselves gently; drop yore hardware to the floor. Remember—yo're covered front and rear!"

Scar Costigan stood erect with his head turned slightly to the left. His eyes never left the face of Rawhide Runyan. Costigan showed no fear as the sounds of metal striking the planking told him that he faced the bar of justice alone.

"Proceed with the trial, judge," Houston told Doc Bedford.

"I have a warrant for the arrest of one Scar Costigan, your honour," Rawhide Runyan said. "He's wanted for the murder of Sheriff Don Baker of this county. I arraign my prisoner for trial."

"I saw Sheriff Don Baker killed," Doc Bedford said slowly. "But as acting judge, I cannot testify against the accused."

"*I* can!" Joe Houston shouted. "Sheriff Don Baker had Faro Powers under his gun, but Costigan took the play away from Powers. Costigan claims to be the fastest gun-slinger in Arizona, and he smoked Don Baker down."

"Who drawed first?" Costigan asked.

"Don did, you red-handed killer!" Joe Houston roared. "You let him clear leather before you made your pass. Then you smoked Don down before he could ear back for a shot."

"I acted in self-defence," Costigan told Doc Bedford. "Baker drew on me first; I shot only to save my life."

"Don Baker was the duly elected sheriff," Bedford argued thoughtfully. "You interfered with an officer in the discharge of his duty. The indictment still stands."

"I have another witness, your honour," Rawhide Runyan interrupted. "Cowhide Jackson will take the stand for the State!"

Scar Costigan glared. Cowhide Jackson walked from the jury room, his left arm in a bandanna sling. Costigan's black eyes began to glow with anger.

" You," he whispered hoarsely. " I should have killed you instead of waiting for you to mend that busted wing ! "

" Silence in the court ! "

Doc Bedford rapped on the desk with his own .45 six-shooter and glared at the boss outlaw. Then he turned to swear in Cowhide Jackson, who raised high his right hand proudly.

" Did the accused, Scar Costigan, kill Don Baker in self-defence ? "

" He made it look that away," Jackson answered steadily. " I heard Faro Powers and Costigan framing the play agin' Sheriff Don Baker ; he never had a Chinaman's chance ! "

Doc Bedford stared at Costigan, but there was no merry twinkle in the doctor's blue eyes now. Regular law procedure had long since been forgotten in the town of Boothill, and the doctor was taking his new role seriously.

" You have heard the testimony against you, Scar Costigan," Bedford said quietly. " Are you guilty, or not guilty ? "

Scar Costigan remained silent for a time. He knew that he was a prisoner ; certain death faced him if he was proven guilty. He squared his wide shoulders proudly and answered in a deep voice :

" Guilty as charged, croaker. I'm waiting for you to pronounce sentence ! "

Scar Costigan knew what the sentence would be. He turned slightly to face Rawhide Runyan. The ivory-handled gun on his right leg was pitched out for a fast draw. His right thumb was hooked in his shell-studded belt. He showed no visible emotion as Doc Bedford passed sentence upon him.

" I hearby sentence you to be hanged by the neck until you are dead, Scar Costigan. Sentence to be executed immediately, upon the gallows erected by your late contemporary, Faro Powers, now deceased. Deputy Runyan, take your prisoner ! "

" I arrest you in the name of the law," Runyan said, without moving.

" Fair enough," Costigan answered steadily. " I've had a fair trial, like I promised you would have. I also made you *another* promise. Remember ? "

Rawhide Runyan nodded slightly. Costigan had offered him another trial before the court of old Judge Colt. A square-shooter could offer his opponent no less, and Rawhide Runyan was a square-shooter.

" Suits me, killer," he answered Costigan. " We'll let Judge Colt decide the issue. If you're the best man, you ride out free so far as I'm concerned. Any suggestions ? "

"Let the croaker sitting on the bench give the go-ahead," Costigan answered without hesitation. "He's another *honest* man; he won't cheat. The doc will rap three times with that six-shooter he's been using as a gavel. He can shoot the first man who jumps the gun. You and me will unlimber when he hits the third count!"

"Suits me," Rawhide Runyan murmured. "Give the go-ahead, doc."

Doc Bedford frowned. His hands began to tremble. He could cut off a man's leg without a quiver of emotion, but this was something different. Then he remembered his position. He raised the gun in his right hand.

Doc Bedford did not trust himself to speak. The muzzle of his .45 struck the top of the bench. Both Runyan and Costigan fell into the gunman's crouch.

The signal gun struck the bench for the second count. It rose slowly again, and poised for the stroke that would be a death toll for the man who shot second.

Then it banged down sharply.

Scar Costigan made a lightning pass for the ivory-handled gun in his tied-down holster. Rawhide Runyan was also in action; his hand blurred with the speed of his draw. His gun spilled sidewise from the holster against his hip, belching flame and smoke just as Costigan eared back the hammer of his leaping gun.

Costigan triggered a shot into the wall not more than a foot from Rawhide Runyan. Runyan was leaning against his bucking .45 Peacemaker watching the face of Scar Costigan. Costigan grunted and pitched forward. A smoke ring made a gun-slinger's halo above Rawhide Runyan's head.

Unnoticed by the men in the smoky court-room, a tall man stepped inside. His hair was white like the clipped moustache on his upper lip. The badge of a United States marshal rode on the left side of his short coat. Rawhide was the first to notice the stranger.

"Marshal Charley Snow! I didn't know——"

"You did a good job, Deputy Runyan," the marshal told him quietly. "You spoke the only language Scar Costigan and his gang could understand. I passed a little graveyard out in the valley as I rode in. The owlhooters can be planted there. Costigan was right when he said that Boothill is for outlaws!"

Charles M. Martin was born in Cincinnati, Ohio. In 1910 he worked for the California Land and Cattle Company. In 1915 he fought in Mexico as a mercenary soldier on the side of Pancho Villa. Later he worked on cattle ranches in various parts of the American West, sold paint products in Japan and China, was briefly a cowboy singer in vaudeville, and was a rodeo announcer in such places as Madison Square Garden in New York City and the Cow Palace in San Francisco. He began writing Western stories for pulp magazines in the early 1930s and continued to do so until the 1950s, something that in terms of his authentic background he was certainly capable of doing with a degree of verisimilitude. He published his first novel in 1936, *Left-Handed Law*, and followed it with *Law for Tombstone* (Greenberg, 1937). These novels introduced his character, Alamo Bowie, a Wells Fargo trouble-shooter and gunfighter. The character appealed to movie cowboy, Buck Jones, and both novels were made into motion pictures by Buck Jones Productions, *Left-handed Law* (Universal, 1937) and *Law for Tombstone* (Universal, 1937), with Buck Jones as Alamo Bodie. Martin was personally a brawling, hard-drinking individualist after the fashion of many of his fictional heroes. He carried on feuds with magazine and book editors as well as other writers. He worked so hard at his writing—at one time producing a million words a year for the magazine market—that on at least one occasion he suffered a nervous breakdown. In 1937 he began signing his name as Chuck Martin. He believed so passionately in the characters he was writing about that in the back yard of his home in southern California he created a graveyard for those who had died in his stories and by 1950 there were over 2,000 headstones in this private boothill. His stories always display great energy and continue to be read with pleasure for their adept pacing and colorful characters.